Unholy Ghost

Unholy Ghost

James Green

This edition is published by Accent Press

ISBN: 9781909624542

Chapter One

'Good heavens, Mr Costello, there is absolutely nothing life-threatening about what I'm asking you to do.'

Jimmy gave her what his mum would have called an "old-fashioned" look.

'No, there never is, is there?'

Professor McBride didn't answer. Jimmy didn't expect her to. On her last non-life-threatening outing he'd got a knife in his side. But his real reason for kicking was the way she had summoned him, like some bloody junior office clerk. 'Come to my office': no 'please', no explanation, just the command to be there.

'You are, of course, at liberty to refuse, although I have to say …'

'No you don't. You don't have to say anything.'

They sat in silence. The office was at the top of a tall block in a modern business suburb and through the windows Jimmy could see the sun shining on the distant blue hills of Frascati. It was a lovely view made all the lovelier by the glory of the April day. After a moment Jimmy pulled his mind back from the glories of nature. Yes, he could refuse. But if he did, what else was there? This woman was all he had, without her his life had no point, made no sense. She had given him some sort of life back, so he put away his petulance and gave in.

'What is it I'm supposed to do?'

'Simply what I said. Find a missing person.'

'What missing person?'

'I don't know.'

He threw up a hand in frustration.

'You see! There you go again. You give me a hurry-up call because you say there's a job. I come running and you tell me that I'm to look for a missing person, but you don't know who it is. What is it about you? Why can't you be straight? Why can't you just tell me …'

Professor McBride's voice was sharp. Jimmy almost expected her to lean forward and rap her knuckles on the desk.

'Mr Costello, I've heard all that before. You don't trust me, you think me, in your own words, a devious bastard. Very well, I agree you may have grounds for thinking as you do …'

Jimmy sat in silence as she went on. It didn't matter what she said. Whatever it was, she was right, she was always right, so he sat and listened and, when she was ready, she began to explain what it was he was going to do for her, the job that absolutely couldn't be life-threatening.

Next day, early, he packed a cheap black holdall with essentials and left his apartment. He lived in an ultra-respectable district not far from the Vatican, on the top floor of a four-storey building which looked just like all the other four-storey buildings that lined either side of the street except that beside his main entrance there was a small restaurant, the Café Mozart. He went in and bought his breakfast; a coffee. Then he walked to Lepanto where he caught the Metro. He was going to Fiumicino airport and a taxi was out of the question during the Roman rush-hour. It wouldn't be quicker to walk, but it would be close. At the airport he boarded a scheduled flight to Paris and by lunch-time he was sitting in a bar overlooking the Seine.

It was April in Paris. People wrote songs about it, got romantic about it, came here just to be part of it. Except that today the rain was running down the café window distorting the view so that the buildings on the far bank were almost indistinguishable from the dark sky above them. Outside the bar cars and pedestrians alike passed in little more than a blur. The wind strengthened and threw even more hard rain against the big window, and what little was visible momentarily dissolved.

It was as if some sort of animal was trying to get in. It was Paris in the spring.

Jimmy looked down at the cup of coffee on the table and thought about his meeting with Professor MacBride the previous day in Rome. Too bloody true he had grounds, she *was* a devious bastard, and the more she said nothing should go wrong the more he'd felt sure something not only could but would go wrong. But he'd still got on the plane. He picked up the cup but the coffee was almost cold, he'd nursed it for too long. He looked at his watch. There was still an hour to kill before the meeting she'd arranged. He looked at the window again. The view, what there was of it, had returned. It was no day to be out strolling on the boulevards. It was a day to stay inside where it was dry and warm, but inside a bar with the rain hammering at the windows wasn't his idea of discovering Paris. He might be anywhere, Rome, Copenhagen, Lübeck, even London.

Funny, he thought, when I've passed through Paris before, when there was no time to see the place, the sun always shone and it all looked terrific. I was sorry I couldn't stay and look around. Now here I am and it's no better than a wet Sunday in Kilburn. And he let his mind drift back to London, to Kilburn and his childhood. But his memory, as it does with everyone, played him false. It told him that when he was a child playing with his friends in the narrow terraced backstreets the sun had always shone and the days had always been warm and bright. There had been no cold, wet days, not until he'd grown up, when suddenly the warmth and sunshine somehow got switched off at the plug and a cold greyness had begun to seep inexorably into his soul.

Shit. Forget it, what's done is done, it can't be mended or changed. It's finished and gone. What was it Danny said? Let the dead past bury its dead. His mind went back to a dirty, side-street bar in Rome and a big West Indian who hated coffee, wouldn't drink alcohol, and had a laugh like a bass drum.

Jimmy smiled to himself. Good bloke, Danny, but too clever for his own good. Even so he wasn't wrong, leave the dead alone and maybe they'll leave you alone. He got up from his table, went to the bar, paid, and left the café.

He pulled his collar up as far as it would go, pushed his hands deep into the pockets of his light raincoat, waited at the kerb then crossed the road and walked alongside the wall below which was the embankment and then the wide, muddy Seine. He was headed for the bridge which would take him over the river onto the Isle de la Cité. He didn't want to be out in the rain so he was heading for somewhere inside that couldn't be anywhere but Paris. He walked on quickly hunched up against the rain, a stocky, crumpled, middle-aged man with short, grizzled hair. He might not like the weather, but it fitted him. A cold, grey day for a cold, grey man.

Chapter Two

Once over the bridge he kept going down a straight, tree-lined road. The small spring leaves seemed to be able to defy the gloom of the day and almost shine as their branches swayed, but maybe it was just the rain easing and the clouds lightening. After a short while the road opened out on the left side onto a big square. Jimmy turned. There were plenty of people here who had braved the weather because beyond the busy square rose up the massive, marvellous front of Notre Dame Cathedral, the place where Jimmy had been heading. Jimmy wasn't surprised the square was so busy, after all, if you've travelled all the way from the US or China or Japan you didn't let a little bit of rain stop you. He passed through the tourists who, under umbrellas, in waterproofs and hats, or just getting wet, were laughing, talking, looking, snapping themselves and each other on their cameras and smart phones. They were doing what all visitors did in Paris on wet days, ignoring the rain and enjoying themselves.

Jimmy made his way towards the small entrance in one of the great doors at the foot of the cathedral's glorious façade. He went in, dipped his finger into the holy water stoop, and blessed himself. The soaring space of the interior was filled with the busy hum of voices, lines of tourists were being led through the aisles and people stood in groups, or in twos and threes, or by themselves, gazing at the glory that surrounded them and flash lights gave sudden, brief bursts of bright light. Only a very thin scattering of people knelt in the pews and up the main aisle the great main altar stood aloof, silent and empty. To most of the visitors this wasn't a church, a place of prayer and worship. It was high culture, serious history, a building of almost miraculous beauty the like of which, somehow, we couldn't manage to make any more.

Jimmy looked around and walked to a statue in a quiet corner. It was a woman, a nun. He didn't know who she was nor did he particularly care. He needed someone to pass on a message. It didn't matter who the messenger was so long as it was a saint, someone who was already on that other inside, the one he'd been told about as a child and now found it so hard to believe in. He slipped some coins into the black box below the tray of burning candles, picked up a new one, lit it, and placed it in a holder among the others. Then he took a step back and looked up at the statue.

'Saint whoever you are, I want you to pray that …' But the next bit was always difficult but finally he managed a few words. '… ask God not to let me slip away. Tell him I don't want to just slip away. Ask him to keep me, keep me …' But the words petered out. It never got any easier. He knew it never would. Maybe that was because he wanted to believe, wanted it so badly to be true, and wanting it so much he could never be sure that if he believed it would be no more than self-delusion. He shook his head. If that was how it was then he would never get there. How had Bernie managed it? How had her faith been so simple and so strong, even to the end?

He crossed himself, turned and walked away from the plaster image. It wasn't much of a message and he wasn't sure it would get through, or that anyone was there if it did. But he still tried, tried to hold on for the sake of Bernie, because Bernie had stuck with him and looked after him while he … but again the words petered. Let the dead past bury its dead. It was over, gone, couldn't be changed or mended, so let it go.

Outside the rain had stopped. The umbrellas were coming down. The clouds had noticeably thinned, the gloom of the dark clouds had lifted, bringing a hope of the sun breaking through. Maybe the day wouldn't be so bad after all.

Jimmy turned down the collar of his coat and walked away,

heading for the nearest Metro to go see and talk to another nun, a real one this time, not a plaster image.

He was half way back along the tree-lined road when the clouds suddenly parted, the sun came out, and the dreary dampness of the streets changed magically. The drips on the leaves began to sparkle, the wet pavement glistened as the sun hit it, the dark roofs took on a wet brightness, and the window shutters and black ironwork balconies on the upper floors of the buildings on either side no longer looked grim, but now offered a happy and elaborate counterpoint to the light colouring of the Empire frontages so quintessentially Parisian. The red, wet pantiles of the roofs seemed to come to life and glow as the sun streamed into the streets. All around him the place seemed suddenly alive, full of light. What was it that name they used? *La Ville Lumière*. City of Light. Jimmy instinctively lost some of his crumpled look, straightened up, and walked on with a livelier step.

The Seine flowed heavily under the bridge as he crossed but even the dirty water managed a few glistening twinkles up at him as the sun caught its ripples. The clouds were clearing fast and there was the promise of a fine afternoon to make up for the foul morning.

Jimmy left the bridge and crossed the main road. The café was just down on his left. Maybe he'd come back later and sit outside in the sun, have a beer, and watch Paris go by. His whole mood lifted. He felt better. Perhaps this time it really would be something easy, something straightforward, just find a missing person. Nothing evil, nothing life threatening. Nothing that would get him or anyone else killed. He looked around and brightened. April in Paris, Paris in the spring, all as per the brochure. All very ooh, la, la. Oh yes, all very much ooh la bloody la.

Chapter Three

'There are only three of us here now and I am the youngest at seventy-eight. Sister Alphonse has to use a wheelchair if she leaves the convent,' there was a pause, Jimmy waited, 'which she never does these days so it doesn't really matter. Sister Agatha can do nothing because of the arthritis in her joints although, with difficulty, she can still manage the rosary.' The little nun sitting opposite Jimmy suddenly looked at him aggressively. 'Of course there is no question of her kneeling, no one could expect that.'

Jimmy felt as if he had just suggested that Sr Agatha should, at this very minute and despite her crippled joints, be on her knees somewhere, praying.

'No. Of course not. No one could expect that.' The little nun seemed grudgingly satisfied. Jimmy waited but she just sat. He decided to gently get things going again. 'You speak good English.'

'I was sent to Cameroon, the French-speaking part, but then I was moved and they all spoke English so I had to learn. I didn't want to learn but in those days discipline was discipline. Today, of course, it is all different. If someone …'

Having got her going again Jimmy tried, again gently, to steer her back to why he was there.

'You must be sorry the convent is closing.'

'Yes, the convent is closing. It has been difficult. There are only three of us and I am the youngest at seventy-eight. Sister Alphonse has to use a wheelchair if she leaves the convent.' Jimmy worried for a second that she'd got stuck in some sort of loop and would keep going back to the beginning, but she carried on. 'But I'm not complaining, you understand.' Jimmy nodded trying to look as if he understood. 'We are provided with help, a young woman comes each day to see to household matters, there is another woman who cooks, and a nurse who visits regularly each week.' The nun looked at Jimmy who tried to smile encouragingly but the nun ignored him and carried on, talking, apparently to herself, or to nobody. 'When I joined we young nuns looked after the old ones. We were a community in those days. Now there are no young ones so Sister Alphonse sits in her chair, Sister Agatha says the rosary when she can, and I have to deal with whatever needs to be dealt with. But at least I am mobile which is a blessing,' she lapsed into a short silence, maybe saying a prayer of thanks for the blessing of being the one who had to deal with everything, 'although I fully expect that I will find myself similarly placed as Sr Alphonse and Sr Agatha in the not-too-distant future,' she paused, 'if God spares me.'

She said it as if sparing her was the sort of nasty trick she expected God to play on her. Jimmy could see why she would feel that way.

She was small, even in the voluminous black habit and the long, black veil that covered her head and shoulders. She sat facing Jimmy with her hands in her lap. They were in a cold, bare room lit only by what daylight could force its way in through two grimy, lattice-leaded windows. The walls were covered with a dull paper with no discernable pattern except for three bright rectangular patches of pale green with small, faded yellow flowers where pictures had once hung. The carpet was badly worn and wouldn't be going anywhere when the place closed except into a skip. An empty bulb socket hung from a flex in the centre of the ceiling.

'How long before it closes?'

'The house is already being emptied. Most of the rooms are finished. Soon we also will have gone. The Blessed Sacrament was removed from the chapel months ago. We were promised a priest would visit but …'

Jimmy thought he detected a shrug of the shoulders but it was difficult to be sure. He waited for her to continue but her attention seemed to have wandered off. He tried to bring her back.

'Professor McBride said you wanted someone found.'

She looked at him with puzzled frown.

'Professor McBride?'

'In Rome, at the Collegio Principe. She sent me. You asked for someone to come.'

This time there definitely was a shrug.

'I know nothing of any Professor or any Collegio.' She fell silent again. Jimmy felt that at any moment he would either scream or jump up, grab her, and shake her, but then she got going again. 'Still, if you come from Rome …' She suddenly looked at him, studying him for a second. 'If you're a priest you should dress like one. I don't like all this modern nonsense of not wearing proper habits. If you're a priest or a …'

'I'm not a priest, I just help out when things need to be done.'

'Not a priest?'

'No.'

She seemed to lose interest.

'Oh, well, if you're not a priest then I don't suppose it matters how you dress.'

Jimmy tried to get the meeting back on track.

'I was told to come here because you wanted someone found.'

'That is correct.'

'Who? Who do you want found?'

The old nun looked surprised at the question.

'I have no idea.'

'Oh, for Christ's sake …'

The words crashed, unspoken, against the back of Jimmy's teeth. He told himself that he had to stay patient and gentle, that she was a confused old nun who was being kicked out of her convent, that it wasn't her fault. He tried, but it wasn't easy with such a rambling old stick in the mud.

He gathered himself together and spoke slowly and clearly. She wasn't deaf but he felt he had to do something.

'I'm sorry, Sister, I don't understand. I was told you would explain.'

She gave him a withering look as if he was a particularly backward child who was making no effort with what little brains he had.

'Oh I can explain. We want you to find the owner of this house.'

He waited but nothing more came. She sat looking at him. That, apparently, was it, that was the explanation!

'But the nuns own it, it's a convent. Your order must own it if it's a convent.'

The old nun raised a tiny hand and waved away his words. She'd had enough.

'All of that side of it you must get from the lawyers. We are leaving, the convent is closed, finished. Now the building must be returned. Wait.' She rummaged about inside her habit and finally pulled out a letter. She handed it to him. 'The address is the firm who are handling it. Inside is my letter giving you authority to act on our behalf. The lawyers will explain everything.' She stood up. She was only slightly taller than when she was sitting. 'Now I must go. There are still things to do. Good day.'

The meeting was over, he'd been given his instructions and was now dismissed. Jimmy followed her back to the big main door which she pulled open. Jimmy stepped out into the bright sunlight, the door closed heavily behind him, and he heard a bolt being shot into place.

He had never liked nuns, never since he was a child at school where the headmistress had been a nun. A cruel bitch, he remembered. But he felt some sympathy for the one who had just given him the letter. Seventy-eight and being turned out of what she obviously looked on as her home. No wonder she was a grumpy, rambling dodderer. Poor old sod. Still, it was none of his business. His business lay elsewhere, with the lawyers who would explain everything.

Chapter Four

Jimmy stood for a moment and enjoyed the warmth of the sun. It was pleasant after the cold interior of the big, empty convent. He looked at the letter which was still in his hand, then put it into his pocket. The letter could wait, whatever the batty old nun wanted could wait; it was time for lunch, somewhere with Parisian atmosphere. He looked up and down the street. It was a classy part of the city, old and elegant. True, the buildings directly opposite were all offices, but discreet offices with polished brass plates and elegant, restrained lettering in the street-level windows. The sort of offices that no one ever seems to go into or come out of but nonetheless smell of money, old money and plenty of it. He looked at the window straight opposite. *Galvani et cie. Notaires Avocats*. Odd, thought Jimmy, that in a place so French the name he picked out was Italian. He looked up and down the street, the whole place looked quietly wealthy. That was good, he shouldn't have any trouble finding somewhere to eat that fitted what he wanted. Paris class and style, the works. Why not? He could go to the lawyer after lunch, there was no hurry, whatever it was didn't seem urgent or important. He could take his time and enjoy himself.

He went down the steps and joined the other sprinkling of pedestrians walking in the sunshine.

The first restaurant he came to was about four hundred metres away from the convent. It was expensive-looking in the same reserved way as the offices and very much Jimmy's idea of what it was he wanted. He looked in through the window. It wasn't crowded but that didn't mean anything, from what he'd heard nobody hurried their lunch in this city, so it could still be early. He went in.

A young woman in crisp white blouse and black skirt was standing beside a tall stand on which rested the reservations book. She looked at him as he came in. Jimmy had seen that sort of look before. He guessed he wasn't what they were used to or wanted, but it didn't bother him. As a detective sergeant in London he'd turned up in lots of places where people thought he didn't belong. Here, at least, they probably wouldn't take him into the back alley and try to kick the shit out of him.

'*Oui, M'sieur.*'

'I'm sorry I don't speak French. Do you speak English?'

'Yes, sir.'

'Good, a table for one.' The hesitation was only momentary, but it was there and they both knew it. 'Unless you're fully booked.' Jimmy looked around then back at the young woman. 'But you don't look fully booked, not at the moment.'

'This way, sir.'

Jimmy followed and one or two of the early diners looked up at him. They didn't think he fitted either. The young woman came to a table at the back of the room, well away from the door and windows, and pulled out a chair.

'May I take your raincoat?'

Jimmy pulled it off and handed it over. She might be young but she knew her job well enough. The raincoat was crumpled and nondescript but the jacket, although it wasn't Paris chic, was expensive and, she guessed, Italian, Rome or Milan. The rest of his ensemble hung badly but she could see that they had all started life in some shop that didn't put the price-tags on their merchandise. English-speaking in good-quality Italian clothes who was comfortable in high-class places even if he didn't look the part. It made a difference. As she put his raincoat carefully over her arm she gave him a big smile to make up for the doubtful start. Whatever he was he had the right clothes even if they did nothing for his appearance.

Jimmy sat down.

'Anything to drink, sir?'

'A beer.'

'Any particular brand?'

'Just as it comes, and not chilled if you can.'

'Certainly, sir.'

She headed off with his raincoat and his order. A waiter arrived and placed a menu before him, removed the other setting at the table, and left. Jimmy picked up the menu. In Rome he ate very simply but this was his first proper visit to Paris and he wanted to do it right. The menu meant little to him except the figures in the right hand column. They, like the decoration of the place, impressed him. He decided he'd talk it over with whoever served him and put the menu down. The girl arrived with the beer and set the bottle and glass down on the table.

'Leave it, I'll pour when I'm ready.' Jimmy pointed to the menu. 'What would you recommend out of this lot?' The girl seemed not to understand so Jimmy went on. 'This is my first real visit to Paris and this is my first proper lunch here. I want it to be something, well, something really Parisian. What would you suggest?'

The girl gave him a smile of understanding then picked up the menu and pointed to something. Jimmy looked at her choice and even with his limited knowledge of the language saw that what she was recommending was the dish of the day.

'Wherever you eat in Paris I suggest you always look first at the *plat du jour*. It is always freshly cooked and is usually a speciality of the chef. It is only a suggestion, you understand, but it may help.'

'Good thinking, Batwoman.' She looked at him puzzled. 'It's a joke, a way of saying well done. *Plat du jour*, then.'

'No starter?'

'No.'

'Wine?'

Jimmy didn't much care for wine. He drank it more often since he'd been living in Rome but he wasn't so very keen on it. Still, if this was France.

'You choose, a bottle of something good to go with the *plat du jour*. I'll leave it to you.'

She picked up the menu, smiled again, and left. Jimmy poured himself some beer. He liked the place, it was pricey but they were friendly, once they got to know you. He took a drink. It was OK, nothing special, but at least it wasn't chilled. He made a silent toast to himself.

To Paris in the spring.

Then he sat back and got ready to enjoy his first real Parisian lunch. The job, whatever it was, could wait. This afternoon or, if the lunch was really good, tomorrow, he'd get in touch with the lawyers. Today he was busy being a tourist and he intended to enjoy it.

Chapter Five

'All I was told was to find someone, a missing person. I was given no identity, no name, no nothing. What I was given was your name and address on a letter of authorisation, so here I am. That's it.'

The lawyer sat back, put the tips of his fingers together, and looked over them through rimless glasses.

'Hmm.'

Jimmy waited. The lawyer seemed reluctant to get going.

Maybe he's had a better lunch than me, thought Jimmy, and doesn't like someone popping up without an appointment so soon after he's eaten.

Jimmy's lunch, though expensive, had been a disappointment. The wine had been OK but the actual meal had been sort of chicken casserole, not so very unlike something his mum might have knocked up back in Kilburn. He'd expected something, well, different, more French, more Parisian. Chicken stew with extra veg. on the side, that's all it had been really. Christ, he might as well have ordered bacon and bloody cabbage.

The lawyer surfaced again and sat forward.

'Hmm. Yes.'

He was elderly, thin, and bald, with suspicious eyes behind his glasses. He continued to look at Jimmy but said nothing. The lunch had left Jimmy feeling dissatisfied and vaguely angry and the lawyer's manner wasn't helping. His let his voice express his mood.

'The person who sent me didn't know who I would be

looking for, neither did the nun who gave me the letter this morning. If I'm going to go on with this I hope you know who I'm supposed to find.'

The lawyer slowly shook his head. His English was good, very good and very accurate, but accented, as if he was saying, 'I speak your language as well as you, but I remain French and therefore not like you'.

'No, Mr Costello, I'm afraid I cannot give you that information either. I have no idea who it is you will be looking for.'

Jimmy decided he'd had enough.

'Look, sunshine, I don't like being pissed about, and I get the feeling I'm being well and truly pissed about so either tell me what this is all about or bloody well …'

The lawyer took it very calmly.

'No, not "pissed about" as you put it, Mr Costello, merely being answered accurately. I do not know who you will be looking for. Nobody does.' And he raised a hand as Jimmy was about to speak. 'Let me explain. The sisters have had their convent here in Paris for many years. You visited it this morning so you will know it is closing down. I was approached by a priest friend to assist them. You see they, or more accurately their order, do not own the convent, they rent it. The house was the property of a lady who left Paris at the end of the war and the house was given to the sisters at a peppercorn rent. When the lady died some years ago, in Switzerland, she left everything to her daughter. Unfortunately there was no trace of this daughter. The lady's will made the sisters executors of her estate and allowed them to continue on in the house on condition that the daughter was found. Once found, the daughter would be free to decide what was to be done with her property. The sisters instituted enquiries through a firm of lawyers in Basel, also through a firm in Paris. No information on the daughter could be found. The matter, shall we say, lapsed – until now. Now the sisters are leaving, like many religious orders their numbers in Europe are diminished almost to the point of extinction, but in South America, apparently, they thrive. Their Paris convent will be closed, so the search for the missing daughter must resume and if no daughter can be found then we must look for the deceased lady's nearest living relative. That is your missing person, Mr Costello, the rightful heir to Mme Colmar, our deceased lady from Switzerland.'

Jimmy relaxed, he was off the hook. He could go back to being a tourist for a few days, see the sights, get some proper French cooking, and then go home.

'It's not a job for me, I'd be no good to you or the sisters. I wouldn't know where to begin. It's a legal thing.'

'Would you say so?'

Jimmy smiled, he felt better.

'I just did, sunshine.'

'You feel you must decline to assist?'

Jimmy decided to get a little bit of his own back. He couldn't do a French accent very well, but he did his best.

'Yes, decline to assist. I feel I must.' He reverted to his normal voice and was about to stand. 'Now, sunshine, if there's nothing else …'

'Before you make a final decision, Mr Costello, may I urge you to check with Rome, with Professor McBride?'

Jimmy sat back.

'You knew she sent me?'

'Of course. I was told to expect you. The letter you were given was a confirmation not an introduction. I am told Professor McBride most strongly recommended you.'

'You spoke to her?'

'No, to the superior of the sisters' order. It was she who first raised the matter once the decision to close the convent was finalised. She was in Rome and was advised to talk to Professor McBride. Professor McBride recommended you and the superior contacted me to say that I should expect you to get in touch. That was about two weeks ago. I do not normally see visitors who arrive without an appointment but in your case I made an exception. That should indicate to you how seriously I regard this matter. I hope you will come to see it in the same light.'

Jimmy thought about it. It all sounded right and the lawyer seemed straight enough even if he was a snotty bugger. But why had McBride got herself involved? It was just a missing heir, wasn't it? Or was it? McBride might be a devious bastard but she never did anything without a reason. In fact she never did anything without several reasons, all very good ones. The problem was, you never knew which one was the real one.

Jimmy stood up.

'I'll talk to her, but don't get your hopes up.'

There was almost a self-satisfied smirk around the lawyer's mouth as if he had scored some sort of point.

'Good day, Mr Costello. Thank you for coming.'

The lawyer didn't get up or offer to shake hands. He sat back and put his fingers together again and let the rimless glasses play over Jimmy.

Jimmy looked down at him.

'Hmm.'

'I beg your pardon, Mr Costello. Did you say something?'

Jimmy managed a smile. He thought it would annoy the lawyer. It did, so Jimmy kept it going.

'I said, "hmm".'

'And that means?'

'It means, hmm.'

Jimmy turned and left. He didn't bother to close the door.

Outside the offices the sun was still shining and Jimmy tried to get back the feeling he'd had before lunch, of Paris in the spring. So what if the lunch had been nothing special? There was still the Eiffel Tower, the Louvre, and all the other stuff. Most of all there was Paris itself, just enjoying the place.

He set off walking. Time enough to get in touch with McBride tomorrow. She'd probably planned it that he would have to call her, so she would be waiting. OK, let her wait. Tomorrow, or maybe even the next day. Right now he had more important things to do. He had to walk along the Seine, see some of the sights, visit Sacré Coeur. And he had to leave enough time to plan his dinner. He didn't want to take pot luck again with any dish of the day. This time he wanted to get it right. He headed back the way he had come to the nearest Metro.

In the office the lawyer was on the phone.

'He was very much as described, Professor, not an easy man nor particularly pleasant. I told him to get in touch with you as I had been instructed. Very well, I will wait to hear from you.'

The lawyer replaced the phone.

He had not communicated directly with Professor McBride before, and, as he was a thorough and a careful man, as soon as he had been told about her involvement he had given her and the Collegio Principe some careful attention.

The Collegio was an obscure college founded in the late sixteenth century from a bequest in the will of one of the minor Borgias. The income from several farms had been given over to its support. The Collegio was originally staffed by Dominican friars and its purpose, apart from praying for the soul of its founder, was to study the relationship between politics, power, and religion. Through the centuries the Collegio became a secular institution and its farmland became modern office blocks, the income from which meant that the small Collegio, unlike so many other bigger and better known academic institutions, never had any money worries. In fact it was wealthy.

Apart from its history, the lawyer's enquiries had indicated that the Collegio, in the person of a Professor McBride, seemed to have considerable political influence but in an ill-defined and even shadowy sort of way. In particular it had some sort of relationship with the Vatican, nothing official and nothing sufficiently concrete and demonstrable that any lawyer would consider it suitable for use as evidence into a court of law. Nonetheless the lawyer was convinced that a definite relationship existed.

He looked down at the phone he had just replaced. The man who had left, this Englishman, was no ordinary private investigator. His manner was all wrong and his attitude abrasive. He was more like a policeman, a detective. Or perhaps a criminal. Both? The lawyer mused for a moment on Jimmy then decided that whatever he was, he was someone well used to trouble and trouble would undoubtedly attend whatever involved him. He then moved his mind to Professor McBride. Her accent was American. That had surprised him and, in his opinion, did not bode well. This Englishman Costello had unsettled him. Any connection with the Vatican, no matter how remote, unofficial, or unintended, unsettled him. And now an American. The Vatican was bad enough, but if the Americans were involved …

He would have to tread very carefully in this matter for he seriously doubted if it was at all as straightforward as he had been led to believe. Yes, he doubted it very much indeed.

He sat back and put the tips of his fingers together and uttered softly to himself.

'Hmm.'

Chapter Six

Jimmy finally made his call to Rome the following night at eleven. Since his visit to the lawyer he'd been a tourist and he'd enjoyed it. But enough was enough. Paris might be another place, a new place, a different place, but he was still the same, he wasn't any different just because he was in a different city. He'd had his break, now he had to get on.

He was standing on the small balcony outside his room, recessed into the steeply sloping roof among the red pantiles on the top floor of his hotel. If Professor McBride resented the delay in his calling or the lateness of the hour there was no trace of it in her voice.

'Yes, Mr Costello? All is going well in Paris I hope?'

'All is going as you expected it would.'

'Which means?'

'Which means I'm calling you because the lawyer told me to. Don't expect me to believe you two haven't spoken since I visited him.'

'He called me, yes, and he doesn't seem to like you.'

'That's all right, I don't like him. But that apart, what's going on? Why am I here? And don't screw me around with that missing person crap.'

'No, Mr Costello, it is not, as you put it, crap. M. Joubert was quite accurate in what he told you. The sisters are leaving, the convent is being closed. They need to find the rightful owner, the heir to Mme Colmar. I was asked to help the sister superior and I sent you.'

'And?'

'What do you mean, and?'

'And the rest? The bit that tells me why I'm here.'

'The rest. There has to be the rest?'

'Oh yes.'

'Well then, the rest. Briefly, Mme Colmar was a well-known collaborator with the Germans and lived in that house as the mistress of a Waffen SS officer during the Occupation. Just before Paris was liberated she left and moved to Switzerland. She gave the house to the sisters at a nominal rent to use as a convent. It is generally believed that her motive was nothing to do with any goodness of heart or religious conviction but rather a way of ensuring her property was not confiscated and remained legally in her possession. All of that is in the public domain. What is not in the public domain is in a short dossier which I sent to M. Joubert. The dossier will provide you with information which will, having read it, help you to understand why you are there.'

'Why couldn't you just tell me before I came?'

'Because I wanted you to behave naturally, to be yourself.'

'You didn't have to hide things. You could have trusted me.'

'No I couldn't. You behaved exactly as I wanted you to behave. I'm sure you were very convincing. The sister you spoke to will tell anyone who asks that you were exactly what you said you were, as indeed will M. Joubert. It sounds like you made exactly the right impression on him. All you have to do now is go back to M. Joubert's office, pick up the dossier, read it, and get on with the job in hand.'

'Which will be?'

'Find an heir to Mme Colmar.'

'Any particular one?'

'No, it matters not at all who inherits her estate, so long as we are the ones who find whoever it is. Just do a thorough job, one that will stand up to close, legal inspection. Goodbye.'

And she was gone.

He slipped his phone into his pocket and looked down. Across the road from his hotel were the lights and bustle of the Gare de l'Est. The headlights of the traffic still flowed busily and the cafés and restaurants, of which there were many, poured light out onto the streets. This part of Paris looked nowhere near like going to sleep. He looked across at the dark roofs opposite. Beyond them, under the night sky, he could see the Paris landmarks which were lit up. Away to the left, high on its hill like a large, white, celebration cake, was Sacré Coeur. He hadn't made a visit to it yet, he'd spent too long in other places. He looked across the dark city and decided that he liked Paris, it hadn't disappointed, apart from that first lunch, and you can forgive any city one disappointing lunch.

He went back into his room, closed the French windows, and began to get ready for bed. He'd had a good time over the past two days, he'd seen a lot, eaten well, now he was tired. Being a tourist was all very well but it wasn't something he could do for long. He needed to get working, to be up and doing. Tomorrow he would get the dossier and he had no doubts that, having read it, he would understand why he was here and what it was he was supposed to do. If McBride said that's how it would be, that was exactly how it would be. Although it probably wouldn't be all that it would be.

Chapter Seven

The following morning at ten thirty M. Joubert was not in the office. The receptionist said he was away on business but he'd left an envelope to be collected by a Monsieur Costello whom he had said would call. She knew who he was from his previous visit but just as a formality he showed her his passport, which he always had on him, and she handed over the envelope. It was the big, strong padded sort with no label or writing. He took it, left, made his way to a nearby café, and, after ordering a coffee, opened it. Inside there was a plastic folder containing two sheets of paper and copies of three old photographs. One sheet was covered with print and the other had a couple of lines of handwriting. Jimmy pushed the photos and the short note to one side and began reading the page of printed text.

The woman known as Mme Colmar was born Alicia Müller in the German Alsace in 1912. She was the second child of a wealthy industrialist. The family were ruined during WW1. Her father committed suicide shortly before being arrested for selling substandard materials to the German army which cost the lives of a considerable number of troops. After the war ended Alicia, with her mother and an older brother, left Germany and went to America. Nothing is known of Alicia's life there until a Boston police report of 1928 that stated her brother had died in a knife-fight in a brothel. Alicia was named as one of the girls working in the brothel and the brother was identified as part-owner. The next report of Alicia appears in a confidential file from the Boston Mayor's Office dated 1931. Local politicians, senior police officers, and important local businessmen were named as regular clients of a local madam who ran a high-class establishment. The file indicated that blackmail of clients was strongly suspected and that evidence of considerable sums from clients had been paid into accounts which were indirectly controlled by the madam. There was a reference to an appendix containing statements from some of those clients who were suspected of being victims of this blackmail. That appendix seems to have been removed at some point from the report. The file was stamped as inactive with a note that no official action was recommended. This note was initialled by the then chief of police and countersigned by the deputy mayor on behalf of the mayor. Alicia was the madam. Nothing more is known of her until she registered the birth of a daughter, Thèrése , born at a private hospital in 1934. No father's name appeared on the birth certificate.

Alicia next surfaced in Paris in 1937 where she bought a large house in a fashionable neighbourhood. By that time she had become Mme Colmar. From the records of various transactions and from other reliable sources it seems that she presented herself as an American widow with one daughter, wealthy and a devout Catholic. Before Paris fell to the Germans in 1940 Mme Colmar sent her daughter to the US. Shortly after her daughter left a young Waffen SS officer attached to the German Paris Headquarters staff moved into her house and Mme Colmar openly assumed the role of his mistress. From Paris she made frequent trips to Switzerland. A short time before the D-Day landings in June 1944 the officer was transferred to the Eastern Front. Soon after the allies had landed in Normandy Mme Colmar closed her house and left for Switzerland. Through lawyers in Switzerland she rented her Paris house to an order of nuns who took up residence at the end of the war. Mme Colmar lived on in Switzerland until she died in 2000 aged 88. In her will she left everything to her daughter, Thèrése , and made the nuns in Paris her executors on condition they instituted a thorough search for the daughter. They were given permission to stay at the house until her daughter was found and could decide for herself what would happen to the property.

No trace of the daughter could be found. An examination of what records are available show that she was sent to the US by her mother in 1940 at the age of six and was placed in a convent boarding school. All fees and other expenses were paid by a lawyer's office in Manhattan. She appears to have had no visitors and spent her holidays at the school among the nuns. School records show her as a talented pupil who could speak four languages fluently by the age of twelve and loved music, especially the singing of Gregorian chants. She ran away from her convent school at 16 with a black musician in 1950. How she met him no one knew. They disappeared. If she is still alive there is still no trace of where she is or if she had any children.

As far as can be ascertained Mme Colmar, née Müller, had no other known relatives. If no heir can be found within a reasonable time her considerable wealth will be disposed of through a Swiss court.

Jimmy put the sheet of paper down and picked up a photo. It was a woman in her mid-twenties. She was beautiful but her looks were diminished somewhat by the severity of her black dress and the way she looked out of the picture, unsmiling, with eyes that told you nothing. It was a posed portrait probably in a photographer's studio. He turned over the photo. Handwritten on the back was:

Mme Colmar 1937 location unknown.

The other photo was of a young German SS officer in dress uniform. Jimmy looked at the back. Also handwritten was, *Obersturmführer Erich Streubel 1939. Promoted Hauptsturmführer 1940 and posted to Paris HQ. Promoted Sturmbannführer 1942. Promoted Obersturmbannführer 1944 and posted to the eastern front. Died in 2006 as the result of a hit and run incident in Munich while in his wheelchair outside his care home.*

Jimmy turned the photo over, looked at the young soldier, and did a quick calculation. If he'd been around twenty when he was in Paris then in 2006 he'd have to have been in his eighties. How the hell does somebody survive the whole of a war, including a spell on the Eastern Front, and then get killed over sixty years later in his wheelchair outside his care home? He went back to the writing. The ranks meant nothing but one date did – 1940. Promoted, posted to Paris HQ, and shacked up with Mme Colmar all in one year. Good going even for wartime.

Jimmy picked up the last photo, a sad-looking, pretty young girl in her early teens in a school blazer and tartan skirt, standing beside a smiling nun in full old-fashioned rig-out. On the back was written,

Thèrése Colmar and an unknown sister 1947.

That was all. He put it down beside the other two photos and picked up the short note which was handwritten in the same hand as the writing on the backs of the photos.

Gathering this information has almost certainly alerted other parties to our involvement in this matter. The value of the inheritance is substantial and we must presume others know about it and are interested, especially in the light of the death of Erich Streubel. We must act accordingly.

Jimmy pushed everything together, put it all into the plastic folder and back into the envelope.

He liked the way she said 'our involvement' and 'we must act accordingly'.

He spoke almost silently to himself.

'Sod the "we". I'm the only one out in the open on this. Anyone interested will be watching Paris not Rome which means they'll be watching me.'

But she was right about one thing, he would definitely have to act accordingly.

He took a sip of his coffee. It was cold so he left it. He had only bought it to be able to sit at the table and go through the dossier.

He let his mind go through what he knew so far.

Colmar was put on the game by her brother from a very early age and it must have taken plenty of guts to get off her back and set up in business for herself. And she was shrewd, she had brains. She didn't set up just any old cat-house, it was high-class with the right kind of customers, ones who would make sure she and they were left alone. But they were also the ones who would be most vulnerable to blackmail.

Yes, thought Jimmy, a strong, smart lady. A lady who knew how to take care of herself. A lady who was trouble even from beyond the grave.

Chapter Eight

The waiter passed and Jimmy ordered a beer. It was still a bit early but he wanted to sit and think and he didn't want another coffee.

Colmar had used her business to burrow into the underbelly of Boston's establishment and that had probably given her a fair share of powerful friends. But her sideline in blackmail must also have given her plenty of equally powerful enemies. Running a brothel and blackmailing your best clients was a very dangerous game so maybe, if the enemies started getting too close, that was why she jumped over to Europe. Or maybe she decided she'd milked enough from her racket and wanted some sort of life for herself and her kid while she was still young enough to enjoy it. If that was how it was then she wouldn't stay in America. In America she could never be sure of being safe. But even living in Europe she would have made sure she'd got some solid insurance tucked away somewhere in case anyone decided to come looking for her.

The beer arrived. Jimmy poured some into his glass and took a drink.

But Colmar didn't stay retired, did she? She may have meant to become a comfortable, pious bourgeois lady and mother, but the war got in the way. And she obviously still hadn't got her old habits out of her system. She was up to something during the occupation of Paris and it wasn't just rumpy-pumpy with a dashing Young Hitler from the SS. And whatever she was up to in the war had surfaced again and was important enough to get McBride involved, which means somehow it involves the

Church.

Jimmy pulled out the printed notes and checked them. She'd died in 2000 so that would be when her goods, whatever they were, came up for grabs. Whatever she had amongst them it seemed no one was in any hurry to get hold of it during her lifetime. However she'd done it, the old girl had made sure that as long as she was alive she and her property were left alone. But if someone was interested why not make a move as soon as she died? Why not put in some sort of claim? It wasn't as if the daughter was sitting on the lawyer's step waiting to collect her inheritance.

He let his mind circle the question. Maybe they wanted to see if the legitimate heir, the daughter, would surface. No, they'd have been watching and as soon as the nuns gave up they'd have made a move to stake their claim, and nobody had made any move. The thing just lapsed. Then, six years after Ma Colmar hands in her chips, somebody pops Young Hitler while he's outside his care home sitting in his wheelchair. That had to be a planned killing. Who the hell gets killed in an accident like that? In a wheelchair parked outside a care home. How weird is that for a way to die, for God's sake?

Jimmy lined up the questions.

Why wait so long? If there was something important in the estate why not manufacture a claim when the daughter didn't surface? And why kill Young Hitler? He had no claim on the estate, did he? Or did he? Maybe he had some sort of claim but didn't know it.

As Jimmy's mind circled the questions came, plenty of questions. As for answers … there were none. Yet.

Jimmy took a drink and poured the rest of the beer from the bottle into his glass. There was no doubt that Young Hitler, he checked the name, Erich Streubel, had been murdered, '… as the result of a hit and run incident.' Some bloody incident.

Jimmy put the papers and photos back together and closed the folder. OK, he'd read the dossier. What was he supposed to do? McBride said he'd know.

He called the waiter and ordered another beer. This needed

thinking about. One thing was certain, it wasn't going to be easy or straightforward and at least one person had already been killed. The more he looked into this thing the less happy he felt. Not life threatening?

If it looks evil, smells evil, and makes evil noises, then it has to be evil, and he didn't want to be the one in the way when whatever it was it broke loose.

The beer arrived and as he poured it and took a drink he suddenly realised that McBride had been right as always. He now knew exactly what he had to do. It would indeed life-threatening to somebody but, if he was careful and made the right moves from day one, he should be able to make damn sure it wasn't his life that got put in the frame and was threatened. That he would leave to somebody else.

Chapter Nine

He knew it as soon as he got back to his hotel room. They were out there all right and they were watching. It had been well done, very professional, but there was no way you could turn over a room, even a hotel room, and not leave signs for anybody who was used to looking, which meant they didn't mind him knowing he'd had visitors. Maybe they even wanted him to know to see what he would do about it.

OK, what was he going to do?

First things first, ditch the dossier.

Jimmy went down to the reception.

'I'd like something delivered by courier. Can you arrange that?'

'Certainly.'

'Can you make it now, immediately?'

'I will try, sir.'

The man pulled out what looked like a directory, thumbed through it, found what he wanted, and made a call.

'What is it you wish delivered?'

Jimmy put the big envelope on the desk and the man went back to the call, finished, and put the phone down

'The rider will be here shortly.'

Jimmy wrote the lawyer's name and address on the envelope clearly in block capitals and then borrowed a roll of tape and taped it up securely.

'What's the name of the courier company?' The man told him a name. Jimmy picked up the envelope. 'Thanks. I'll wait over there.'

Jimmy walked across the small entrance lobby to a chair and sat down. Nobody came in or went out. It wasn't a busy place, fairly cheap, fairly central, fairly comfortable. It suited him, but it didn't seem a busy place. While he was waiting he thought about his situation. 'Gathering this information has almost certainly alerted other parties to our involvement in this matter.' Well it had certainly done that. 'We must act accordingly.' Fine, but what was *accordingly*? Stick it out in Paris and carry on asking questions? But who was there to ask? The old nun knew nothing and neither, if he could be believed, did Joubert. And even if he did know more than he was telling how did you get it out of him? He wasn't exactly someone you could take into a back alley to persuade, and anyway where was there a good, quiet back alley to use? He didn't know the Paris all the tourists knew never mind the bits that the tourists didn't want to know.

Jimmy went over what he actually had and looked for something to act on, to follow up, preferably something away from Paris. He didn't like the feeling that he was a sitting duck with someone watching him who probably knew all the best back alleys of Paris.

The motorcycle rider walked in and crossed to the reception, pulled off his leather gauntlets, lifted his visor, and spoke to the man behind the desk. He had a stained fluorescent safety vest over his leather jacket with the right company name on the back. Jimmy went over to the desk. There was no way anyone could have slipped in a ringer so well turned out at such short notice, not even if they'd guessed at what he was going to do. The man at reception pointed a pen at Jimmy and the courier turned round. Jimmy held out the envelope.

'By hand to the person it's addressed to. Be sure and hand it over to him,' he pointed to Joubert's name, 'or his secretary if he's not there. Nobody else. Understand?'

The face looked blank from out of the helmet. The rider shrugged and looked at the man behind the desk who said something rapidly in French.

The rider turned back to Jimmy nodded and held out his

hand.

Jimmy held on to the envelope.

'Does he understand? By hand to the name or his secretary, no one else?'

'Of course, M'sieur. It has been explained.'

Jimmy handed over the envelope. The rider took it, put it on the desk, and said something.

Jimmy looked at the man behind the desk.

'Payment, M'sieur.'

'Oh, yeah, of course. How much?'

The reception man told him. Jimmy pulled out his wallet and handed over the notes. The rider stuffed them into his jacket pocket and took out a notebook which he put on the desk beside the envelope. He wrote in the book, tore out a page, and held it out to Jimmy. Jimmy took the page and looked at it. It was his receipt headed with the name of the courier firm.

'Thanks.'

The rider put away his book, picked up the envelope and left. Outside stood a motorbike with a pannier. The rider opened the pannier, flipped the envelope in, closed it, then got on the bike and rode off. Jimmy stood in the doorway and watched him go. There was no way of telling if anyone was following him, the traffic was too busy, it swallowed up the bike as soon as it had pulled away from the hotel.

Jimmy walked back across the lobby to the lift, went up to his room, sat on the bed, and made a call.

'Is M. Joubert in? OK, this is Mr Costello. I've sent a package over by courier. You should have it soon. Tell M. Joubert it is to go straight back to Professor McBride. You understand? That's right, at once using whatever way M. Joubert feels is quickest and safest. Good, thank you.'

He put away his phone and looked around the room again. It was nearly half past one. He thought about a quick lunch but decided he'd have to give it a miss, he could grab something later. It was time to move. He got up and began packing. He always travelled light, one holdall which would be cabin luggage on a flight. He never carried anything which would have to go in the hold and make him hang about at the baggage carousels when the plane landed. It was a habit he'd got into.

Once his packing was complete he went down to reception, settled his bill, then crossed the road to the Gare de l'Est where he got into a taxi at the rank outside the station. He told the driver Charles de Gaulle airport and sat back.

The taxi pulled away and joined the traffic. Jimmy looked out of the window, not that he was looking for anything in particular. If they were following him he wouldn't see them. He was just looking, saying goodbye. It hadn't been a great start to the job but at least he had one piece of solid information worth following up. An old Nazi killed in his wheelchair outside his nursing home in Munich in 2006. It didn't sound too promising but it was somewhere to start and it got him away from Paris and the searchers, whoever they were.

The taxi was caught up in the traffic and moving in that stop-start way taxis do in big cities. The general traffic noise got joined somewhere behind them by a police or ambulance siren. At first the traffic around them ignored it but as it got closer drivers began to slow and then part to make way. A big black Citroen with a blue light on top pulled past them and then across the front of them and stopped. Both back doors opened, two men got out, and walked quickly to the taxi. One pulled the back door open, looked in and said something in French. The taxi driver turned and also started to talk. The second man shouted at the taxi driver who turned and shouted back. The man by the door spoke again to Jimmy. Jimmy didn't know what he was saying but he guessed he was being invited to leave the taxi and join his new friends. The taxi driver and the second man from the Citroen were carrying on their shouted conversation. Vehicle windows were going down, heads were turning towards them. People on the pavements were stopping. A couple of oriental tourists were busy taking pictures. Paris in the spring and free street theatre.

Jimmy got out of the car and the man by the door immediately grabbed his arm. The other man stopped his conversation, came to the back, reached in, and took Jimmy's holdall. All three headed for the Citroen. The driver was now out of his taxi and shouting loudly to everyone and no one. He certainly was pissed off and Jimmy didn't need a translator to interpret. No one had paid him and he was letting everyone know what he thought of it.

The men bundled Jimmy into the back of the Citroen and got in either side of him, the siren started again, and the car reversed and then pulled out into the traffic. The show was over and the traffic began to move again.

Chapter Ten

The siren was now silent and Jimmy sat quietly in the back of the car. He thought about it. The police picking him up was good and bad. It was good that they were coppers but it was bad that they had been watching him and saw him leave his hotel. It was good they didn't mind anyone seeing them lift him but it was bad that it wasn't a regular police car and they weren't uniformed. It was good that he hadn't done anything or really knew anything but it was bad that they must think he'd done something or thought he knew something. And there he stopped. He'd know soon enough when someone told him what it was all about, then he'd really know whether it was good or bad. He sat back and watched as the car muscled its way like every other vehicle through the Paris traffic.

No one spoke and the car left central Paris, travelled on through the suburbs then through the outskirts until Jimmy noticed they had been following the signs for Charles de Gaulle Airport.

Bloody hell, he thought, is that good or bad? It was good that it looked like he was getting a free ride to where he wanted to go, it was bad that the free ride was courtesy of the French police. Still, he'd already decided that whatever McBride had got him mixed up in wasn't going to be easy or straightforward but, as it was the coppers who had lifted him, it shouldn't be life-threatening, not at the moment. Not good, but definitely not so bad, and he looked out of the window as the car headed to the airport.

'You are not desirable.' Jimmy looked at the man speaking.

He didn't need to wear any badges for Jimmy to see he had the senior rank. It was partly the way he spoke and partly the way he carried himself, but mostly it was the way the others called him 'chief'. 'You're not a desirable person, Mr Costello.'

Jimmy's mind went back to another copper in Santander, an inspector, a good-looking blonde with long legs and soft skin. She had found him desirable, but she was dead.

'No, I'm not at all desirable.'

Jimmy sat in front of a plastic-topped office table. The ranking man stood beside the table looking down at him. Another officer stood behind him by the door and one was by the window flossing his teeth. The cops at the door and window were the ones who had picked him up in the Citroen.

The room was modern and anonymous like everything you got in airports, clean and impersonal, somewhere to pass through. Outside the afternoon sun was shining but the blinds were closed and the light was on. The man by the table bent a little so as to be closer.

'I want you to understand that when you leave it would be best to stay gone.'

His English was good enough but heavily accented.

'Better.'

The man by the table pulled himself back upright and looked puzzled.

'"Better?" What do you mean, "better"?'

'Better I stay gone. You shouldn't say best. You need at least three options to use best. Stay or go is only two. Better I stay gone.'

The ranker looked at the other two and said something in French. Neither answered but the one with the floss shrugged his shoulders for both.

Jimmy wondered why he was winding up this bloke. It wouldn't help yet he still went ahead and did it. Why was that?

The senior man went to the door and opened it and stood to one side.

'The message is delivered. You are not wanted in France. Best you stay gone.'

Jimmy didn't move. He'd been given his cue to get up and leave. But he stayed in his chair.

'An undesirable alien, is that what you mean? Am I being deported as an undesirable alien?' The man waiting at the door said nothing. 'Only you never took my passport. Usually they take away your passport if you're getting deported, or so I'm told. I've never been deported myself so I'm not certain about it.' The way the man looked at him changed. Jimmy stood up. He'd pushed it as far as it would go. 'Is this official? Am I barred from re-entry?'

The man still didn't answer.

Jimmy went to the door. The man from the car who was standing there picked up his holdall and held it out. Jimmy took it.

'Thanks.'

He went through the door then turned back to the senior man.

'I take it this isn't official then, that I'm not being deported, that I can come back if I …'

But the man in charge wasn't there any more. He'd gone back into the room and the door had closed.

Jimmy walked down the corridor where over an hour ago he had arrived with his escorts. The one they called chief had kept him waiting to make a point – I can have you picked up, I can keep you as long as I like, I can do what I like with you. It was a good point, well made and well taken, but what had actually happened? Bugger all except telling him to leave. Why all that effort to finish up doing almost bugger all? And why no explanation, no paperwork, nothing except 'sod off'?

It wasn't right, it wasn't the way the police did things, even the French police. But they had to be police, who else could swan around central Paris in a car with a siren and requisition office-space in an international airport? Jimmy gave it up. What did it matter? He was leaving, which was exactly what he'd wanted in the first place.

He walked on and eventually came out of a staff doorway into the main concourse where he looked around for the nearest flight information screen. There was an Air France flight to Munich due out in just under an hour. He went to the Air France desk, bought his ticket then went through security into the Departure lounge where he went to a bar, bought a beer, and sat down at a table. He took out his phone and made a call.

'I read the dossier.'

'Good.'

'Not so good.'

'No?'

'No. My hotel room got turned over and I got picked up by the law.'

'The law? What sort of law?'

'I don't know what sort, just plain-clothes coppers. I'm at the airport now, they're bouncing me out.'

'Good heavens, Mr Costello, what on earth have you been doing?'

'Nothing. I went to the convent then the lawyer and did a bit of sight-seeing in between, that's all.' He paused wondering whether to go on. Then decided why not? 'I assumed it was something you'd arranged.'

'Me! Why would I arrange for such a thing to happen?'

'Well who else is there who might have set it up, Joubert, the old nun, my hotel clerk? All I did was go to the convent, got sent to Joubert, took in some sights then picked up your dossier. Next thing I know, blam, my room's turned over by somebody and then I'm bounced out of the country by the police.' There was a silence. 'You didn't arrange it then?'

'Mr Costello, I sent you to Paris to do a job. Even supposing I could do such a thing, why would I arrange for you to be ejected by the French police only days after your arrival when you've hardly had a chance to get started?'

It was a silly question coming from her, why did she do anything? Jimmy ignored it.

'Whoever tossed my room must have known I was coming, so did the police. They were both waiting. They must have been. Somebody tipped them off,' he paused, 'like they did in Santander.'

There was silence for a moment. His point had got home, he could tell, because when she spoke again the sharpness that had been in her voice was gone and was replaced by concern.

'I assure you it wasn't me this time. Where is the dossier, was it taken from your room?'

'No.'

'Do the police have it?'

'No. I read it in a café after I'd picked it up from Joubert's office. As soon as I got back to the hotel and saw my room had been done I sent it back to him by motorcycle delivery with a message to get it safely off to you as quick as he could.'

'I'll check with M. Joubert.' There was another silence. 'Are you coming back to Rome?'

'I can, but I thought I'd follow up on the bloke in the hit and run in Munich, Ma Colmar's ex-lover. It gets me out of Paris and it's all I've got so far. There's nothing else.'

Another silence.

'I have something.'

'Oh yes?'

'A woman.'

'What sort of woman?'

'A woman who may be what you're looking for.'

Jimmy smiled to himself and shook his head. She was indeed a devious bastard.

'You had her up your sleeve all along, didn't you?'

'Yes. I was going to introduce her into the matter when I thought the time was right but as it is …'

'As it is you'll have to tell me the truth instead of giving me the usual run-around.'

'Yes, unfortunately I can see no other way.'

'So, do you want me to come back to Rome and give Young Hitler the elbow?'

'Young Hitler?'

'Ma Colmar's SS lover-boy.'

'No, follow that up. I doubt it will give us anything but my woman isn't ready to be put into the picture yet, it's too premature. Really, Mr Costello, I thought I might have been able to rely on you simply to do as you were told for a few days at least.'

'Not get turned over and bounced out? No, well, if it's any consolation, I wasn't expecting it myself.'

'No, I suppose you are not altogether to blame but please do try not to make any more ...'

She paused looking for the right words. Jimmy offered a suggestion.

'Fuss?'

'Any more complications. This is a delicate enough matter without you making it more so.'

Jimmy was about to say something but thought better of it. Just get on with the job.

'What about your woman?'

'I'll tell you what I decide about that when you report in from Munich. I wanted all this to happen quietly in Paris but now .... Really, Mr Costello, you do complicate things sometimes.'

'I know, I get knifed, beautiful blondes die because of me, and I get deported without reason. I guess I'm unlucky. I can see how it would all be a nuisance for you.'

'Yes, I'm sorry, I can see that it probably isn't altogether your fault. But please try to keep a low profile from now on. I am almost certain that I will need you to go back to Paris and that has now become a problem. Well, I will just have to deal with it. Get on with the Munich thing.'

'If that's what you want.'

'I do.'

'Can you get me the address of the care home? It'll save a lot of time and nosing about.'

'Yes. Call me when you arrive. I'll have the address and anything else I can find which may be useful to you.'

And she was gone.

Jimmy put his phone away and took a drink of his beer. It didn't taste of anything in particular, it was too cold. Devious she may be, but she was also efficient. He'd get his address and anything else she could dig up.

He looked at his watch and then at the departure board. The plane would be boarding soon. Oh well, onwards and downwards. At least now he knew that at some point McBride was going to slip in a woman to claim the inheritance and this time he knew in advance. That was good. But he still didn't know what it was really all about and he still didn't know who had turned over his hotel room. It wasn't the police, they weren't shy about such things, they just kicked the door in and got on with it. They certainly wouldn't have waited till the room was empty. He went over what he knew again and came to the conclusion that all in all he knew damn all. And that was bad.

His flight number clicked over to 'Boarding'. He took another sip from his beer and decided to leave it. He'd probably be airborne before it lost enough chill to see what it tasted like.

He picked up his holdall and headed in the direction of his gate. A crumpled man again, with no spring in his step and no spring in his heart. A man who was letting go, slipping away, from Paris and from everything else that he had tried so hard to cling on to.

Chapter Eleven

It wasn't a particularly large living room but it was definitely too small for the way it was furnished. In the centre was a heavy, dark wood table on a bulbous pedestal with ornate feet. Against a wall was a large Welsh dresser affair in the same dark wood which was littered with china ornaments except for one shelf which was filled with photographs in silver frames. On the walls there were more framed photographs and three pictures. One was a landscape in oils mounted in an elaborate, gilded frame, the other two were prints in simpler frames. Both were religious monstrosities, a vacuous Madonna in blue robes staring upwards presumably to heaven, and a garish Sacred Heart almost identical to the one he remembered form his childhood which had hung in his own and almost every other Catholic living room. Under the Madonna and the Sacred Heart was a chest of drawers in the same wood and style as the dresser. Almost every available surface was home to something: bowls, statues, and assorted knick-knacks.

The furniture was old, ornate, and solid, but most of the china ornaments and statues looked new. Dominating the wall opposite the fireplace was a large, dark cross with a twisted, mutilated Christ-figure hanging on it. An uncomfortable thing that spoke of violence and pain yet strangely, Jimmy felt, not altogether out of place. Definitely out of place, however, were the state of the art television which filled the recess on one side of the fireplace and the modern recliner which faced it.

To Jimmy it was the room of a devout old woman who had collected her memories about her but still enjoyed her comforts.

Jimmy's eyes went back to the crucifix, it was a symbol of a fallen world, a place full of sin and pain and it gave not even the slightest hint of any resurrection or salvation. He was sitting on one of the four upright chairs which were around the table in the centre of the room on auto-pilot, the woman, who was sitting in the recliner continued to talk.

'… when I was younger but everything changed after the war …' Jimmy let her ramble, she probably didn't have many visitors so she was taking the chance to talk about the old days while she could. '… and they murdered my father, but of course nothing was done.'

Jimmy was suddenly listening again.

'They?'

She seemed surprised that he needed to ask the question.

'The Jews.'

'The Jews!'

'Of course. Who else would want to kill him?'

Of course, who else indeed, thought Jimmy.

The old lady had sparse, blue-rinsed hair and wore too much makeup, inexpertly applied. Her pencilled eyebrows had been put on slightly too high and gave her a surprised look which contrasted dramatically with the grim red slash of her mouth in a powder-pale face. Her dress was a shiny material with lots of flounces. To Jimmy it looked cheap and gaudy but he guessed it had probably cost a packet.

'Tell me about it.'

'They are still everywhere, in politics, finance, the police. I sometimes think that not even the Church is free of their …'

'Why did they kill him?'

She stiffened.

'Because he was loyal to the Füh …' she changed the word that she had so very nearly spoken, '… to the Fatherland. Because he was a brave soldier who knew how to do his duty.'

'He was in the Waffen SS?'

'Yes.' She was unapologetic, proud. 'An Obersturmbannführer.'

'I'm sorry, I don't understand SS ranks.'

'A major.'

'Had they tried to kill him before? Did he ever get threats?'

'Oh yes, there were threats. Soon after the war men came, officials, foreigners. We lived in what was left of Berlin, in the American Sector. The whole city was split up and run by foreigners, all gangsters and cheats.' She sneered. 'The victors.'

'And they threatened your father?'

'They asked questions, made insinuations.'

'Do you know what they wanted?'

'I was only a little girl, five years old. I didn't understand what they said but I knew they were threatening my father. I could tell.'

'But you don't know what it was they actually wanted?'

She shook her head.

'They came again after we had left Berlin and moved here to Munich. My father was a clever man, he saw that the Russians would steal the whole of the East and still not be satisfied. He moved here to where he would be …' What she wanted to say was that he would be in the old Nazi heartland, among his own, but this crumpled Englishman was also a stranger, another foreigner. '… where it was safer. Where I could grow up in peace.'

'When they came here in Munich, were the officials German?'

'There was a German who asked the questions but the other two were foreigners, American.'

'And the questions?'

'They tried to get my father to say he had stolen money from the Jews. They said they knew of his bank accounts in Switzerland, they said that he had put stolen money in them. But he showed them it was a lie. He was a clever man, he was a soldier but he had invested well during the war. He had shares in companies. There was no stolen money.'

'And after they came and questioned him here in Munich they left him alone? There were no more officials, no more men who came to ask questions?'

She shook her head.

'No, no one came. We were left in peace, if you can call what Germany was like after the war peace. The Jews came back and the government was weak. They let the Soviets take the whole of the East and communist agents and sympathisers got everywhere …'

Jimmy went back onto auto-pilot and let her ramble. It was all going too easily. She was an old woman with nothing but her bits and pieces and her memories. She liked talking about her father, about the old days. She didn't much care that Jimmy had arrived about half an hour ago with a badly told story about being a journalist gathering information, a story that wouldn't have taken in a child even if that child had anything it wanted to hide. But she was hiding nothing, that much was clear.

He stood up.

'May I look at the photos?'

She inclined her head so Jimmy went to the dresser and looked at the array of photos.

He picked them up one by one and studied them. Then he picked one up again. It showed two young, smiling, uniformed officers standing by the steps of a big house. On the steps was a woman, a little older than the officers but striking and with a good figure. She looked straight ahead at the camera and there was no smile. He could just make out the twin lightning flashes on the collars of the officers' uniforms He showed the photo to the old lady.

'Your father?'

'Yes, on the right, it was taken in Paris in 1941 while he was stationed there. He sent it to my mother after I was born. I still have the letter he sent with it, a long letter. I read it sometimes, it is so …'

'The other officer? The woman?'

'I don't know. My father told me who they were but I don't remember, just people from Paris. She was somebody he worked with I think, the other officer's name might have been Carl.'

'I thought the woman might be your mother, visiting him perhaps.'

'No, of course not. My mother never went to Paris. The woman was somebody he worked with. My mother had the picture in our house in Berlin. She kept all the pictures my father sent her.'

'What happened to your mother?'

'She died, killed in an air-raid in 1944.'

'But you survived?'

'I was in hospital, a fever, something, I don't remember. I was a little child. They came and told me. There had been a raid, my mother was dead, a direct hit on the shelter she was in. Many died. Even as a very young child I understood death, there was so much of it.'

'I'm sorry. It must have been awful for you, as it must have been for your father, to lose his wife while he was away fighting. He was on the Eastern Front then, wasn't he?'

'I don't know. I was three. Death and destruction I understood, hunger I understood, but the war … that was a thing grown-ups talked about. But when he returned he often told me how much he and my mother loved each other. How terrible it had been that he had not been able to return for the funeral. For some years after the war he would still cry when he spoke of her.'

Jimmy turned back to the photos, leaving her for a moment with memories of a father's tears for a lost wife. He looked at one or two more photos again, put them carefully back then sat down.

'What did your father do after the war? Did he work?'

'Yes.'

'What work did he do?'

'He was a writer.'

'What sort of books did he write?'

She paused, her manner changed.

'One book. He was working on one book.'

Once again Jimmy was listening with real interest.

'Just the one, I see, a sort of life's work. What sort of book?' Suddenly she was reluctant to talk. Her look was filled with a suspicion and distrust she made no effort to hide. Jimmy pressed on. He needed to know about this book. 'It may help me. I think I have a story here about your father, how his side of things never got told and how he and others like him were persecuted for doing no more than their duty, how it went on long after the war ended and, if you're right about the Jews killing your father, how it still goes on. It could be a big story, important, the sort of book he was writing might help.' He could see she still wasn't keen but he was saying the right kind of things. She was coming round. Maybe she did have a secret after all, but just didn't know how big a secret it was. 'Was it a novel, history, war memories?'

'It was about the nature of Jesus.'

Jimmy nearly swore out loud but once again, as with his old nun, it got no further than his teeth.

Oh shit, he thought, not only a bloody Nazi but a religious loony. That puts the lid on it. But he pressed on anyway, he might as well have everything there was.

'The nature of Jesus? What about it?'

'Christ's nature before the Incarnation. He believed that Christ had a human nature as well as a divine one before he was born into this world.'

'I see.' Like hell he did. 'That sounds very interesting, go on.'

'My father tried to explain it to me. He said that if Christ had a human nature before the Incarnation then that proved that there was a perfect humanity, a humanity free from any corruption or perversion. It meant that Adam and Eve shared that perfect humanity, they were the mother and father of what should have been a perfect race. He said that …'

Jimmy had heard enough about the book. He wasn't interested any more, not in the crazy obsession of an unrepentant Nazi SS major who was busy trying to re-invent the dream of an Aryan super-race.

'Did his writing take him abroad, did he visit people or places?'

'No. He spent a great deal of money but not on travel.'

'No?'

‘No. He didn’t trust the sources he said. He said they had been corrupted.’

‘By the Jews.’

If she noticed the mockery in his words she didn’t show it.

‘By the Jews and others, communists, deviants. He taught himself Latin, Greek, and Hebrew, and even some Aramaic. He bought manuscripts and old books that he said were more true to the originals. I found some of them were quite valuable when I sold them.’

So much for a daughter’s loyalty to her father’s memory and his life’s work.

‘There was plenty of money? Your father was well off?’

‘For books and study, yes, plenty of money, plenty for his work. Not for clothes or parties or holidays. He was too busy.’ He could see she was pretty bitter about the way the old boy had spent his money. Whoever had popped Young Hitler had done her a big favour, she had finally got her hands on what was left of daddy’s money. That accounted for the hair, the make-up, the dress, and her collection of modern, gaudy tat. From 2006 she’d had a life-time of pent-up spending to catch up on.

Jimmy stood up. It was over, he’d had enough.

‘Well, thank you. When the story is printed I will send you a copy.’

She didn’t get up, just looked at him.

‘Three copies.’

‘Of course, as many as you like. You have been most helpful.’

She finally smiled. It didn’t do anything for her.

Jimmy walked away from the house. It was a leafy old suburb filled with other, similar houses, comfortable and detached standing in their own gardens with plenty of trees and shrubs. Not big houses but solid and probably very expensive. Young Hitler had had money all right, however he’d spent it. But a rich, ex-Waffen SS major who’d done well out of the war and didn’t need to work would have been looked at pretty closely by the authorities which, by his daughter’s account, was what had happened. If nothing had shown up then there was probably nothing to see. Unless. Unless he'd had friends who could look after him, powerful friends. Perhaps even friends who were on the winning side.

Hmmm.

He set off to the nearest Bahnhof to catch a train back into the city centre and his hotel. As he walked he pulled out the silver-framed photo from inside his jacket and looked at it. It was the two young officers and the woman on the steps. He was pretty sure, but not certain. The house looked like the convent in Paris and the woman on the steps could be Mme Colmar. It looked like the same face he'd seen staring straight out at the camera in the photo McBride had sent him in the dossier. He wasn't certain, he'd need to study both photos more closely, but he was pretty sure.

He slipped the photo out of its frame and put it into his pocket, wiped the frame thoroughly with his handkerchief, and dropped it into the next litter bin he passed.

Not a total waste of time then. He'd got something out of it and it wasn't Jews murdering a nutty old ex-Nazi who was still trying to prove he was part of a master race.

He walked on through the tree-lined street towards the station pleased with himself. It had been easy and straightforward and not in the least bit life-threatening.

Chapter Twelve

The spring sun was still shining and the view of the hills above Frascati was still beautiful but Professor McBride wasn't bothered about the view or the weather and neither was Jimmy.

'I don't know much about care homes. It seemed all right. They didn't want to talk about it and you can't blame them. One of their residents gets hit by a lorry while he's left parked on the pavement right outside the home. It wouldn't fill prospective clients with confidence would it? I told them I was a journalist doing a piece on what was left of the SS officer-class, where were they now, and what influence did they still have if any? I said Streubel was a loose end, nothing important, just one more mid-ranking officer to be accounted for. If he was dead then he was of no interest unless his death had been suspicious. They said they were happy to co-operate, his death was *not* suspicious. It had been an accident, tragic but not in any way suspicious. I hummed and haa'd and …'

Jimmy paused. McBride looked as if she was listening but he got the feeling she wasn't taking very much notice. She noticed the pause. He was right, she hadn't been paying any attention.

'Go on.'

'The place didn't have much in the way of grounds so they used to wheel the residents round the streets when the weather was nice. It was quiet, residential, not much traffic. Leafy streets and neat gardens, a nice neighbourhood. Apparently he'd been taken out as normal but the woman doing the pushing had left him. When she was asked what had happened she said he'd asked her to go back in and get him his glasses which he'd forgotten. She parked him and had gone back in. She never heard the lorry hit and when she came out she saw what had happened but it was too late to do anything. He was dead. It was obviously a set-up and the woman was part of it.'

McBride nodded absently.

'But nobody was interested?'

'No. An old man got hit by a lorry because a care worker was careless, very sad. Couldn't have been suspicious because there was no motive, so it had to be an accident.'

'The police?'

'The care home said the police looked for the lorry but never found anything.'

'The care worker, the woman?'

'She was dismissed for gross negligence, didn't make any fuss, just went. They had no idea where she might be now.'

Jimmy pulled the photo he had taken from the dresser out of his pocket and tossed it onto the desk.

'Check it against the picture of the Colmar woman in the dossier you sent me.'

'I don't have that dossier.'

'No?'

'No. Joubert never sent it.'

'Did he get it, did the courier deliver?'

'I assume so.'

'Did you ask him?'

'No, he is not taking any calls. M. Joubert is convalescing at home. He was attacked and robbed by what witnesses say looked like two north Africans as he left his office. He spent two days in hospital. I'm told the police have it down as a routine mugging.'

'Like hell it was. His office wasn't on the sort of street where anyone gets mugged and two north Africans hanging about would stick out like sore thumbs.'

'Yes, I agree,' she opened a drawer, took out a folder, 'but I have this copy.' She opened the folder and let the contents slip onto the desk. She picked up one of the photos and held it next to the one Jimmy had given her. 'You're right, it's her.'

She handed them across to Jimmy who looked at them then dropped them onto the desk.

'I ask myself why an officer serving in Paris would have sent a picture of him with his mistress home to his wife? I also ask myself why he would keep the picture after the war and tell his daughter she was someone he worked with?'

'You only have the daughter's word for that.'

'Oh, she was straight enough, didn't try to hide anything. She did everything but tell me that she was still a good Nazi like her father and still believes the Jews are behind everything including his death. She also said her parents loved each other, that her father used to cry when he talked about his wife. Does that sound like a man who, if he kept a mistress, would send a photo of them together to his wife just after their baby had been born?'

'People do strange things at the best of times and this wasn't the best of times, it was wartime. He was a young man far from home, maybe …'

But now it was Jimmy who wasn't listening. He was building a picture and he didn't want anyone to change the way it looked.

'He was a bloody fanatic, and fanatics don't do things by half, not politics, not religion, not anything. He was a Catholic, the house was full of Catholic stuff. He was the sort who played by the rules. Once he'd decided to follow Hitler he was in all the way and for all time. It would have been the same with his wife, he wouldn't have cheated on her with some ex-whorehouse madam.'

But McBride didn't like Jimmy's picture.

'Fanatics reconcile the irreconcilable every day. You should know that better than anyone.'

Jimmy stopped. She was right. It wasn't just possible, it could be easy. The best lies, and the biggest, were always the ones you told yourself. He should know, he'd built a life on lies that were not so different from the ones Young Hitler must have told himself.

'Yeah, I know. But look at the whole thing. Apparently he loves his wife but as soon as he gets to Paris he shacks up with the Colmar woman. And look at the timing. He's promoted, posted, and shacked up all in five minutes. It's too neat, it has to be a cover for something else. And if you don't like that then look at the Colmar woman. She gets to America and gets put on the game probably by her own brother. He gets himself knifed and she takes on the family business and does a damn sight better at it than he did. She runs a whorehouse for high-class punters and does a bit of blackmail on the side. She gets pregnant, has a kid, and pulls out. Off she goes to Paris to start a new life as a devout widow, but as soon as the Germans arrive, bingo, either she's fallen in love or she's back on the game. Neither of which makes any sense. Colmar had about as much romantic sentiment in her as a pit-bull and she was rich, why start working on her back again? And according to your dossier she got the kid out of the way before the Germans arrived. Why do that? Why clear the decks? The Germans were no threat to her or the kid, they weren't Jews, they were American and America was neutral. As I see it, she wanted to be ready for when the Germans arrived. Whatever she was involved in was already up and running before the Germans got anywhere near Paris.'

'And do you have any ideas on what she may have been up to?'

'I thought about it on the plane coming back last night. She must have still had contacts in America, political and business. Your dossier said she made frequent visits to Switzerland from Paris once the Germans were settled in and her boyfriend was installed. Switzerland means banks and banks mean money. Either she was depositing it or getting it. My guess is she was putting it in.'

'For the Germans?'

'No, they wouldn't have needed her to do that.'

'For herself then?'

'No, if she'd wanted to stash anything of her own in a Swiss bank she would have done it when she first arrived, not waited until the whole of Europe was at war. But if it was money and it had to go to Switzerland it meant that whoever it belonged to wanted it in a country that was neutral.'

'If not for herself and not for the Germans then who?'

'I think she was some kind of courier for somebody in America, somebody who was doing business with the Germans and whatever the business was they didn't want Washington to know anything about it.'

Professor McBride leaned back in her chair.

'Well done, Mr Costello. Your deductive skills still do not disappoint. She was acting as the agent of a small group of American industrialists and financiers. From before 1939 to America's entry into the war many people thought Germany would win. Once France fell that sentiment increased. How could Britain stand alone? It had to be no more than a matter of time before a German victory in Europe and then some sort of arrangement with Hitler would have to be hammered out. There was plenty of clever money in America which bet heavily on Germany. However, clever money always minimizes risk. What if Germany didn't win?'

'They wanted guarantees?'

'Indeed they did, and not bits of paper, promissory notes signed by Hitler on behalf of the Thousand Year Reich. They required something more tangible.'

'Gold in Swiss banks?'

'Gold or anything as good.'

'Loot?'

'Anything that could always and quickly be converted into cash. The people in America who supplied hard dollars and a lot more besides required guarantees for their investments. They wanted to know that the Reich's promises could be backed up. Mme Colmar was the person who made sure that everything that Berlin said was going to the Swiss banks as guarantees did indeed get there. The deal was that it would all be held until the end of the war. If Germany won then it could honour its I.O.Us in Reichmarks and its property would be safe and sound whenever they wanted to go and get it.'

'And if they lost the Americans got what was in the Swiss vaults.'

'Exactly. But when Japan bombed Pearl Harbour and America entered the war on the side of the Allies the arrangement became considerably more dangerous. A certain type of mind might even have seen their business arrangement with Germany, if continued, as treasonous.'

Jimmy didn't hide his surprise.

'Bloody hell. They kept it going?' McBride nodded. 'But they were at war. You mean they actually kept doing business with Germany even though they were at war with them?'

'Big business, Mr Costello, is never at war with anyone. Countries and governments have wars. Big business, really big business, has no frontiers and admits to no loyalty except profits. Big business has no friends and no enemies and works with whoever will help it to those profits.'

'How did they get away with it?'

'Through neutral countries and dummy companies. They knew what they were doing and how to do it, despite the war, business, like life, went on. They supplied both sides and made handsome profits.'

'Christ. And when Germany lost?'

'The guarantees were invoked and the deposits withdrawn.'

Jimmy tried to let it all sink in.

'But they knew it was loot.'

'Not to them. They didn't steal it.'

'OK, but wasn't it all still very risky? A lot of the stuff must have been identifiable as loot, stolen from Jews and God knows who else. Weren't they worried questions would get asked?'

'Good heavens, no. These were men of huge power and influence. Some of them were at the heart of rebuilding Europe. They were above suspicion and had access to every possible resource. If questions did get asked, they would be the ones doing the asking. It was quite simple for them to realise their guarantees so long as they took their time and decent precautions. Europe was such a mess after the war they could have stolen a couple of small countries and probably got away with it. Stalin stole the whole of Eastern Europe and Britain and the US congratulated themselves on a job well done. As Europe healed and things settled down the Cold War set in. America forgot about Nazis and began looking for Reds under beds. The people who were involved quietly got on with liquidating their guarantees and saving the world for freedom and democracy.'

'So they got away with it?'

'Yes. They always do, don't they?'

Jimmy thought about it for a moment.

'I suppose they do. It must go on all the time. Every so often the whole crappy machine overheats and blows a gasket and there's some bloodletting, but I suppose the really big fish see it coming and make sure it's never their blood that finishes up on the floor.'

'No, Mr Costello, never their blood.'

Chapter Thirteen

They both sat in silence for a moment. Then Jimmy put any thought of right and wrong away from him. This wasn't about right and wrong. McBride hadn't sent him to Paris on any moral crusade. There was something in this Colmar business that she wanted and he was the one who was going to get it for her.

'So how is the convent mixed up in it? The nuns didn't get the place until after the war, they couldn't have been involved. What's the problem there?'

'There is the possibility, an outside one, but still a possibility, that there may still be something compromising hidden away in the convent. We need to be sure the building is swept, thoroughly swept, and anything that shouldn't be there is removed before any new owner takes over. It is entirely possible that Mme Colmar, being the sort of entrepreneur she was, decided to appropriate for herself some of what should have gone into the Swiss vaults. When the Allied invasion made it time to close things down she had to leave Paris quickly and after the Normandy landings things became somewhat dislocated among the German occupying forces. She still had no difficulty, given her connections, in going to Switzerland but she would have had to travel with very little in the way of luggage and would definitely not have carried anything that might compromise her with the authorities, German, Swiss, or even Allied. It is just possible that she may have decided to leave things concealed in her Paris house in the hope that one day she would be able to retrieve them.'

'Which would give her a good reason to lease the place to

the nuns. Apart from making sure it didn't fall into any unfriendly hands the nuns weren't likely to do any serious redevelopment without asking her first.'

'Exactly. If there is anything hidden in the convent and it were to come into the light of public scrutiny that would be unfortunate. We need to be sure that anything of a compromising nature is quietly removed. To be able to do that we need total and unrestricted access with full authorisation which means we need to produce the heir to the Colmar estate.'

Jimmy understood, or at least he thought he understood. But it didn't fit together as well as it should, not if McBride was the one putting the pieces together.

'Isn't that all a bit over the top? If anything's there then it would be down to Colmar. No one could possibly think the nuns …'

'Mr Costello, public relations is obviously not your field but I will try to explain. Even after all these years anyone found to be in possession of Nazi loot immediately becomes headline news. That would be especially so if that "anyone" happens to be a part of the Church. After the war far too many ex-Nazis slipped away from justice through the help of Catholic clergy or religious. The last thing the Church needs at this time is to find compromising material in a Catholic convent. The Church, in the face of considerable opposition, is in the process of trying to canonise Pope Pius XII.'

'Didn't someone call him Hitler's Pope?'

McBride almost scowled, but only almost.

'I believe there was a book of that title. If it came out that a convent in Paris was found to be the repository for ex-Nazi loot what do you think forces antagonistic to the Church would make of it?'

'They'd have a field day.'

'The beatification of Pope Pius XII is no small matter. It will be a symbol of the Church's rejection of Nazism and all other godless ideologies. If it is frustrated it will be a serious blow to the prestige of the Church, the Vatican, and the Papacy.'

'Not to mention Pope Pius himself wherever he is.'

'Please don't be flippant, Mr Costello. I hope you now see why we must find a suitable heir to Mme Colmar's estate or at least prolong the process until we can be sure that all that needs to be done is done.'

'Yes, I suppose so. But if the nuns are moving out why can't the Church quietly move in and do what they want?'

'Because the matter, unfortunately, is not in the Church's hands. There are lawyers and procedures, unfortunately they are already in place and active'

'Yes, I see. If the Church sent people in to pull the place apart questions would get asked.'

'Nothing could be properly done without attracting unwanted attention and enquiry. We need to be able to look thoroughly and without interference and then dispose of whatever is found, if anything is found, with the minimum of fuss.'

'If you say so.'

'Good. I hope you now have some sort of grasp of the seriousness of what you are doing.

'I suppose so.'

'Then I will send for you when I decide what is the best way to proceed.'

'You mean when you think it will be best to slip your woman in with her claim?'

'That among other things, but as I have already said it has become difficult. After the assault on M. Joubert it is likely that the matter of the owner of the convent will be passed into other hands. When that happens I will need you in Paris and after your last visit that presents certain difficulties. Stay available and ready to move at short notice.'

Jimmy stood up and waited but McBride ignored him, she was busy putting away the copy of the dossier so he left the office, went down in the lift and walked out into the sunshine. It was about a fifteen-minute walk to where he could pick up a bus which would take him to the nearest Metro station but he didn't mind. The morning sun was pleasantly warm and it gave him time to think.

She'd told him a lot, but had she told him all of it? She usually didn't so she probably hadn't, only what she wanted him to know to get the job done. So, what was the job? And he suddenly realised she hadn't actually told him. Apart from all the kerfuffle about American business playing both sides during the war she hadn't really told him anything. And even if all of it was true it was all ancient history now. And the Pope Pius XII stuff? No, it wasn't right, it didn't feel right.

As Jimmy walked and thought he began getting a bad feeling about it all. McBride might be devious but she didn't normally lie outright, just bent the truth to suit her own aims. But what were her aims? Planting her candidate on whoever was responsible for finding the Colmar heir? Or was it something else as well?

He'd flown out of Munich to Rome late and after he'd arrived in Rome he'd only had time to grab a quick breakfast before setting off to meet McBride. He decided he was too tired to give it the kind of attention it needed so he walked on to the bus stop, caught a bus to the Metro, and went home. Once back in his flat he took a shower and made himself a cup of coffee. He wanted to think but he also wanted to sleep. He was caught between the two. He sat and tried to think but his brain kept closing down.

When the phone woke him he didn't know how long he'd been asleep in the chair, a few minutes or a couple of hours. He answered the phone and recognised the voice. It was a Monsignor that McBride used.

'Hello.'

'Mr Costello, I have some bad news. Professor McBride has been shot.'

Jimmy sat up wide awake and the cup of cold coffee on the arm of his chair fell to the floor.

'Dead?'

'Not when she was in the ambulance but I'm afraid it was very serious.'

'How?'

'Two men on a motorcycle as she came out of the office

block. They were waiting for her.'

'Can I see her?'

'No. She is in surgery and then, if she survives, she will be in intensive care.'

'Do you know what her chances are?'

'The hospital say she is unlikely to live. One bullet nearly severed her left arm and they had to amputate above the elbow, a second grazed her heart. But she is a woman of great courage and faith, Mr Costello, great courage and faith. We must hope and pray for the best.'

Jimmy swore quietly. His wife Bernie had been a woman of great courage and faith all her life, but he'd still had to sit at her bedside and watch her die.

'Let me know if there's any news.'

'Of course, Mr Costello.'

'And thanks.'

Jimmy put the phone down.

Christ, if she died where did that leave him?

All of a sudden it had become life-threatening, only it was McBride's life, not his, at least not yet. But it soon could be. Whoever was out there knew about him, had been waiting and watching in Paris. This had to be them again and if they'd made a try for McBride he could be next. He stood up and listened to the voice in his head drumming the same message over and over.

Run, Jimmy, run fast, run far, and hide well.

The voice was right, one down and one more to come if he wasn't fast and clever.

He grabbed what he needed, put it in his holdall, then left the apartment, went down into the street, and began walking quickly.

The first church he came to was dark and empty. He went to the nearest statue, it looked like a Madonna and child.

He grabbed a candle, lit it, and put it with some others. This time the words came quickly and the message was clear.

'Look after her. It's all down to you now.' He left the church and headed for the Metro station. In his head his prayer continued. 'If you're there, God, bloody well get it done right this time. Don't let her die.'

Jimmy was running and McBride was dying or already dead but for Rome the late morning sun was warm and golden. It would soon be lunch time, time for a drink and a meal. Life was simple and straightforward, except for the crumpled man in a hurry that nobody noticed.

Run, Jimmy, run far and hide well and hope that your message with the candle got through and there was somebody there to listen.

Chapter Fourteen

The hotel was nothing special, clean, reasonably comfortable, but cheap and quiet because it was well away from the centre of Rome in the Quadraro district in the south-eastern suburbs.

Jimmy had run fast but in the end he hadn't run far. He'd caught the Metro and headed for Ciampino airport where the budget flights came and went. But once on the Metro he had changed his mind. He didn't want to run. He'd done too much running and it had never solved anything or got him anywhere except where he was now. He had nowhere else to go so he got out at Porta Furba Station. He chose it because he knew the district slightly. He'd been there with a local detective inspector when on his first job for McBride a few years earlier. He found a hotel and booked in.

The next morning things still seemed the same, nowhere to go and no reason to go there. He found a church and lit another candle but this time he had no words to go with it. It was a gesture, a bit of his past that he wouldn't let go.

After an aimless morning walking, drinking coffee, and more walking, he took an early lunch. He sat at a table under a big awning outside a restaurant and watched the traffic on the busy Via Tuscolana. He ate out of habit not hunger and after he had finished his meal ordered a coffee. He didn't want it but it gave him a reason not to get up and leave. The coffee came and grew cold at his elbow while he sat thinking, not that he could make much sense of his thoughts.

Whoever had turned over his room had been waiting for him when he went to Paris or picked him up after his arrival. Either they knew he was coming or had found out he'd arrived in double-quick time. If they had been told about him who told them and why? McBride? But somebody had gunned McBride. Was it the same people or someone else? Then there were the police, they also knew he was in Paris. Who told them? And why did they bounce him out so promptly and in such a very non-police way? Then there was Lawyer Joubert, immobilised but not dead. Nobody had tried to kill him, just knock him down to get the dossier, roughed up enough to be scared off. Again who and why? Who knew Joubert was involved? And that took him back to Professor McBride. She hadn't been roughed up and nobody had tried to scare her off. Somebody definitely wanted her dead.

And it all had to do with the Paris convent, an old whore who was also a blackmailer, a missing daughter, and Nazi loot with a very nasty American connection. He absently picked up his coffee and quickly put it down. It had formed a cold skin. He took out his handkerchief and wiped his lips. There were too many unknowns and what little he had got in Munich didn't help him with any of them. And on top of all that he didn't know how much of what McBride had told him was important or even true, nor what sort of game she was playing. Was it political or financial? Both or neither? He didn't know who 'they' were or if 'they' were one or more. He didn't know why the French police …

The high revs of an approaching motorbike grabbed his attention. The bike pulled in sharply at the curb opposite his table. On it were two leather-clad riders with full-face, black visors. Both were closed. The engine was still running as the pillion rider pulled the zip of the leather jacket down. Suddenly Jimmy found his legs wouldn't work. He couldn't move. The pillion rider got off the bike. Jimmy tried to think of a prayer but nothing came. Then the rider pulled off her helmet and shook out her long brown hair. The one on the bike took off his helmet, they kissed and the girl turned and walked away swinging the helmet by its strap. The rider put on his helmet and the bike roared back into the traffic.

Jimmy looked down at his hands, his fists were clenched and his knuckles white. Slowly he moved his legs under the table. Now, too late, the words came, Dear God … but now they didn't matter. He unclenched his hands and picked up his cold coffee. His hand was shaking but needed to do something, anything, to tell himself he still could function. He took a sip of the coffee and put the cup down, used his handkerchief on his lips again, wiped the sweat from his face then sat breathing deeply but slowly. Finally his mind unfroze and he asked himself the last question of all. Why the hell was he still alive?

The waiter appeared at his elbow and looked at the coffee. 'More coffee?'

'No.' But he needed something and it wasn't coffee. 'Grappa.'

The waiter nodded and took the cold coffee away.

OK, he'd listed all the things he didn't know. So what did he know?

He tried to think of who might be his friends in all of this but came up empty so he went to the other side of the ledger. Enemies? That wasn't so difficult. If he went on looking then probably everyone involved, known and unknown.

The waiter arrived, put the glass on the table, and left. Jimmy took a sip, it tasted harsh like all spirit tasted to him. He wasn't used to it and didn't like it, but after a couple of pulls it seemed to work.

He finished what was left in the glass, beckoned the waiter, and asked for another. It might only be Dutch courage, but as things stood he'd take whatever courage he could get however it came.

The first thing he needed to decide was, should he go on with this, whatever it was? He looked at his hands then held them up with fingers outstretched. There was no shaking. He shuffled his legs, they also seemed back to normal and he hadn't wet his pants, thank God.

So, back to the question, go on or give up?

But could he go on with it even if he wanted to? He knew damn all for certain – no, wrong, not damn all, he knew a little.

The convent was real, Joubert convalescing after a kicking was real, Young Hitler's death was real, and McBride dead or in a critical state was real. The Colmar woman … No, never mind the Colmar woman, not yet. The first thing he needed to be sure of was where he stood. Was he a target like McBride? There was only one way of answering that, to put himself out in the open. If they were after him then he had to make it easy for them to get him. And if they did – well, that was that.

The waiter came and went and Jimmy took a good drink.

Sitting in a café feeling philosophical about dying after a couple of drinks was one thing. Actually going through with it was another. The motorbike had shown him that. Still, he had to start somewhere and all he had at the moment was himself. Did it matter so much if they shot him? Probably not. If they'd killed McBride then they'd pretty much killed him as well. Without McBride to give some crazy sort of reason to his life he would be just going through the motions, like lighting candles to prove there was something to believe in. He looked at his drink but left it untouched. McBride. Maybe he wasn't on his own. She wasn't dead when he last heard. Maybe she'd make it and if she did he wanted to be ready.

If he put himself out in the open and nothing happened it meant they weren't looking for him and he could get on with trying to find out what all this madness was about. He pushed what was left of his drink away. It had done its job and now he knew what to do.

He picked up the bill and put the money and tip on the plate and walked back to his hotel and settled up. Then he went to the Metro station and set off back to his apartment. Sitting on the train he felt surprised. He wasn't scared any more. He might die but he wasn't scared, not like he'd felt when he saw the bike stop. Was that was something to do with McBride or was it the grappa? Or both? One thing he was sure of, he couldn't leave her dead or dying and not try to do something. And if she made it then he wanted to be ready, to show her something, to let her know he'd done all he could. She'd been there for him, now he had to be there for her.

But then a small voice whispered to him.

'No, Jimmy, no lies. You're not doing this for her are you? You're doing this for the only person you really care about, Jimmy Costello.'

And he knew his conscience was right. He needed a reason to keep going and at the moment McBride, dead or alive, was his only reason.

The Metro rattled on. Jimmy changed lines at Termini and got out at Lepanto where he'd started his brief attempt at escape the day before. Back in his apartment he had a thorough look around. If it had been turned over he couldn't spot it.

Oh well, give it two or three days and if you're still alive, you stupid old sod, get back to work. Find out which bastards shot McBride and, if you find them, kill them. Now, phone the hospital and find out how things stand.

The news was good. For once God had held up his side of the deal, or the medics had, or McBride had done it on sheer will power and bloody-mindedness. She was alive, still in intensive care but alive.

And she'd asked for him.

Chapter Fifteen

When Jimmy got to the hospital the doctor tried to speak in his most serious voice. He wanted Jimmy to be absolutely clear how much he disapproved of the visit.

'She is really far too unwell to have any visitors, even close family. Not even a priest.'

'I'm not family and I'm not a priest.'

The doctor shrugged. He didn't really care who Jimmy was.

'She asked for you.'

'I know, that's why I came.'

Jimmy waited. The doctor seemed unwilling or unsure how to go on.

'She is fighting.'

'Isn't that good?'

'Under certain circumstances, yes, but in this case, no. She is fighting and the drugs cannot do their work properly. She needs to rest and let the medication work, she needs to let her body heal.'

'Give her something.'

'We have to be careful, at the moment she is stable but her condition is still critical. We have done all we can. We cannot, as you say, give her something. All that can be done has been done. Now she needs to rest. But she is a strong woman, not strong physically, not in her present condition that would be impossible, but …' he tried to find the right medical words but the best he could come up with were, '… strong spiritually, you understand?'

'No.'

'No? No, neither do I. She fights, not to live you understand, not to cling on to her life, but for some other reason, and this fighting will kill her. She says your name, more than once, so finally we ask that you be found and that you come. Whether it will help …'

He shrugged again and stood looking at the floor. Jimmy waited a moment.

'So do I see her?'

The doctor was young and looked tired. Jimmy guessed it wasn't easy for him. Let her have a visitor and it could kill her. Keep this visitor away and it could also kill her. Either way he would get the blame.

'Any strain, any strain at all … you understand?'

'No.'

The doctor looked annoyed.

'She must not be …'

But Jimmy was also tired and he was no longer young and he didn't give a fuck any more about who got any blame.

'Look, Doc, I know she was shot, twice. As I understand it she's lost an arm and should be dead. The medical side is up to you lot here. If you let me see her you let me, if you don't, you don't, but spare me the words, will you? I didn't ask to come, she asked for me. You're the man who gets to decide. It's your decision so make it. Do I see her or don't I?'

The doctor didn't like it but he couldn't argue with it. It *was* his decision. But he still didn't like it. She shouldn't be alive but she was; she shouldn't be holding her own, but she was. She definitely shouldn't be having a visitor. But apparently she was.

The doctor took Jimmy to the door of a room.

There was only a low light but Jimmy could see the bed clearly. McBride lay there with a plastic bag of clear fluid hanging from a stand and a tube going down to her arm. There were wires leading to machines on trolleys where screens turned her life into numbers and lines. He looked at her. She seemed dead. He could see no sign of life whatsoever. In one wall of the room there was a window beyond which was another room with a light on and the head of a nurse who looked up when Jimmy and the doctor appeared.

The doctor pointed to a chair that had been put at the bedside.

'Please, as short as possible and as little strain. Press that button if anything, anything at all happens. The nurse in the next room will come immediately if you press the button or make any gesture of concern.'

He stood to one side and Jimmy went and sat down in the chair.

God, she'd changed. He'd only ever known her turned out crisp, clean, and totally in control. This wasn't her. This was a tired, old woman who had pain and suffering written into her face. Her tight, curly, black hair had flecks of grey amongst it. One arm lay on the white sheets with the pale palm half up and fingers slightly bent. It looked useless, as if the fingers would never close on anything ever again. This was a worn-out, old black woman waiting to die after a hard life. This wasn't McBride.

Jimmy waited but her eyes remained closed. He couldn't see any evidence of breathing. He wondered if he should call the nurse but decided against it. As he sat and waited his mind went back to another bedside, one in a London hospital where another tired woman was waiting to die. Nobody had shot her, it had been cancer that had killed her. He had waited by her bedside as useless then as he was now.

The head on the pillow turned slightly and her eyes opened. She didn't try to smile or show any sign of recognition or welcome. Jimmy bent close to catch whatever she might say.

'Keep going. Even if I die don't give up.'

The head turned back and the eyes closed. He was dismissed. She had finished with him and had gone back to the business of trying to stay alive.

Jimmy looked around the small room, full of complicated kit and most of it seemed connected to her by tubes or wires. But he knew it wasn't all this medical kit that was doing the real work, that was being done by the woman inside. The woman inside was the one keeping the woman outside alive.

Jimmy got up quietly and looked down at her. In his head he said, Christ, you're a stubborn old bastard.

And in his head he heard her voice reply, 'Sometimes you have to be.'

It was his imagination of course, but that didn't change anything. He knew exactly what she meant. And she wasn't wrong.

Chapter Sixteen

'I work for Professor McBride.'

The young receptionist nodded.

'I know. Is she …?'

But she couldn't say the words because she didn't want to hear the answer.

'No. I left her in hospital about an hour ago.'

The young woman said something under her voice and made a quick sign of the cross.

'I didn't see it. I didn't even hear it.'

'The shooting?'

She nodded and got a small white handkerchief from somewhere. She'd had it ready. She wiped her eyes.

'A man ran in and told me to call an ambulance. I thought there'd been an accident or something.'

'And you called an ambulance?'

'Yes. Then I went out to see if I could help. I am fully trained in first aid. But when I got to her …'

She stopped and got to work with the handkerchief.

Yes, thought Jimmy, one arm nearly blown off and a bullet to the chest isn't really a case for an amateur, even one fully trained in first aid. But what she said interested him, no sound of shots meant a silencer and no roaring away either to attract attention. He remembered the bike revving up to him as he sat at the café. Don't let the target know you're coming. Just cruise up, do the business, and leave. All very professional. Still, that part of it was someone's else's pigeon, he hadn't been a copper for a long time and he wasn't going back to it now, not even on an amateur basis.

He waited a moment until the girl lowered the hanky.

'I have to go to Professor McBride's office. There's something there she wants me to get, some documents concerning work I'm doing for her.' The young woman looked at him doubtfully. She knew him, that he visited McBride, but she didn't know him well enough to let him into the office. 'Is there someone who can take me into the professor's office? It's quite important and I'm afraid it's a little urgent.' He pushed the lie as far as it would go. 'She asked for it, for me to get it.'

The girl gave a weak smile, made a call, and then turned to him.

'Professor Scolari says he will be with you in a minute.'

'Fine. I'll wait over here.'

Jimmy walked away from the reception window. He didn't want to talk any more. The girl knew nothing that could help him. He stood and waited until the lift door opened and a man in his thirties came across to him. He was good-looking and casually dressed, nothing like Jimmy's idea of a professor.

'Professor Scolari?'

'Yes.' He held out a hand. Jimmy took it. 'You want to get something from Professor McBride's office?'

'Yes.'

'Could you tell me what it is and perhaps I could get it for you?'

'No.'

Professor Scolari waited for more, an explanation, something. But nothing came. Jimmy just stood and looked at him.

'You understand, Mr Costello, I cannot take you into Professor McBride's office and allow you …'

'Let's go upstairs, shall we? You can tell me up there what you can't do.'

Scolari hesitated then gave a non-committal shrug.

They went into the elevator and up to the top floor. Scolari stood by the doors as they opened.

'Now, Mr Costello, perhaps you could explain.'

'I've already explained. I was sent to get something by Professor McBride.'

But this wasn't a tearful receptionist.

'No. Professor McBride is in intensive care, we follow her progress carefully. She is not allowed visitors and would certainly not send for anything from her office.'

'She asked to see me.' Jimmy ploughed on as the professor was about to speak. 'The medico didn't like it either when I turned up but she'd asked for me, more than once. He didn't like going along with it but I still saw her.' But Scolari still wasn't buying it. 'I know it sounds all wrong but there it is. She asked for me, the hospital sent for me and I saw her. I'll wait while you check with the hospital if you like.' That helped. 'I have to get a file from her desk.'

But Scolari still shook his head.

'No, Mr Costello, as I said, she is in intensive care. I doubt if she would even be conscious or, if she was, that she would make any kind of sense. She would certainly not send you to bring her any file.'

'She didn't. It's not for her, it's for me. For something I'm doing for her. Something we were working on before she was shot and almost certainly related to her shooting. As you say, she's in intensive care and not allowed visitors but she still made them let me see her. Look, phone the hospital.' The professor thought about it then took out his phone and looked at it. Jimmy gave him a nudge. 'It's important or she wouldn't have sent for me. It cost her a lot to do that, the doctor told me it might even have killed her.' Then he gave it his last shot. 'He was the same as you, he didn't like having to make a tough decision either.'

The professor gave him a look, he didn't like the crack. Jimmy didn't think he would, that's why he'd made it.

'What is it, this file?'

Jimmy could see he was coming round so he decided to tell him the truth.

'It's a dossier containing information on some people. One has already been murdered, an old man in Munich a few years back. Another, an old woman, died in Switzerland also a few years back. I have no real idea what it's about other than it involves the woman's legacy which may or may not involve crimes committed during the war. Professor McBride sent me to Paris to begin looking for the dead woman's legal heir. Then she got shot so I came back. She sent for me and told me to keep looking. To do that I need the dossier. Now you know as much as I do and if you finish up dead or in intensive care don't blame me, it will be your own fault.'

That was the clincher, Scolari didn't need any more persuading. If Professor McBride could be shot in broad daylight right outside the building then the sooner this man, whoever he was, was gone the better. Scolari put away his phone and they set off along the corridor to Professor McBride's office. At the door he stopped, pulled out a key from his pocket, and unlocked the door.

'I will go into the office with you. You are to touch nothing. If what you want is there I shall get it for you.'

'Sure.'

They went in and crossed to the desk.

'It's in there, that drawer. A folder with a few pages in it and some photos.' Scolari opened the drawer then looked at Jimmy. 'OK, my mistake, try the other one. The folder's green.'

Scolari opened the other drawer and took out the green folder. He put it on the desk and they both looked at it.

'Well, do I get it?'

Scolari continued looking at the folder. Then looked at Jimmy.

'No.'

It was Jimmy's turn to shrug.

'Why bring me in here then?'

'You may look at it but you may not take it. When you have looked at it I will return it to the desk.'

Jimmy could tell that was as far as he would get, Scolari wouldn't budge any further. A look was all he was going to get.

'OK, open it.'

Scolari flipped the folder open.

Jimmy reached over and pulled the folder to him. The top pages were the ones he had seen before but there was one sheet that was new to him. Clipped to the top left-hand corner of the sheet was a passport photo of a woman, sad-looking, plain, with mousy hair and glasses. A face it would have been difficult for even a professional photographer to flatter and whoever had taken this photo hadn't tried. Jimmy picked up the page. There was a name, date and place of birth. *Veronique Colmar, 5th February 1965, Saigon*. Jimmy looked at the face again, he could see no trace of anything oriental. He looked at the notes under the name, date, and place.

Daughter of Thèrése Colmar. Father unknown. Present whereabouts ...

Jimmy stopped reading. He didn't want to know where she was. If he knew he could be made to tell so he didn't want to know. He looked back at the photo. This was McBride's woman, the one she was going to put in the frame. This was the old whore's inheritor, or the candidate McBride was going to put forward for the job. He closed the folder and pushed it back.

'Finished?'

Jimmy nodded.

'I may need to see it again.'

Scolari picked it up, dropped it, into the drawer and pushed it shut. The fear had evaporated, common sense had returned.

'That will not be up to me.'

'Who?'

'Professor McBride.'

'If she lives.'

Scolari went to the door and waited.

'If she does not live then it will be up to the governing council of the Collegio or perhaps to the Collegio's lawyers. Perhaps even the police.'

'That sounds like it would take a long time.'

'It would, probably a very long time. But if you know Professor McBride at all well you know that if she has survived so far then the probability is that she will live.' Jimmy wanted to believe that, but somehow he didn't share Scolari's faith. But the professor didn't care one way or the other. He was already regretting what he obviously considered to have been an error of judgement and for that error he blamed Jimmy. 'If you want to visit this office again for any reason please bring with you written permission from Professor McBride when, of course, she is well enough to give it to you. Now you must go. I have work to do.'

They left the office and went down to the ground floor. Jimmy left the building. Scolari stood and watched him all the way out. They didn't shake hands.

Jimmy walked away from the building. McBride had given him a way in. God knows what it must have cost her to get him into the hospital and give him her message. It must have come bloody near to costing her life so it had to be enough to do more than just get in. It had to be enough to get him off and running and keep him going.

So, back to Paris to do what needed to be done. And maybe find the bastards who'd put her where she was now.

Chapter Seventeen

Jimmy's flight landed at Charles de Gaulle airport at eight fifteen in the morning. He had reported to security and asked to speak to someone, explaining that when he had last visited Paris he had been expelled by the police and didn't want any trouble on his return. He had already been waiting for over an hour and a half to see anyone who might be interested in what he wanted and who was prepared to speak English. Two French-speaking-only guys had come to see him and gone away again. Now he was parked in a room almost identical to the one the police had used when he was bounced out of the airport, although this time there were no closed blinds at the windows through which the bright morning sun poured in. Finally a tall man in a smart white shirt, blue tie, and impeccably creased trousers came into the room and sat down at the desk where he had been waiting.

'I understand you want to speak to somebody about a friend who was deported from this airport …'

'No.'

'No?'

'No. I was deported. It was me.'

'I see.' The man was very black, spoke beautiful English and didn't seem in any hurry. Jimmy waited. 'Or perhaps I don't see.'

'I came to Paris on business, private business.'

'From where?'

'From Rome. I live in Rome.'

'But you are English? You have an English passport.'

Good, thought Jimmy, at least he did a bit of checking

before he came to see me. Now I might get somewhere.

'I live in Rome but I'm English. As you say I have an English passport.'

'And you came to Paris on private business?'

'Yes.'

'Yes. Our records show that you came to Paris from Rome.' He smiled. He had beautiful teeth and he still didn't seem to be in any hurry. 'And you say you were deported?'

'Yes. By the police from this airport.'

'But now you are back and you have come from Rome.'

He waited so Jimmy tried to help him along.

'Yes, I'm back.'

'You previously had business?'

'Yes.'

'And that business is unfinished? Is that why you have returned?'

'Yes. Before I could finish my previous business here I was picked up by the police, brought here, interviewed by what I assumed to be a senior police officer who told me I was to leave the country and not come back.'

The man nodded and thought for a bit.

'But here you are again. Why were you told to leave?'

'I wasn't told.' The man's eyebrows rose in surprise, real or pretended Jimmy couldn't tell.

In fact he wasn't at all sure whether this bloke was really confused or pissing him about. He suspected the latter but he didn't want to lose his temper, so if this guy really was pissing him about he would just have to live with it. 'I was told to leave but I wasn't told why I had to leave. OK?'

'Ah, I see, yes now I see.' Another pause and Jimmy waited. 'And what is it, exactly, that you would like airport security to do?'

At last, a sensible question.

'Tell the police I'm back. Tell them that I'm staying at the same hotel …'

The man held up a hand.

'Wait, Mr Costello. Wait, please. We are airport security,

not a message service. If you want the police to know you are here I suggest you go and tell them yourself.'

'No. I think it's best if I tell you, so I'm telling you. And I want you to remember that I told you as soon as I arrived. Remember that. I did it before I did anything else.'

'I'm afraid what you think is not the issue. We are still not …'

Jimmy decided a little pushing would help.

'Look. I was picked up by an unmarked police car, brought here and bounced out of this airport and out of this country just over a week ago by a senior plain-clothes copper. Maybe I'm a security risk, maybe I'm a danger to the French state, maybe I'm an undesirable alien. I don't know, I wasn't told. But now I'm back and if I get picked up by the police I shall make it very clear to them that I reported my arrival to airport security as soon as I got here and asked that they be informed. Clear?' But he didn't wait for a reply, it was clear all right. 'And if you haven't passed on the information about my arrival then it'll be your arse in your nicely pressed trousers that will be on the line, sunshine, not mine.' Jimmy got up. The man on the other side of the desk didn't move or say anything. 'Right, I've officially reported in, now I'll be on my way.'

Jimmy walked to the door of the small interview room and opened it. An armed, uniformed man was outside, he turned and blocked the doorway. Jimmy looked back at the man behind the desk who said something in French. The guard turned away and moved to one side. The black man looked at him for a second before he spoke and when he did there were no more smiles.

'You are free to go, Mr Costello.'

So Jimmy went.

Chapter Eighteen

It was still Paris in the spring, but Jimmy wasn't interested in the sights or the weather any more. He wasn't a tourist. He wasn't sure what he was except for one thing, he was working. He took a taxi from the airport into Paris and booked into the same hotel opposite the Gare de l'Est. As soon as he was in his room he went out and stood on the little balcony set into the slope of the roof and looked down at the road below and, across the road, the station. People going somewhere, people whose lives had purpose, people who mattered. They'd shot McBride because she mattered, she was important, she had a purpose. But him they could ignore. He wasn't important. To them he had no purpose in whatever it was that had almost killed McBride.

'Well, fuck you,' he said to the empty air, 'I didn't matter, but I will. I'll find you and when I do …'

But the futility of flinging words into nowhere silenced him, empty words into the empty air. Don't talk about it, get on with it. He went back into the room, sat on his bed, and made a call.

'Good morning, I'm trying to contact M. Joubert. He is? I'm sorry to hear that. I hope he soon recovers. I had an appointment with him just over week ago, he was helping the sisters at the convent of Bon Secours to trace somebody and I've been assisting in the search. Yes, Mr Costello, that's right. I came from Rome, visited the convent, and brought a letter of authorisation. You remember, good. There was also a dossier which I sent to M. Joubert by courier to return to Rome. Did it arrive safely and was it sent off like I asked? It arrived but you don't know if it was sent on. I see. Will M. Joubert be continuing to act for the sisters when he recovers sufficiently? No. Then perhaps you could tell me who is acting for them now. One minute, I need to get a pen and paper.' Jimmy pulled a notebook from his jacket pocket and a pen from another pocket. 'Go on.' He wrote down the information as he got it. 'And I should ask for?' He added a name and a direct line number. 'Thank you, you have been most helpful. Please tell M. Joubert I asked after him. A sad comment on our times, I'm afraid. Goodbye.'

Jimmy put his phone down and looked at the name of the lawyers who had taken over from Joubert. It meant nothing to him except it wasn't French – Parker and Henry International. He picked up his phone again and dialled the direct line he had been given.

'Good morning …' The voice at the other end replied and he glanced at his watch. It was two minutes past twelve. 'Quite right, good afternoon. My name is Costello, James Costello, I have been asked by the Sisters of Bon Secours to assist them in the matter of finding someone. I was working with a M. Joubert but unfortunately he has had an accident and his office gave me Parker and Henry International as the firm who have taken over. I was told to ask for a Nadine Heppert. Thank you.' He waited until a voice came on the line. 'Miss Heppert, Nadine Heppert? My name is Costello, James Costello, I was given this number by … Ah, you know what it's about. Good, that saves us both time. Would it be possible to meet? Thank you, that would suit me fine. I'm afraid I don't know Paris, which would be the best Metro station? La Défense, Line One, or RER Line A and it's the thirty-first floor of the Tower Initiale. No, don't bother, I'll ask directions when I get there. Thank you, and I look forward to our meeting.'

Tomorrow nine thirty. That was quick. He doubted she was someone with a lot of spare time so she must really want to see him. Why? As soon as he'd given her his name she knew what it was about. How did that work? Jimmy decided that tomorrow's meeting with Ms Heppert was going to be most interesting. One more call, then a beer and then somewhere for lunch.

Jimmy's call was to the hospital in Rome and the answer was "no change", the non-committal bulletin he would go on getting until there was a change. But at least it meant she was still alive.

When Jimmy returned from lunch the receptionist told him there was someone waiting for him in his room.

'You do that in Paris, you let callers wait in people's rooms?'

The receptionist ignored the irony of the question.

'Yes, if they are the police and they say they have been asked by the guest to call.'

'Did I ask this one to call?'

The clerk shrugged disclaiming any responsibility and looked down at some paperwork.

'He said so.'

'And you just took his word.'

The clerk looked up with dead eyes. He didn't care and nothing could make him care.

'Why not? He is the police.'

Jimmy went up to his room and let himself in. Sitting in a chair by the balcony windows was the same man who had bounced him from the airport. He didn't get up as Jimmy closed the door. Seeing as how the policeman had the only chair Jimmy sat on the bed.

'You got my message then?'

'What do you want, Mr Costello? I am a busy man and I have no time for games.'

'Deporting me was a game?'

'You were not deported, merely asked to leave. You left of your own free will.'

The policeman was about forty with short black curly hair. He wore a dark suit with a tie hanging loose at his open collar. He looked worn rather than sloppy. Jimmy guessed he was more a working copper than a desk-jockey.

'You're a busy man and I have a job to do so let's not jerk

each other about. You got told to kick me out and warn me off, which you did. Now I'm back. Are you interested or not?'

The policeman waited before he answered.

'Go on, Mr Costello. I'm listening.'

'I got asked to do a job of finding a missing person for the Sisters of Bon Secours here in Paris. I was sent by my boss in Rome as a favour to the superior of the nuns' order.'

'Your boss?'

'Professor Pauline McBride. She works for an institution in Rome, a College …'

'She works for the Vatican?'

'No, not that sort of College, Collegio Principe, an academic institute. When I got to Paris I met with a nun at the convent who sent me to a lawyer, M. Joubert. All clear so far?'

'Go on, Mr Costello, I'll ask if I have questions.'

'Right, because this is where it all becomes very unclear and the questions start for me as well as you. My room in this hotel gets turned over by experts. Very neat job but I spot it. I decide to leave. I get a taxi from across the road and head for the airport but the taxi gets stopped by your lot and we meet at the airport where you deliver your message. When I get back to Rome my boss, Professor McBride, gets gunned down by somebody who knew what they were doing, silencer, motorbike, the whole works. But she lived, she lost an arm, and is in intensive care, but she lived. Next thing I hear is that Joubert has been mugged, put in hospital for a couple of days, and has dropped the case. Now that is what I would have called in my days as a police detective a set of connected circumstances indicating criminal activity, perhaps involving police corruption.'

The last couple of words juiced up Jimmy's visitor considerably. He had guessed it would.

'Are you making some sort of accusation, Mr Costello?'

'Oh yes. I'm saying that there must be a connection between the attempted murder of Professor McBride, the criminal assault on Joubert, and the instructions you were given to see that I left Paris. Unless you can explain that connection I'd say that at the very least there is a criminal conspiracy between the perpetrators of the crimes and someone high up in your police. That's my accusation.' He paused for a second, then went on. 'But I'm making it to you, privately, in this hotel room, not to anyone else and not in any way that it might go public.'

Jimmy waited. He'd chosen his words carefully, now it was for his visitor to think and make a decision. It was still a tricky call. Jimmy had hung out his message through airport security in the hope it would find its way to this man, the policeman who kicked him out. He also hoped that Paris was no different to how London used to be, that the police and those who worked closely with the police looked after their own. It seemed they did because now the man was in his room.

So far so good. But now he had to wait and see if this copper wanted to know why he was back. He needed him to be interested enough to want more, but not frightened enough to do anything silly, like have him killed. He wanted to bring him alongside. But would he come, or would he decide that Jimmy was too much of a risk? He needed to find a way into this thing and it only opened from the inside. He needed to acquire a friend for his side of the ledger, a friend who was part of that inside.

So he waited to see which way his visitor would jump.

Chapter Nineteen

Parker and Henry International had a suite of offices on the thirty-first floor of the Tower Initiale. From the windows you got a view of the other, bigger, more modern skyscrapers that had sprouted up all over the district known as La Défense, the financial heart of Paris which, unlike London's City, beat in its western suburbs.

Nadine Heppert met him at the elevator. From a distance she looked in her early twenties, but close up you realised that a considerable part of that illusion was the way she was turned out. But the special effects were justified because even Jimmy, who was no expert on women's fashion or beauty, could see she was something a little special.

'Good morning, Mr Costello, thank you for coming.'

Her English was excellent but with a background accent that didn't sound French. Dutch? Belgian?

'Thank you for fitting me in so quickly.'

She led the way down a corridor to her office. They went in and sat down.

'I fitted you in, Mr Costello, because if your time, like mine, is valuable I don't want either of us to waste it.'

'Waste it?'

'Yes. You were asked to find the legal heir to the estate of Mme Colmar, were you not?'

'Yes.'

'That will no longer be necessary.'

'You firing me?'

'No. How could I do that? We never hired you. Any charges

or fees you wish to claim for your services must be made to M. Joubert's office or to the Sisters of Bon Secours, whichever you feel is your employer in the matter.'

'So how come you're telling me I'm surplus to requirements?'

'Because we are handling the matter now and we have found the heirs to Mme Colmar's estate.'

'Heirs?'

'Yes, two brothers, the sons of Mme Colmar's daughter. She married a musician named Henry Budge when she was sixteen, they had two children, boys. There are no other known members of Mme Colmar's family and, as the brothers' parents are both dead, they are the nearest living relatives. We shall be processing a claim to the estate on their behalf. So you see, your services, though they are excellent I am sure, are no longer required in this matter.'

'Are they black?'

'Really, Mr Costello, their ethnicity is hardly any …'

'The musician Colmar's daughter ran off with was black.' She tried, and failed, to keep the surprise out of her face. So, thought Jimmy, not so perfect after all. 'Was this Henry Budge, who you say was supposed to be their father, black?'

'There is no supposed about it. Mme Colmar's daughter married Henry Louis Budge in the Baptist church in Choquette, Fern County, Florida in February 1951. They moved to Chicago in 1953 and the boys were born there in 1956 and 1958 at the city hospital. The papers are all in order, I assure you. We have been very thorough.'

'I congratulate you, and considering you've only just taken over the case from M. Joubert, I'd say your success borders on the miraculous.'

'Our head office in New York located the brothers. M. Joubert was acting for the sisters here in Paris. We were acting for parties in the United States. The two lines of enquiry crossed only recently.'

It was crap, of course, and badly cobbled together, but that was good. It meant it had been done in a hurry which meant they weren't expecting him and didn't yet know how to deal with him.

'I'm afraid I'll have to see the brothers for myself, maybe ask them a few questions, and see all the papers of course.'

She took it well, nothing in the face or voice this time. Her story might be lousy but she wasn't.

'I'm sorry, I cannot see that you are entitled to any of what you propose and I cannot agree to it.'

'You mentioned papers relating to the marriage and the births but you never mentioned death certificates for the parents or any will that either of them might have left.'

'There were no wills.'

'No wills?'

'That is not at all uncommon.'

'No, I suppose not. What about the death certificates?'

She'd let him push her as far as she was going to.

'I'm afraid I'm not prepared to go any further, Mr Costello. As I said, I presume you value your time and don't want it wasted. I assure you that pursuing the matter further would prove a complete waste of both time and effort. I had hoped to be of some assistance to you by providing you as promptly as possible with the information I have given, but if you decide to continue I must make it clear in the strongest possible terms that we intend to progress our clients' claim and you must not expect any co-operation from this office in whatever inquiries you choose to make.' She stood up. She was dismissing him. 'Good day, Mr Costello.'

Jimmy stayed seated.

'What if I told you I had also found an heir to the estate?'

She sat down slowly.

'I would doubt it very much.'

'Very much, eh? I wonder why?'

She knew she'd made a mistake and he could see she didn't like it. He could also see she blamed him for having provoked it. Now she was more guarded. Perhaps now she took him a little more seriously.

'As I said, our New York office took considerable time to

locate our clients and establish that they had a supportable claim. As I understand it you arrived in Paris only recently?'

This woman wanted to know about him as much as he wanted to know about her so he decided to do a little fishing.

'When I arrived in Paris doesn't mean that's when I started looking. New York isn't the only place that's been acting for parties other than the sisters and your American clients aren't the only ones keen to get their hands on the Colmar estate, which , by the way, I would say is a more accurate description of both our efforts.' He waited and let her play with the bait but she didn't seem to want as to bite so he jiggled it about. 'And I have to say I think we have more confidence in our claimant than you seem to have in yours.' He tried to put on an accommodating smile. He couldn't do it well and he knew it. That was why he did it. 'If you make an official request, disclosing who it is you are acting for and your instructions in this matter, we would be happy to make a full disclosure of our client's claim.'

She bit.

'And who is this supposed claimant?'

Now he had to see how far he could play her.

Jimmy shook his head.

'Sorry. I can't tell you anything about it without permission from my boss.'

'Your boss?'

'Yes, my boss.'

'And your boss is?'

'Sorry. I can't tell you that without permission from my boss.'

She was fighting hard but Jimmy could see she was hooked.

'Oh really, Mr Costello. I asked you here with the best of intentions and you make absurd demands, then you invent this claimant and hide your lack of substance behind some fictional boss. On your own admission you were acting for the Sisters of Bon Secours and your only other contact was M. Joubert who, because of a regrettable accident, has now withdrawn from the matter. Do you really expect me to believe in some shadowy organisation which has an heir to the Colmar estate tucked away somewhere. Why, it took us over …'

And she stopped.

He'd landed her.

'Yes? You were going to say?'

'Nothing.'

'Oh no, surely not nothing. You were going to say how long it had taken you to find your boys and I got the impression it took some time.' She remained silent. 'Weren't you?' Still silence. But he had her. She'd made a slip, a bad one, and she knew it. 'I tell you what. Let me see these brothers and ask them a few questions. You or anyone you like can be present. If you do that I'll give you the name, date, and place of birth for our contender. That's as far as I can go at the moment. If, after I've seen your boys, I think we might be able to do further business together I'll get in touch with my boss and see what I can do.'

She thought about it.

'That depends.'

'On what?'

'This person whom you call your boss. What is his interest in this matter?'

'Sorry. I can't …'

'Tell me anything about that without his permission?'

'That's right.'

'Do you have a contact number?'

'For my boss? Really, I don't think …'

But she wasn't in the mood for any jokes.

'For yourself.'

'Hotel Français, opposite the Gare de l'Est.'

'A mobile?'

'No, sorry, I don't use one.'

'I see.'

She stood up again but this time it was a polite invitation to leave not the order of the boot.

'Good day, Mr Costello. I will see what I can do, if anything. When I am in a position to do so I will get in touch to let you know one way or the other. Will that be satisfactory?'

Jimmy stood up and smiled.

'Sorry. I can't tell you that without …'

But she didn't see any funny side.

'Good day, Mr Costello.'

Jimmy left the office. Once outside the building Jimmy took out his mobile and made a call.

'Can we meet? I have something for you. There's a bar I know.' Jimmy described the location of the bar where he'd sat and looked at the rain on the morning of his arrival and meeting with the old nun. 'Fine. I'll be there as soon as I can.'

Back on the top floor Nadine Heppert was also making a phone call. She was speaking in German.

'No it didn't go well. It went damn badly. This guy is going to be trouble. Well that's your problem so you'll have to deal with it any way you can. What do you want me to do? My advice? My advice would be to let him see the brothers and ask his questions. If nothing else it gives us time, time for you to decide how you're going to deal with him. My further advice would be that you get your homework done properly from now on. I was told he was a nobody who would fade as soon as things looked like getting tough for him. Well he didn't fade and I don't rate him as a nobody so I suggest you find out who the fuck he really is. I think it would be a help, a real help, if I knew a little something about the guy seeing as now I have to be the one stalling him, don't you? OK. I'll set up the meeting for a couple of days' time.'

She put down the phone.

This wasn't going to plan any more and she had developed a bad feeling about it. She would have to think about that. Yes, indeed, she would have to think about that very carefully. She picked up the phone again and told the switchboard to get her the head office in New York.

The meeting with her visitor had gone badly and she needed to take it out on someone. Why not New York? Why not the stupid bastard who hadn't bothered to check what colour Thèrése Colmar's musician husband was?

A voice came on the line and Nadine Heppert got ready to give someone hell, perfect hell.

Chapter Twenty

'What's your patch like?'

'The usual, this and that, drugs, illegals, vice. The usual.'

'That would be tough in a big city.'

'In a big city which patch isn't?'

'Some are better than others.'

'I'll settle for what I've got.'

'Yeah, I know.'

They were sitting in the bar overlooking the Seine where Jimmy had started. The man with him was a detective inspector, the one who had bounced him out of Paris. He was also the one who had turned up at his hotel as a result of Jimmy's interview with airport security. His name was Serge Carpentier and in the hotel, Jimmy had told him about the convent, Joubert, and McBride, and as a result Carpentier had opened up a little. He'd been told to go to the airport. A man, an Englishman called Costello, would be picked up and brought there. He was to give the "goodbye" message and make it strong enough to see that Costello not only left but stayed gone. There was to be no violence and the less the airport authorities were involved the better. He'd told airport security to have a room available but to stay out of the way. He didn't know either of the men who had done the actual pick-up but he was sure they were genuine police. He didn't know anything else and certainly not why he had been chosen, all he could think of was that an inspector was senior enough to know how to do the job properly but not so senior that it had to be explained to him. The message had come down from somewhere high but nobody knew, or was prepared to admit they knew, who had originated it. He had asked, oh yes, he had asked, before and after, but there was nothing doing. All he knew was, 'kick Costello out and be sure he stays out'

'Then I got the message from airport security that you were back and wanted the news sent to the police. I'd done the kicking out so it got passed on to me. Your coming back isn't good news and announcing it like you did makes it worse. Like I said, I had no idea what it was all about in the first place so I decided to pay you a visit in my own time at your hotel. There's no diary entry and nobody knows I'm here.'

'OK, you're on your own time, you're here, and nobody knows except you and me. Now what?'

'I'm involved. I don't want to be but I am, so I want to know what was going on. I thought you might tell me.'

That was Carpentier's story and Jimmy had to admit it was a good one. It made some sort of sense, fitted the known facts, and kept Carpentier more or less in the clear. Jimmy had stalled him at the hotel and said that he needed a couple of days, then they could meet and he'd tell him what he knew. If Carpentier was telling the truth, that he was on his own time and the visit unofficial he didn't have much choice, either he did like he was told or he had to make it official. Jimmy was glad he'd done as he'd been told. It meant his story might even be true. He'd taken Carpentier's number and that was that, until now. Now the question circling in Jimmy's mind as they exchanged small talk in the bar was, is he really a good guy who got used or is he being clever and telling a good story? Jimmy knew all too well that the really clever coppers always has good stories, especially when the shit might hit the fan and spray it in their direction.

He looked out of the bar window across the Seine. It was a beautiful spring day, a day to enjoy yourself. A day to fall in love. A day to …

'It was raining last time I was here. Paris in the spring, I thought, what a bloody washout.'

'You shouldn't believe the films, they make the real thing a disappointment.'

They both had beers and both were drinking slowly, finding words to say that said nothing. They were sizing each other up. Each had the same question – how far can I trust you, if I can trust you at all?

Jimmy made up his mind. When you came right down to it he didn't have any choice either. He decided it was time for one of them to get the thing going.

'Look, one of us has to get started so I'll tell you everything I know then you decide if we can work together. I need you more than you need me because this is your town and you're a working copper here. But that also means that you have more to lose. If things go pear-shaped I can walk away from it, if I can still walk. It'll be different for you. You married?'

'A partner.'

'Kids?'

'No. His name is Jules.'

A pause.

A lifetime of Catholic prejudice tried to surface but he stamped it down. What the hell, it didn't matter, he was going to work with the guy not … Well, he was going to work with the guy so his private life was his own business.

'In the hotel I didn't give you anything to see which way you'd jump. You jumped the right way so now you can have the rest.'

And Jimmy told him all he knew or had been told about Mme Colmar, the convent, the hit and run in Munich, Young Hitler's Nazi's daughter. All he left out was the woman in the passport photo on the extra page in the dossier in McBride's office.

'… and that brings you up to today when I get to see Nadine Heppert over in La Défense.'

And Jimmy told him about the meeting, the brothers, how she tried to kick him off the case, and how he wouldn't go.

'And she sat there and took it?'

'She didn't want to.'

'So what was your leverage to make her take it?'

'I told her I had a claimant as well. That we'd been looking here in Europe just like they'd been looking in the States.'

'And have you?'

'No, but she can't be sure I haven't, and it looks like she isn't prepared to take the chance that I'm bluffing.'

'But you are bluffing?'

'Sure.'

Serge called the waiter and ordered two more beers.

'You're telling me everything?'

'Everything. I said I would.'

'Is that because you trust me?'

'Sure.'

'But you don't know me.'

'No, but I have to trust you. I told you, I need you more than you need me.'

'OK, you need me and maybe I'm prepared to stick with it for the time being.' He finished what was left in his glass. 'I will call you Jimmy, not because I trust you or want to be your friend, but to show you I am prepared to work with you. And you can call me Maillot.'

'Maillot?'

'It's a nickname, it means shirt, sports shirt, you know, *le maillot jaune*, the yellow shirt that the leader of the Tour de France wears. I was a bicyclist, a good one. I wanted to be a professional.'

'But you became a copper.'

Serge spread his hands.

'Being good is not enough, to be a professional you have to be the best so, as you say, I became a copper, *un flic*. And now we work together and we try to trust each other. I call you Jimmy and you call me Maillot.'

Jimmy tried it inside his head but it wouldn't work.

'No, it would sound daft if I said it.'

Serge laughed.

'Then make it Serge. But only if you don't lie to me any more as you have just done. What was it that you so carefully did not tell me?'

The beers arrived. Jimmy took a drink. McBride had told

him often enough that he couldn't act. He shouldn't have bloody well tried so he gave it up.

'The claimant. It wasn't a bluff. There's a woman, right age, right name, born in Saigon.'

'Did you find her or was she given to you?'

'Given. My boss in Rome, the woman called McBride at the Collegio Principe. It was in a file in her desk.'

'The woman who got shot?'

'She was in intensive care, but she still managed to tell me to get on with the job. You should have seen her, she was …' but he stopped. This bloke didn't need to know about McBride, that was for him to worry about. 'I went to her office and the picture was in a dossier with the name and the rest. That's why I came back to Paris.'

Serge looked doubtfully at Jimmy.

'I thought you said your boss was dying maybe.'

'Sure, but she still got them to send for me so I guess it must be important, important enough for her to nearly croak herself to give me the message.'

Jimmy wasn't acting any more so Serge believed him.

'Could the lawyer you saw this morning, this Heppert, have been the one who ordered your boss shot?'

'No.'

'Why so certain?'

'Because she knew nothing about her. Didn't even know she was a woman, didn't know she'd been shot, nothing.'

'And the brothers, the ones she's acting for? Could they be real claimants.'

'No, absolutely not. She said that Colmar's daughter and the musician were married when she was sixteen in a Baptist church in Florida in the fifties. Can you see that happening?'

'Why not? Sixteen is young but in America in the fifties …'

'It was nothing to do with her age, Thèrése Colmar's musician was black. Can you see a black man and a sixteen-year-old white girl marrying in a southern American state ten years before the civil rights movement got going?'

Now Serge saw why not.

'No, I can't. But why make up a story that falls down straight away?'

'Because Heppert didn't know that the musician was black, which means whoever did the research didn't do it properly. They needed someone who fitted the dates and had the right kind of paperwork and they came up with these blokes who, I guess, are both white. All they wanted was a couple of guys who would let themselves be used, probably not too bright, a couple of blokes who would settle for what would be, for them, a lot of money and keep their mouths shut when it was over. They needed the paperwork and the bodies to put before the authorities in Switzerland. Changing a name to Thèrése Colmar on a marriage licence in some obscure country church register wouldn't be too difficult and the Chicago birth records could be genuine, probably are. The paperwork will say Thèrése Colmar married Henry Louis Budge and the birth certificates will show the two blokes Heppert has in tow are Mr and Mrs Budge's little boys.'

'But if someone challenged their claim? Could you prove that the musician was black?'

'I don't know. But it's true, so if New York goes back and does its homework like they should have done first time round they'll find out for themselves. And if the brothers are white and couldn't pass for mixed race they daren't go to a Swiss court and take the risk of the whole thing blowing up, especially after me turning up.'

Serge decided that Jimmy must have come as a nasty surprise to Nadine Heppert.

'Are you sure that this Heppert woman couldn't have had your boss shot?'

'Yeah, pretty sure, why?'

'Because if you're wrong I think you've given her a great reason to shoot you as well.'

Jimmy went over it again in his head.

'No, she's not behind any killing. She's on the fiddle with this claim and it's possible she may have got someone to organise a couple of street lads to give Joubert a tickling to get the dossier and get him off the case. But she's not the one who put the gun on McBride. That's linked to whoever had the old Nazi run down and that was in Munich in 2006. By the look of her she'd still have been at college maybe even still at school.'

'Well I hope you're right because if you're wrong then it isn't healthy to sit too near you. Now, if you've told me everything …?'

'Everything, you're up to date. Now it's your turn to bring something to this party.'

'Yes?'

'Heppert knows I'm back and knows I'm going to make trouble. We have to assume others will know soon enough so I need to get going quickly which is where you come in. You're the working copper in this town so how do I get inside this thing?'

Serge beckoned the waiter and ordered more beers. Jimmy hadn't asked for another and Carpentier's glass wasn't anywhere near empty. He was doing what Jimmy would have done, giving himself some time to work things through. Carpentier waited until the waiter brought the beers.

'OK, Jimmy. What we need to get on the inside of this is someone who can write a good story.'

Chapter Twenty-one

'I'm not with you. What sort of story?'

'That article you promised the old Nazi's daughter. We get it written up by a journalist so that it makes her father look good, you know, hounded for doing what he saw as his duty. Hints of Jewish bully-boys against a brave old soldier. Anything that will sweeten the daughter. Then we get him to tell her that to make the article fireproof, to show everyone that her father was more sinned against than sinning, he will need to show that the income from his investments was absolutely legitimate. If she goes for it and gives him access to the right kind of paperwork we get to know where his money was coming from. She inherited so what he had she now has, she should have, or be able to get hold of, all the paperwork we need.'

'Sounds good. Tell her the story right and she may very well drop. She didn't strike me as any too bright and the chance of a bit of good publicity for a loyal servant of the Third Reich should be like catnip to a cat.'

Serge smiled, he was pleased with himself and Jimmy's response. He went on.

'And whoever killed the old man maybe did it so that they could deal with the daughter. If they wanted something and he wouldn't play along.'

'Knock him over and then approach the daughter.'

'Yes. If that's how it was then she'll be able to say what it was she sold, what it was they got from her that they couldn't get from her father. If our journalist can get that then we'll really be on the inside.'

Serge sat back, still pleased with himself. He took a drink and waited for Jimmy's response. Jimmy lifted his glass in salute and decided now was as good time as any to give the self-satisfied sod a little prod.

'Well done. For someone who's new to this particular piece of action you've cottoned on very quickly. It's almost as if you knew what to expect. That you'd already done some heavy thinking on it.'

Jimmy took a drink as the smile dropped from Carpentier's face.

'I'm a detective, I pick things up fast.' He leaned slightly forward. 'And if they're not what I want I can drop them just as fast.'

Jimmy was pleased; he'd got him edgy which was how he wanted him.

'Keep your shirt on, Maillot,' Jimmy smiled in support of his little joke. Carpentier didn't smile back. 'All I meant was that, considering you're new to this Colmar business, you think quick. But there's a big hole in your idea.'

'Hole?'

'What does our journalist get out of it?'

Carpentier was still sulking but he managed an answer.

'Money, what else? We pay him.'

'No, money by itself wouldn't do it, not if we want a good job done. We'll want a real journalist and one who knows what to ask for and can make sense of the figures if he gets them. That's going to limit the field and on top of that any really good journalist will want to get the whole story and that would mean another body poking their nose well in.'

'So what do you suggest?'

'We tell him a story of our own. We say we think Young Hitler stashed away money made during the war while he was here in Paris. That he had a private thing going whereby he seized shares, bonds, and financial stuff like that from wealthy French citizens in return for seeing their names didn't appear on certain lists.'

'Death camps?'

'That sort of thing. That he stashed them in Switzerland and after the war lived comfortably off what he had taken. After all this time there can still be SS officers who are living off their ill-gotten gains.'

'But he's dead.'

'All right, the families of officers, who the hell cares? The story will be that there's still wartime loot, stolen from Paris citizens, in Swiss banks and it's going into Germany to the relative of the high-ranking officer who stashed it.'

'He was only a major.'

'For God's sake, it doesn't matter.'

'And what's our interest?'

'I'm working for a group who wants to get the stuff back and see that it goes to the families of the people it was stolen from.'

'And me?'

Jimmy paused as if he was thinking about it.

'You can beef up the French angle. The French angle is what makes it good. We could tell the journalist that there are high-placed people today who don't want the whole thing raked up again, who want to forget the war and everything that happened during it.'

'What people? We don't know any …'

'Tell him about your bloke upstairs, the one who passed down the order to have me bounced.' Jimmy could tell Carpentier wasn't expecting it and didn't much like it. 'Tell him that even in the police, right here in Paris, there may be people with pull who don't want this particular SS officer looked at too closely, dead or alive.'

'No. Anybody in the force today, even close to retirement, wouldn't have been born at the time. It won't work.'

'If the money's still coming out of Swiss banks maybe pay-offs are still being made to keep the whole thing quiet.'

Carpentier gave a dismissive laugh.

'That's ridiculous. You might get away with crap like that in Hollywood but not with a reporter, not today and certainly not in Paris.'

'Why not? It doesn't have to be true, it doesn't even have to be believable. All it has to do is give the journalist the smell of a real story. There *was* an SS major and he *was* topped in Munich. There *is* a daughter and, if we're right, there is or was stuff in Swiss banks. A solid citizen, a lawyer, has been beaten up and put in hospital. A college professor in Rome has been shot and damned near killed. And on top of all that I did get bounced out and you got told to do it. That should be enough to get a reporter on board, wouldn't you say? If he doesn't altogether swallow the story we tell him, so much the better. It all helps make him believe that there's a real story in there somewhere and that a high-up in the Paris police is part of it.'

That was the pitch made, so Jimmy sat back and let Carpentier chew on it. He didn't chew for long.

'No.'

'Why not?'

'If the Paris end is what gets us the journalist we can't deliver. I'm a cop here and I couldn't get anything about who gave the order. I said I tried, remember?'

'We'll get it.'

'You sound sure.'

'I am. Heppert wouldn't have anyone gunned down in the street or run down by a lorry but she definitely fits the bill for slipping a copper enough money to get a couple of small favours. Once the journalist has got our Munich stuff, or even if he doesn't get it, we can use him to squeeze Heppert. She won't be a happy girl if a reporter starts to ask her questions about possible links to the mugging of a lawyer and an unofficial police action to kick someone out of the country. If I'm right and she was the one who put Joubert in hospital and the fix on me then I'm pretty sure she'll sell her high-up police friend to save herself.'

'And the journalist?'

'We'll sort him out when the time comes. Leave that to me. What do you think?'

Jimmy watched Carpentier.

The Heppert angle wasn't so badly cobbled together. It made

some sort of sense. But it would only convince someone primed to believe it, someone who already knew it was true. If Carpentier swallowed it that meant Heppert had indeed been behind getting him bounced out. It also meant that the copper she'd got to do the bouncing was sitting opposite him thinking over what to do.

'This must be very important for you, Jimmy. To go to all this trouble I'd say it was more than just a job, that it was personal.'

He was playing for time again.

'Whether it's personal doesn't matter a damn one way or the other. This Colmar thing isn't any smash and grab, some slam-bang and have it away on your toes job. They waited until the Colmar woman died, then left it a few years before they topped the old guy in Munich. Then they left it again until they thought they could get the estate with little or no fuss. This is a very slow-burn operation. How big does a thing have to be to run on a time-scale like that and what sort of villains do you know who work that way?'

'So what do you think kicked off this latest round of violence?'

Jimmy relaxed, Carpentier wanted to be on board. He'd guessed as much as soon as he found him waiting in his hotel room. Now he was sure, and now he knew why. Carpentier was hooked up to Heppert in whatever game she was playing.

'The convent started it off. The nuns closing down and suddenly asking again who the real heir was. That's when my boss got involved and that put me in the frame. The convent set everything going, Joubert, McBride, you bouncing me, everything. We need a way in and your idea about the journalist gives us our best chance. There has to be some sort of answer in what the old guy's daughter sold or passed on. If you're right and they killed him so they could deal with her she'll have a record of what she sold and who she sold it to.'

'You think the old Nazi had something worth killing him for?'

'Yes, something he wouldn't give up.'

'What about the Colmar woman's estate? Isn't it more likely that's what it's all about, something the Colmar woman had?'

'Perhaps, but we can't get at that. My boss might have found a way. For all I know she's already done it and knows what everybody is after. But she's not going to be any help for quite a while so I'm stuck with what I can get at, which is the old guy's stuff.'

'So you think stick with the old Nazi's daughter?'

'Who else is there?' He took a sip. 'Unless you think we should go straight for Heppert.'

Carpentier picked up his glass and took a sip.

'No, not Heppert, not yet. Let's see what we can get out of Munich.'

'OK, Munich first it is.'

Now it was Jimmy's turn to smile and be pleased with himself, because now he had Serge Carpentier and Nadine Heppert, which meant with or without Munich he was finally on the inside.

Chapter Twenty-two

Jimmy sat at one of the café's pavement tables, looking over the river, keeping a cup of coffee company while it went cold. He had time to kill. There was nothing he could do except wait so he kept his coffee company and did nothing. The day was warm and sunny and the streets were busy as locals and tourists went about their business. It was Paris in the spring, like in the films or the brochures.

Serge had found them a journalist. They'd fixed a price and, as Jimmy had expected, it was the Paris police angle that he'd been most keen to follow up on, but he'd listened to what Jimmy wanted then gone away and written the outline of a good article. That is, he had written the outline of a lousy article saying what a good but misunderstood bloke Young Hitler had been. Jimmy thought it would soften up the daughter nicely. Now the journalist was in Munich trying to get the information they needed and all Jimmy could do was let the time pass. It wasn't a great plan, it wasn't even a very good plan, and it would probably get nowhere, but it had already done its main job, it had confirmed for him that Heppert and Carpentier were in this together and given Carpentier a reason to be alongside him. He thought again about the journalist. A keen, bright, young bloke who asked the right sort of questions but also knew when to stop asking. Jimmy guessed he'd have a rosy future in journalism, unless of course he hit a snag along the way. And that, thought Jimmy, was beginning to look like it might have already happened. The journalist had been gone three days and there was no report, nothing. That was too long not to hear anything at all. The whole thing was beginning to look like a bust. Either the daughter wouldn't play or something else had gone wrong, and if that was how things stood, he'd need a new way of keeping Carpentier interested.

He looked down at his coffee; it had nothing to suggest. He'd pushed Carpentier as far as he could without actually saying out loud, 'I know you and Heppert are tied up together in this'. He looked across the river and let his mind go over the ground but again he came up empty. He'd have to leave it alone until an opening came up, if one ever did. What else could he do? He'd asked himself that question regularly over the last couple of days and always come up with the same answer: nothing.

His phone went off on the table. He picked it up.

'Good morning, Mr Costello.'

'Good morning, Ms Heppert, nice to hear from you at last. You got something for me?'

'If you come to my office I will show you copies of the marriage record and the birth certificates.'

'And the death certificates for the parents?'

'Only those papers I have mentioned.'

'And the brothers?'

'No, it has been decided that you should have no direct contact with them.'

'It's not good enough, Ms Heppert. My boss wouldn't …'

'I'm not in the least interested in your employer, Mr Costello, in what she does or does not want. I am offering you this chance to examine the documents in my office this morning before midday. After that, whether you take up the offer or not, I consider all necessity for communication between us to have come to an end. Good day.'

And she hung up.

Jimmy put his phone down. So, tough guy all of a sudden. This is my offer, take it or leave it, and no sight of the boys at any price. Well, he didn't want to see any papers, if she reckoned they were going to be good enough for the Swiss authorities they'd certainly look like the genuine article to him.

When he'd left her office a couple of days ago she was prepared to think about dealing. Now she was freezing him out. She had something now that she didn't have before.

His phone went off again. It was Serge and he didn't waste any time.

'Our journalist is dead.'

'Dead?'

'Dead. Suicide. Threw himself under a train at the Bahnhof near where the daughter lived. He must have been coming away from seeing her.'

'Who says it's suicide?'

'The police, there was a witness standing near him. She says he shouted out something in what sounded like French as the train came then threw himself under it.'

'Bollocks.'

'Maybe, but that's what the Munich police have got it down as. You're not going to try and tell me they're in this as well? One bent policeman in Paris, possibly. The Munich police force? No.'

No, thought Jimmy, the Munich police aren't part of it. If they say they have a witness to a suicide then they have a witness.

'Did the driver of the train see anything?'

'What they usually see I suppose, a body going under at the last minute. He couldn't have heard anything from inside his cab and he wasn't looking for anyone to throw themselves off the platform.'

'Who was the witness?'

'No idea. I only found out this morning. I was worried that we hadn't heard anything so I checked. It happened yesterday, middle of the afternoon. Quiet time, only one other person on the platform, the witness.'

'It's got to be a fix. Get anything you can on the witness, whoever it is has to be part of it. Unless your journalist really was suicidal?'

'No, he wasn't about to kill himself when he left Paris.'

'OK, let's find out about this witness.'

'I'll see what I can do.'

Jimmy put the phone down.

'Shit.'

But it wasn't said to anyone in particular.

He picked up his phone and made a call. There was still no change with McBride.

'Shit.'

It was becoming very apparent to him that on his own, without McBride pulling the strings, he was only managing to go round in ever decreasing circles and would all too quickly disappear up the only avenue of escape that would be left to him.

'Shit.'

He went back to his thoughts and absently put his cup to his lips only to put it down quickly. The waiter was clearing another table so he ordered another coffee. The waiter took the one from his table and left.

It was now two killings in Munich and McBride as near as dammit dead in Rome. Somebody was playing for bloody high stakes. He was still sure Heppert was up to her neck in it but now she looked like a blind alley. So was the daughter unless he wanted to go under a train or a lorry himself. All that was left was the witness to the suicide and the only way he could do that was through Carpentier. But Serge couldn't drop everything and go with him to Munich and Jimmy was sure he'd get nowhere with the Munich police on his own, except maybe thrown in jail.

The waiter arrived and left and Jimmy took a sip of his coffee.

He gave it some more thought but decided that all he could do was to wait and see if Serge could get anything on the witness. He didn't like waiting, doing nothing, but he'd done enough of it in his working days so he waited.

Serge phoned at two thirty. Jimmy was lying on his hotel bed staring at the ceiling. He'd been thinking and his thoughts had not been comfortable.

'Did you get something?'

‘Yes. The witness was a woman, local, worked in a care home. Absolutely clean as far as the police could see. No record, nothing known, not even a parking ticket.’

‘Worked in a care home?’

‘Yeah, why?’

‘I think I might know her and if I do we’ll have a solid lead to follow up at last.’

‘Who is she?’

‘Well, unless she’s an innocent bystander and it really was a suicide I think there’s a good chance she’s the one who left Young Hitler out in his wheelchair for the lorry to run over him. If I’m right and I can find her then I might be able to get a line on who’s doing the killing in this.’

‘And where would that get you except maybe killed yourself?’

‘I don’t have a lot of choice. I got a call from Heppert. She’s decided to freeze me out. She knows what this is about but she won’t unbutton unless I can get more leverage than I’ve already got.’

‘And you think you’ll get that in Munich from this witness woman?’

‘Maybe, maybe not. Heppert works for an American firm. Colmar came to Europe from Boston and worked for American friends in Paris during the war. Let’s say Heppert represents the American interest in what’s going on but she’s up against interested parties on this side of the pond competing for whatever Colmar had. If I can give her a good line on the opposition, if I show her I can be of help, then she may change her mind about keeping me out in the cold.’

‘I’m still not convinced that this is worth the candle. All we’ve managed so far is to get a good young journalist killed. That might not bother you but it sure as hell bothers me’

‘For God’s sake, Serge, you’re a copper, of course people get hurt in this sort of thing.’

‘But not by me. I’m supposed to be one of the good guys, remember?’

‘Look, Heppert represents someone heavy from the US,

political, big money or both. Someone else, we don't know who, is also heavy because they kill people. Both sides want whatever Colmar was sitting on. How big do you think this thing has to be to get all the action we've had so far? And that's only the action that we know about.'

Serge didn't need to think too long about it.

'So?'

'I want to be on the inside, that's where the money is, not pissing about round the edges. If I can bring Heppert information about her opposition I might find out where the real money comes from.'

Jimmy waited to see if the point would sink in. When Serge spoke he could see that it had.

'And see if any of it is lying about loose for you to pick up?'

'Why not? Whatever's going down will keep going down whether I'm in or out. I'm not doing anything criminal.'

'Not yet.'

'Look, I was sent to do a job. I'm doing it. I was told to find out what was going on. I'm finding out. I didn't make it messy and I didn't kill anybody.'

'No, not yet.'

'I maybe I won't have to so don't come the boy scout on me until I do. At the moment I'm like you, I'm still with the angels.'

'Sometimes angels fall.'

'Fuck you. Will you help or not?'

Jimmy waited for his answer.

'You sure about this woman in Munich?'

'No.'

'But you think you're right?'

'Yes. They needed someone to put the body where the lorry could hit it. Now they needed a witness who could make it suicide. Why not use the same woman? The care home work pretty much nails it, wouldn't you say?'

Jimmy waited again. It would make sense to any copper with more than five minutes' detective experience. Once might be chance, twice meant guilty, so go and get evidence or a confession, preferably both, and get them any way you could.

'Yes, I agree. If they already had a woman in Munich they'd use her again. All right, I'll find out who she is and I'll try to get an address for her, home or where she works. But you'll have to go carefully, if they think you're on to her they'll kill her.'

'And then kill me, I know. Don't worry, I'll be careful.'

The phone went dead so Jimmy put it down, sat on the edge of the bed, and put his shoes on.

Three days of nothing then slap-bang-wallop, the thing goes bananas. Well, that's how it was sometimes, but at least he'd moved on. The daughter was no good for the moment but the woman in Munich might help put her back in play. Then there was Heppert. To get at her he'd need something that she couldn't refuse. And then there was Serge. Yes, he'd have to think of some way of dealing with Serge when the time came, if the time came, which he rather thought it would.

Chapter Twenty-three

Jimmy finished his drink and decided to take a walk. He couldn't face the idea of another coffee and he didn't want anything else. After about twenty minutes of aimless wandering he stopped and got some lunch. Then he walked back to his bar overlooking the Seine. He'd had two beers with his lunch and he didn't want any more, also he'd got fed up with buying coffee just to let it go cold, so he ordered a glass of red wine. After a few minutes his phone went off. It was Serge.

'I've got what you want on the woman in Munich, the witness. A name and an address.'

'Good, give me them and I'll get going.'

'No, before I give you anything we need to talk.'

'Do we?'

'Oh yes. I've been thinking about what you said, about getting on the inside. I don't like it. We already suspect that Heppert paid off someone in the police to get you out of the way. Your boss was gunned down, Joubert put in hospital, now my journalist has gone under a train …'

Jimmy interrupted.

'Make your point.'

'We need to talk before you go to Munich. I need to know exactly what you intend to do. I'm in this now, up to my neck. I made all the enquiries to the Munich police. They think it's all official. You and I know different. I got us the journalist, he will have told people something, he had to say why he was going to Munich. I need to be sure where I stand in this so I think we should talk before you go to Munich. I want to be sure what it is you'll do when you get there.'

Serge waited.

Jimmy wasn't sure. Either this bloke was a bloody good actor or he really was worried that he might be in deep shit. But he wasn't sure which it was. Had he pegged him wrong? Was he really one of the angels? He picked up the glass of wine and took a sip. No. No, he couldn't be wrong. Everything fitted too well. The way Carpentier had handled the bum's rush at de Gaulle airport, the way he came running as soon as he knew Jimmy was back. The way he'd agreed to everything and come alongside so easily. He had to a be a wrong 'un and the next question was, how dangerous could he be? How far would he go?

'OK, Serge, I can see what you mean. I'm at the bar, the one near Notre Dame where we went the other day. Come here and we'll talk over anything you want.'

'No, I'm busy now. I'll pick you up in two hours. Be outside the Gare de L'Est where I can see you.'

There it was. If that wasn't an invitation to a set-up then nothing was. Jimmy wasn't sure whether to be pleased or angry. For God's sake, he'd done it himself often enough, but at least he'd done it properly, better than this – give me a couple of hours to sort things out then stand out in the open where I can see you. For God's sake it might as well have been printed on a card.

'OK. Two hours outside the station. I'll see you then.'

Jimmy put his phone down. It was still a warm, sunny day. The weather was being extra kind. He looked at his watch. Ten to three. He had a couple of hours to fill and he didn't want any more wine. He picked up his phone and made a call.

A slight improvement. If it continued they would be able to operate again and her chances would look much better.

Jimmy put some notes with his bill and got up. He crossed the road and headed alongside the Seine for the Isle de la Cité. He had another appointment he needed to keep and now was as good a time as any to get it done.

In Notre Dame Cathedral he found the statue of the nun

where he had lit a candle on his last visit. He put his coins in the box, picked up a candle, lit it, put it with the others, and looked up at the blank, plaster face.

'Say thank you for me, will you, she's a bit better. She may even make it all the way although she'll be minus an arm if she does. I'm not complaining, you understand, I'll settle for her alive and, if possible, back at her desk.' He stood for moment then bent down and put a note into the box. He picked up three more candles. He lit them slowly and put them on the holder. Then he went to the rows of seats nearby and knelt down. He wanted to say the right words, the words Bernie must have said so many times for him. Now he wanted to say them for her, for their son Michael, for Eileen and the grandchildren, but no words came so he fell back as he always did on the ancient formula from his childhood.

'May the souls of the faithful departed, through the mercy of God rest in peace. Amen.' For Eileen, her husband and the kids it was easier. They were alive. 'Look after them, God, keep them safe and happy if you can. Amen.'

Jimmy stood up, left the row of seats, and genuflected towards the altar. A column of tourists led by a woman holding up a yellow, folded umbrella, snaked round him as he bent his knee and crossed himself in salute to the Blessed Sacrament reserved in the tabernacle at the back of the altar. They didn't look at him, just went round him. A man praying or acknowledging the presence of God in this place wasn't what they'd come to see. They wanted history, culture, beauty, not faith nor any of the faithful.

Well, why not? You could see and touch the history and the beauty here. Faith was more intangible, elusive. That was because it probably wasn't there however much you bent your knee or crossed yourself, lit candles, or said the words.

Jimmy left the soaring Gothic space and went out into the sunshine and the crowds. He'd go back to his hotel and wait for five o'clock and then go across the road and meet Serge. And once he'd got the name and address he'd let him know exactly what it was he was going to do.

Chapter Twenty-four

Two hours later Jimmy stood by the kerb of the main road which passed the Gare de l'Est where any approaching car could clearly see him. Then his phone rang. It was Serge.

'Hello, Jimmy. Where are you?'

'I'm waiting for you at the Gare de l'Est. What's the matter can't you find your way here?'

'Change of plan. Can you meet me at the Gare du Nord instead? It's not far from where I am now and I'm on foot.'

'Sure, anything you want. I'll see you there in a few minutes.'

Jimmy put his phone away. Somewhere close by Serge was watching him to make sure he was alone, but it didn't matter. Let the bugger think he was on top of things. Let the bugger follow to make sure there was no one else tagging along.

Jimmy joined the early evening crowds heading home. He went up the Rue d'Alsace, across Rue Lafayette, and into the Rue Dunkerque. There he stopped as people poured past into the Gare du Nord behind him.

Serge appeared at his side.

'Hello, Serge, why no car?'

'I prefer it that way. Let's just be part of the crowds shall we? Come on.'

They turned and walked back down the Rue Dunkerque, crossed a road, and went into an RER station; Magenta. They joined the line at one of the ticket windows.

'Where are we going?'

'Somewhere I'm sure no one will recognise me. I don't want

to be seen with you at the moment. I've decided that maybe it wasn't a good idea to listen to you in the first place and a bad idea to get involved after I had.'

Serge bought two tickets and Jimmy followed him until they came to a platform. There was a train waiting, already crowded. They got on and stood; neither could see any available seats.

'Where are we headed?'

'Out of town, to the suburbs.'

They stood in silence as more people boarded the train. It was the end of the working day with crowds of workers going home. When the doors closed and the train began to move the carriage was packed in the way that only happens in rugby scrums, subways, and commuter trains the world over. The train travelled quickly through central Paris on out into a landscape of grim suburban sprawl. At the first few stops a miracle occurred and more passengers got on. But the crowding began to ease as at the next few stations as more people got off than got on and after a few more stations they even got seats. A few stops later the pressure had thinned out considerably and at a place called Gagny sous Bois the train stopped and began to empty. Serge got up and Jimmy followed.

Outside the station it wasn't a pretty sight.

This was still Paris and it was still spring, but what Jimmy saw around him was another world, about as different as you could get from anything you might see in the brochures. It wasn't the Paris the tourists saw or would want to see. This was where Paris' immigrant community had settled, urban living on the edge, in every sense of that word. Rising up around them were tower blocks of monotonous, modern flats that had never been a pleasure to look at and now, dirty and in disrepair, were more than just the eyesore they had originally been. It was as if they had contracted a disease from which they were slowly and painfully dying. And beyond the main road they almost filled the skyline, they were everywhere. At street level there were shops, some boarded up, some open but with broken windows, some so busy that the goods, staff, and customers spilled out of the doors onto the street to blend in with the other rubbish which also seemed to be everywhere. This was high-rise, high-density living, and Jimmy guessed that the poverty, crime, and unemployment also came in high density.

Jimmy felt unsettled and he knew it showed. Serge had said he wanted to go somewhere he wouldn't be recognised, but most of the faces that streamed past them outside the station and those filling the street were black and brown. It didn't seem to be such a good place to choose for a couple of well-dressed, white-faced strangers to wander about in. Not unless one of the faces fitted, a face that would be recognised because it was a police face. This had to be somewhere Carpentier knew and was known.

Carpentier seemed pleased with the effect the place had on Jimmy.

'Not the Paris our visitors want to see, eh, Jimmy?'

'No.'

'We'll walk and you can tell me what it is you're thinking of doing when you get to Munich.'

'Sure. Why not?'

Serge began to walk so Jimmy fell into step. If this place was his beat then these people wouldn't be foreigners, immigrants, North African or anything else to him. They'd be people trying to get on with their lives, mostly honest, but with enough of the other sort to keep more than one copper busy. No different really from the Irish in Kilburn where Jimmy had been born and had grown up. Where he'd become a copper.

They walked, and while they walked Jimmy talked.

'The woman in Munich must be tied in to whoever killed the old Nazi. The best guess is they killed him to get at what they wanted through the daughter. But the Paris thing happens, the convent gets closed, and McBride gets involved and suddenly there's a problem for them, a new player. Then I turn up asking the daughter questions. They're not expecting me so I'm gone before they can do anything. But they do their homework and decide to gun McBride. Dead or not she's out of it, but they're not taking any chances so when someone else turns up asking the daughter questions they're ready. Your journalist throws himself under a train and their tame witness tells the police it's suicide. It's well planned, neat, and professional, just like with McBride. If I'm right the woman who stooged as their witness can tell me enough to get a line on who they are. I can also try to use what I know to scare Young Hitler's daughter to find out what they're after. Once I've got that I can do a deal with Heppert.'

'A deal?'

'I think she doesn't know who the other lot are, if I turn up enough I'll be able to help her find out. Also I'll know what she's after and maybe help her get it.'

'Help her how?'

'By giving her a better claimant than the two clowns she was going to put up for it.'

'Are you sure yours is better?'

Jimmy snorted a laugh.

'She can't be worse. No, she'll be better all right. My boss doesn't cock things up. If our woman isn't actually the real thing she'll be close enough to do the job properly.'

Serge stopped and stood looking into the window of a dingy café. It was busy. Several faces turned and looked at him and, having looked, quickly turned back to whatever they were doing. His face was known all right.

He turned to Jimmy who stood waiting.

'You know where this woman is?'

'No, but it's in a dossier in my boss's desk. Everything Heppert will need will be there for her.'

Serge walked on and Jimmy walked on with him but with the distinct feeling that he'd just been put on display, that Serge's casual pause in their walk had not been so very casual. Jimmy also felt that before they had gone very far a couple of those brown faces would come out from the café and take a slow walk themselves. He didn't look back, he didn't need to.

'And can you get your boss's dossier?'

'Sure. I have a letter back at the hotel which gives me full access to her records. All I do is wave it at the girl on reception and go right on up.'

‘And in return for all this Heppert will give you what?’

‘Money, and lots of it. She’s a corporation lawyer working for some outfit in the US and although she’s up to paying a friendly copper to get me bounced out of Paris and maybe arranging for a local lawyer to get a small smacking she won’t want to go up against anyone who goes in for multiple murder. She’ll want my help all right and she’ll be prepared to pay for it, pay well. I could finish up very well off and maybe I won’t even need to kill anyone and can stay on the side of the angels.’

‘No one?’

‘No one that anyone will notice. See, nothing criminal or, at least, hardly criminal at all. A straight business proposition, or as straight as any business proposition ever is.’

They walked on. The place didn’t get any better as you got away from the station, it stayed pretty much the same. Litter-strewn, run-down streets with shabby shops and lines of grey tower blocks behind them which seemed to taint the perfect blue of the sky. The people going home or doing the shopping looked run down as well, they had that tired, defeated air of poverty, that greyness which wasn’t failure but was very close to it. The only exceptions were the young men who walked together or stood about in small groups, talking and laughing. That was youth, still believing in today and looking forward to tomorrow. Hope or stupidity? Jimmy thought probably both.

‘All right, Jimmy. Like you say there’s nothing there that would bother me, if it all stays like you say it will.’

‘So how about the info on the woman in Munich?’

Serge slipped his hand inside his jacket and pulled out a folded sheet of paper.

‘It’s all there.’ Jimmy took it and read it. ‘Satisfied?’ Jimmy nodded and slipped the paper into his pocket. ‘Good. Now let’s get away from this *pissoir* of a place to where we can have a drink.’ They were by a narrow passage, no more than a back alley running at right angles to the buildings they had passed. ‘This way, it’s quicker and the quickest way out of this dump is the best. Come on.’ Serge led the way. Even though there was still bright sunshine in the street this back alley was a gloomy place of shadows, strewn with filth that smelled of decaying rubbish. 'They are animals out here, Jimmy, animals. Look at all of this filth. They …'

Jimmy's fist hit him hard on the side of the head.

Serge staggered away but stayed upright and managed to turn so Jimmy hit him full on the face twice. The first punch knocked him back and the second sent him hard against the high, blank, concrete wall that was one side of the alley. Serge's head bounced off the wall and he sagged but remained upright. Jimmy stepped up and hit him hard under the heart. Serge gasped and folded and the gun he'd managed to get into his hand fell with a clatter to the floor. Jimmy bent down and picked it up. He stood up, turned looked back down the alley. The two dark-skinned men who had come in stood looking at him. Jimmy pointed the gun at them.

'Fuck off or I'll kill you.'

They didn't need to understand English to know what he'd said, but they didn't move.

Serge was propped against the wall bending down holding his stomach, struggling to breathe. Jimmy went to his side and kicked out his legs from under him and Serge collapsed to the ground with a stifled cry. Jimmy kicked him hard in the face. It jerked his head back and bounced it once more hard against the wall. Serge slumped sideways, unconscious.

Jimmy stood away from him and began to walk towards the two men. They stood for a second then turned and ran off. Jimmy waited for a moment then turned and went back to Serge. He felt through his pockets until he found his mobile phone. He slipped it into his own pocket. Then he took out his handkerchief and gently rubbed down the gun, enough to smear any prints. He pulled up Serge's left arm, took his hand, and wrapped it around the butt of the pistol. Then he held the hand so the gun was touching Serge's temple and manoeuvred a finger onto the trigger and pressed. The shot rang out around the alley and Serge's head jerked sharply sideways. Jimmy let the hand fall, stood up, and waited. It was only seconds but to Jimmy it was a long time. No one came or looked into the alley so he walked across to some rubbish piled against a large bin and picked up a couple of half-soggy cardboard boxes. He went back to what was left of Serge, broke the boxes apart, and draped them over the body. He hunted round the rubbish and collected what he wanted and soon the body was pretty much hidden from view to any casual passer-by of the alley entrance. He stood up and waited. Still no one. The body would be found soon enough but not before he was on his way back to Paris. He walked back to the road, turned left, and began to re-trace his way to the station. There would be plenty of trains bringing the workers home which meant plenty of empty ones going back. He should be in his room at his hotel in almost no time at all.

He passed the café where Serge had let the two brown faces see their man; he didn't pause or look in. If Serge's friends were going to do anything it would have been done by now. He walked on.

Shit, he thought, he'd left his ticket in Serge's pocket. Oh well, the police wouldn't have it down as suicide anyway. No one beats himself up before he shoots himself in the head, do they?

Jimmy arrived at the station, bought his ticket, and was soon on a train back. The carriage was empty so he took out Serge's phone and went through the address book, found the number he wanted, and made a call.

Chapter Twenty-five

Jimmy had his story all worked out by the time Nadine Heppert arrived at the bar in the Gare de l'Est station. She came to the table where he was waiting and sat down. Everything about her was impatient and dismissive. She refused anything to drink.

'Thank you for agreeing to meet with me, Ms Heppert.'

Jimmy had called her on Serge's phone and told her that Serge had a problem, that he was in trouble and it wasn't the sort of trouble you could discuss over the phone. Also he had a message from him for her.

'Just give me the message, Mr Costello.'

Jimmy leaned forward and spoke distinctly but quietly.

'Serge Carpentier is dead.'

That took the look of superiority off her face.

'What?'

It was shock in her voice that made it too loud. The rush-hour was about finished and the bar wasn't busy, but nor was it empty.

'Can we keep this quiet please, Ms Heppert? I chose a table where we could talk without being overheard but we will have to keep our voices down or go somewhere else.' She nodded. 'You understand? Carpentier is dead.'

She looked at him half stupidly, half disbelievingly, but when she spoke she leaned forward and her voice was low.

'Dead?'

'Shot in the head in an alley at a place called Gagny sous Bois.'

The shocked stupidity stayed but the disbelief evaporated

and although she managed to keep her voice low Jimmy noticed the tremor of fear.

'Did the police tell you? Who told you? How do I know you're telling me the truth?'

'No one told me and, believe me, I am telling the truth.'

'How can I be sure?'

'Because I shot him.'

Jimmy watched as she visibly deflated. Tears came into her eyes. It was as if he had just told her that her husband or child had been killed.

And then it hit him.

Oh my, God, they weren't just cronies in this scam. They were bloody lovers. The silly cow was sleeping with the bastard. Shit. The bugger swung both ways, Jules at home and Heppert on the side.

He had to get her out of the bar, away from anywhere public. He couldn't have her fall apart with Paris goggling at her. He stood up and went round to her chair and took her arm. She looked up at him, bewildered, as if he was a stranger. There were tears on her cheeks but she got up when Jimmy lifted her arm.

'Come with me, we'll go somewhere quiet, private, where we can talk and I can get you a drink. Come on.'

And to his surprise she came.

He managed to get her across the road, into his hotel, and up to his room where he sat her on the bed.

'Want a drink?'

She shook her head. She was getting a handkerchief out of her handbag.

Jimmy waited.

She found the hanky after some fumbling and wiped her eyes then looked at him.

'He's really dead?'

Jimmy nodded.

'And you shot him?'

'Yes.'

She looked down at her hanky.

'Why?'

'He'd set me up. I had no choice.'

She looked at him again but now with a trace of hate in her eyes and a sneer in her voice.

'Self-defence?'

'No. Self-preservation. I killed him in cold blood before he could have me murdered.'

She looked down at her hands again. Jimmy couldn't make it out. She was crying for the death of a bloke who was presumably her lover and sitting in a hotel room talking to the man who'd killed him. He'd come across many strange reactions to sudden, violent death in his life but this was a new one and he wasn't sure how to handle it. He sat down on the bed beside her. She turned to him but the hate and the sneer had gone.

'Why?'

'Why what?'

'Why did you kill him?'

'I told you, he was …'

'Yes but why? Why was he going to kill you?'

Jimmy could see she didn't doubt him. He'd told her Carpentier was going to kill him and she believed him, she didn't seem to need any convincing, so he began to tell her the story he'd prepared. It wasn't too far from the truth and he'd softened her up with the way he'd broken Carpentier's death to her. All things considered Jimmy felt she was ready to swallow his version without many questions.

'He wanted to get on the inside of this thing that's going on, this Colmar estate thing. He knew there was a lot of money involved and he wanted a part of it. I showed him how to do it and as soon as I did that he wanted me out of the way so he arranged a little meeting with a couple of friends of his. Maybe the same two he hired for you, the ones who put Joubert in hospital.'

She didn't try to deny it.

'I see.'

She sat on the bed looking at her hands. Jimmy decided it

would be best to get her talking while she seemed willing.

'Did you pay him to kick me out of Paris as well?'

She nodded.

'We knew Joubert was acting for the nuns and when you turned up it seemed the simplest thing to do. I'd already arranged with Serge to have Joubert removed from the case.' Jimmy was surprised. Even in shock he hadn't expected her to unbutton so easily. She was, after all, a lawyer and here she was admitting to an almost total stranger counts of bribing a police officer and complicity in theft and an aggravated assault. Still, he thought, as I've just admitted to her what the police would certainly count as murder, maybe it all makes some sort of sense. She was looking at him again. 'What now?'

The tears were gone now and so was the shock. The lover was gone, the lawyer was back and was at work. Jimmy changed his tone to suit her new mood.

'Now you'll have to work with me.'

'Oh yes?'

'Yes. Carpentier was on the make and was a ruthless bastard. You two may have been lovers but he was …'

She managed a sort of laugh.

'My God. You make it sound like a romance from a cheap novel. We weren't lovers, we had sex, magnificent, wonderful sex.' Jimmy's face must have shown he had no idea what she meant and she did the laugh again. 'You simpleton, you stupid, naïve, innocent simpleton. You don't think love had anything to do with it. He was … oh, God, what does it matter now and what would be the point of trying to explain it to you?'

She almost spat the last words at him and somehow, he didn't understand how, Jimmy felt he deserved her contempt. In some ways he *was* innocent and naïve and, when it came to magnificent, wonderful sex that had nothing to do with love, he probably *was* a stupid simpleton. He stood up, she looked up at him, still with tear-streaked cheeks but also a sneering smile. He smacked her hard across the face. She fell sideways onto the bed and he reached down and pulled her back upright.

'Now listen and listen well or I'll throw you over that

fucking balcony.'

There was fear now in her eyes, real fear. That was good because he didn't have much time and certainly no time for any crap about sex, magnificent or otherwise.

'I killed Carpentier because he was going to kill me. He was also going to take you for whatever he could get and he meant to get a shed-load. If you got in his way or wouldn't play along he'd have killed you and gone on to whoever would play along. He was a bastard, understand, a ruthless bastard and now he's dead and we're stuck with each other so let's not fuck about any more and do what has to be done. All right?'

The fear was almost gone. She was coming round, thank God. She nodded slowly.

'All right.'

'Sorry I had to hit you but we don't have much time. Gagny sous Bois didn't look like a place where people run for the cops too quickly but a dead body with a hole in the head will get noticed and reported, especially when they find it's a copper. The best thing to do is assume police already have the body now and any idea that it might have been suicide will have lasted as long as it took a detective to look at his face. We need to get things straight. OK?' She nodded again. 'Carpentier told you about my boss, that she'd been shot?'

'Yes.'

'What else did he tell you?'

'You had another claimant to the estate, a good one, maybe even the real one. He told me what you'd said about the marriage in Florida, how you thought it ruled out the brothers.'

'And about the journalist?'

She shook her head.

'No, he never mentioned any journalist.'

'Right. You have to make a choice and you have to make it now.'

'Or you'll throw me over the balcony?'

'No. If we work together you have to be willing. We're no good to each other if we don't do this as a team.'

She thought about it, but only for a second.

'So, what would you say were my choices?'

'Go with me to Rome and vet our candidate, then go with me to Munich and help me find out who the opposition are.'

'Or?'

'Or go to the police and tell them I killed Serge and why I killed him.' She sat looking at him. Damn, the silly cow was thinking about it. 'Of course if you go to the police you'll have to tell them the whole thing. They'll have to know what this is all …'

'Shut up.'

Jimmy shut up and waited. When she spoke he realised he was wrong, she'd been thinking, but not about going to the police.

'Can the police tie you to the killing?'

'I doubt it. There were two witnesses …'

'What?'

'The two blokes he'd arranged to be there. Probably the ones who put Joubert in hospital, so they won't go to the police in a hurry. The police may eventually get some sort of description but it won't be any time soon. The only real connection between me and Carpentier will be from the airport, from the bloke in security who passed the message that I was back. If he sent it straight to Serge we're clear, if not, if it went through channels it'll surface and they'll have a name, my name.'

'How long do you think we have?'

'He's one of their own, they pull out all the stops, TV, papers, everything. We need to go now, tonight, and we need to go by train. No airports, it has to be train.'

'Or car?'

'No, cars are too easy to pick up. How many people knew about you and Serge?'

'A few, not many.'

'He said he had a boyfriend, a partner, Jules?'

'Yes, but it wasn't exclusive. Jules only liked men, Serge liked men and women. I doubt Jules knows anything about me or would care if he did.'

'If you left, now, would you be missed?'

'I could send in something to the office, tell them I've had an urgent call in relation to this case, that it will take me out of town for a few days.'

'And that won't get anyone thinking?'

'No, the thing's under wraps, top priority from head office. I deal with it and only me and I answer to New York personally to the head of the firm. If I said I was going to Rome to kill the pope it wouldn't get anyone thinking, not out loud anyway, not if they wanted to keep their job.'

'So, are we going to Rome to kill the pope?'

'Yes.'

'Good, you've made the right decision, Ms Heppert.'

'Just one thing.'

'Yes?'

'You're doing this for your own reasons and now I know how far you'll go to get whatever it is you hope achieve, so I'll make something clear. Don't think for one minute I am prepared to help you except in so far as it furthers the interests of my firm. I will hand you over to the police the moment I think our interests have diverged so if you intend to kill me at any point out of your sense of self-preservation then you'd better do it now.'

'Why?'

'Because before I go with you to Rome I will make a full and clear deposition, framed to suit my own interests of course, of everything you have told me or I have learned from Serge. It will be deposited safely at my office with instructions to be handed to the police should anything untoward happen to me in the next few weeks.'

'Head office in New York won't like it if does get handed to the police.'

'As I'll be dead then head office can go and …'

And she used an expression the technicality of which escaped him, but was clearly derived from her experience of the magnificent and wonderful.

'Fair enough. Our train leaves the Gare de Lyon at seven forty-two in the morning. It's the TGV to Milan. I've bought the tickets, I'll see you on the platform.'

She stood up. She was fine. All things considered she'd taken it well and come up smiling. She was all lawyer now, just like Jimmy wanted.

'I'm glad I seem to be dealing with someone organised.'

Jimmy shrugged.

'I guessed you'd be sensible that's all.'

'Then I'm also glad I'm dealing with a good guesser.'

'Seven forty-two. Does that give you enough time?'

'I'll be there, Mr Costello, let's hope you're right about the police and you're there as well.'

'Don't worry. I'll be there.'

She left the room and Jimmy went out onto the balcony and looked down into the street. After a few minutes he saw her come out of the hotel and cross the road. She was on her mobile. Jimmy went back into his room. If she was calling the police there was nothing he could do. He was packed and ready, all there was to do now was wait until it was time to get a taxi to the Gare de Lyon.

He thought about McBride's room at the hospital, all those tubes and gadgets working to keep her alive, if she was still alive. Well, one of the bastards down and more to go. He picked up his mobile and made a call. She was in the operating theatre. There had been a complication and further surgery was necessary. If she survived the surgery her chances were improved but first she had to survive the surgery. Jimmy put his phone down the spoke to the empty room.

'Hang in there, God, I'm doing the best I can. Don't let her go now.'

Then he went down to reception and told them he'd be leaving very early next day. He settled his bill then went back to his room where he sat and waited.

Chapter Twenty-six

Nadine phoned Jimmy about an hour and a half after she had left his hotel. She'd sorted everything out with her office and was clear to go. She also told him that if it screwed up on her she had left information which would ensure that Jimmy, if he survived, would go down for murder, blackmail, shoplifting, and all the unpaid parking fines outstanding in Paris. Other than that she suggested they have breakfast at the Gare de Lyon before the train left next morning. Jimmy agreed and then lay on his bed. So far so good, I mean, why arrange to meet for breakfast if she was going to shop him to the police? So he set his phone for an alarm call, closed his eyes, and fell asleep.

His phone woke him next morning and at five he was went downstairs with his holdall. The night porter at reception looked up from his paper, took his key, smiled, and then went back to his reading and Jimmy left the hotel.

Nadine arrived at the station café shortly after six thirty. She looked good, the real business. She was pulling a small, smart suitcase, had her Gucci handbag over her shoulder, and was carrying a severe briefcase. For a woman like her, Jimmy reckoned that was travelling light, and expecting a very short trip. She sat down, arranged her luggage by her, then looked at him with eyes that said "I'm in control".

'Well?'

'Well what?'

'Aren't you going to get me coffee?'

'Sure. Just coffee?'

She nodded and began to fiddle inside her handbag.

Jimmy brought the coffee and put it in front of her. She took a sip.

'I really do have your neck in a noose if this thing turns sour on me. You do understand that?' It was Jimmy's turn to nod but he was still tired so he didn't add anything. 'You said you had the tickets?'

'Yes.'

'First class?'

'No.'

'Oh, God.'

'Sorry.'

She didn't answer, lapsed into silence as she drank her coffee.

Things stayed that way until they were sitting together on the train and it began to slowly roll out of the station.

As soon as it had picked up speed Nadine began to try to make herself comfortable.

'I'm going to try and get some sleep. When I wake you can get me coffee and croissants.' She paused in her preparations. 'With real butter.'

'Got it. Real butter.'

She turned her head slightly to the window, closed her eyes and, as far as Jimmy could make out, seemed to go straight to sleep. Jimmy looked past her at Paris, now moving past fast, and thought about his last train journey with Serge. That had been a bit of a bastard. He hoped this one would turn out better. He looked out of the window and watched Paris go by, then looked at Nadine. If she was pretending to be asleep she was doing a first-rate job.

The rest of the journey passed in much the same way. Jimmy got her coffee when she wanted it but, other than that, they talked hardly at all. They both had plenty to think about and both had lots of questions that needed answers, but they were not the kind of questions you asked or answered anywhere public. Not that Jimmy would have asked her anything of any real interest even if they'd had the whole compartment to themselves. She wouldn't give him any real answers until she was sure that the woman McBride had hidden away was the real thing, or as good as.

The Paris to Milan run was a trip of just over seven hours. Jimmy stared into space or looked past Nadine at the passing countryside. When awake she kept her nose buried in a book she had brought with her. It was by someone called Lee Child. Jimmy had never heard of him.

He looked at her. Why take a window seat if you didn't want to look out of the window, Jimmy wondered. But he guessed she was one of those people who always took what they saw even if they wanted it or not. At Milan there was a twenty-five minute break before the Rome train. They sat in the station café, Nadine had a glass of wine and some sort of salad. Jimmy had a beer and a slice of some sort of flan. Railway station food. They didn't talk. When their train pulled up to the platform Jimmy slipped past her as she marshalled her luggage to get on the train and, by the time she reached their seats, he was by the window. He didn't offer to help her put her luggage up on the rack. She was a big, strong girl, she could manage by herself. She sat down and began once more to read her book, ignoring him.

'Is it any good?'

'No idea, it passes the time.'

And she turned a page.

The train began to pull out, it was the afternoon, the sun was lowering in the sky making the shadows longer and darker. Once clear of Milan there was a beauty about it all for anyone who had eyes to see. The ticket inspector passed through the compartment. If there was going to be a problem, if the Paris police had put out a call, now would be the time it all blew up in his face. But the ticket collector went on, and, after two station stops, nothing had happened. Everything was going smoothly. Whatever the Paris police were doing about Serge nobody seemed to be working hard at locating one James Costello. Or maybe it was just being on the train. Airports could be checked, but with paperless frontiers someone on a train became pretty much invisible. That was why he had chosen it.

Jimmy looked out of the window. The outer edges of another

big city slowly began to emerge from the countryside. He tried to think about how he'd handle Professor Scolari or whoever he came up against at the Collegio. But his brain froze. Suddenly he was too tired to think so he closed his eyes and went to sleep.

He had been asleep for about ten minutes when Nadine stopped her pretence of reading. She had been turning the pages slowly, at the right pace, but ignoring the words, thinking about Jimmy and her present situation. She lowered the book and looked at him. Definitely not a nobody. How would she handle him once she got what she wanted? It was a tricky call. Ditch him straight away or hold on to him? If she got what she wanted would she still need him to handle things until a deal was done? She then let her mind circle Jimmy's interest in this business. How much did he know, what sort of people were behind him, and how much did they want? There was a lot to play for, more than a lot, but not enough to go shares with anyone. There was never enough to let some of it slip away. Jimmy stirred but didn't open his eyes. The book went back up and her eyes looked at the words for a moment. It was a scene in which some tough guy was being tough. She turned the page and slightly lifted her eyes. He seemed still to be asleep so she lowered the book again and returned to her question. Ditch him or keep him? It was a big question.

Chapter Twenty-seven

The train arrived at Termini at six twenty-five. They had snacked on the journey, not eaten a real meal, and Jimmy was hungry. The first thing he wanted, now he was back in Rome, was to get some food inside him. He suggested a restaurant he knew.

'No, we can have dinner after I've got my hotel sorted out.'

'How long will that take?'

'As long as it takes.'

'Do you want me to recommend somewhere?'

She gave a small laugh.

'No, I don't think our tastes would coincide. I'll be staying at the River Palace. I booked yesterday as soon as I knew we were coming. It's on the Via Flaminia.'

'I know where it is and you're right, our tastes don't coincide.'

The River Palace was very upmarket and in a smart-set part of the city, not the sort of place that Jimmy would want to go and probably not somewhere he'd be particularly welcome if he did.

'I'll call you when I'm ready.'

And that was that. He was to wait until he was wanted.

Nadine walked to the taxi rank, got in, and Jimmy watched the taxi pull away. He turned back to the station. He would catch the Metro to his apartment. Maybe he would drop into the Café Mozart for a drink or go straight up and make himself a sandwich. He wasn't sure. Suddenly a man was at his side, close, too close. Jimmy tried to take a step away but bumped into another man standing on the other side, also too close.

'Please, Mr Costello, do not make any fuss. There is someone who wants to talk to you and it would be better if you came willingly. If I use this you will collapse in less than thirty seconds.' Jimmy looked down at the man's hand which he took out of his coat pocket. It held a small hypodermic. 'You will have fainted. It would only make a small disturbance, a small embarrassment, but nothing more, believe me.'

Jimmy looked at the other man, Hypo was big enough, but not compared to his partner. They both had fixed smiles and were looking at him, no one was taking any notice, it was just three friends meeting and talking. Jimmy decided that they knew their business and if they'd wanted to finish him he'd be dead by now, so he shrugged. Why not? It was what he wanted after all, to make contact with the opposition. Now it seemed they'd saved him the trouble of looking.

'It's your party. Let's go.'

The big one attached himself to Jimmy's arm while the other half of the sketch had his hand half out of his pocket so he could use the hypo quickly if he had to. They shepherded him to a black Fiat waiting some way behind the line of taxis. The big one's grip tightened as he opened the door. Hypo got in first and moved across, Jimmy got pushed in and the big one got in beside him. Jimmy was glad it was a big car, in anything smaller he wouldn't have been able to breathe. The car pulled away and as it did the man with the hypo used it in Jimmy's thigh. Jimmy didn't struggle except for a sudden jerk as the needle went in and, just as the man had said, in less than thirty seconds he passed out.

He came round slumped in a big, comfortable armchair with his jacket and shoes off and a warm blanket spread over him. He had a headache and his first feeling was that if he didn't get to a toilet quickly and take a piss his bladder would burst. He struggled to sit up and that made his head worse but he stuck at it. The man who had used the hypo was sitting in an armchair opposite, watching. Jimmy stood up and the man nodded his head to a door.

'Through that door.'

Jimmy went to the door and opened it. It was the bathroom. He stood at the toilet and relieved himself of the awful pressure. He had been kidnapped, shot full of dope, and was now in what looked like a hotel suite with the man who had used the hypo. But none of that diminished the momentary pleasure he felt, a sense of supreme relief. Finished, he rinsed his hands and went back into the room and looked round. It was the main room of an expensive hotel suite. Jimmy and Hypo were the only two occupants. His shoes were by the chair he'd woken up in so he put them back on while Hypo watched. After he'd tied his laces he stood up. Movement hurt but it helped.

'What happens now?'

Hypo shrugged.

Jimmy knew he spoke English so he tried again.

'I said what happens now, shithead?'

The man didn't react except to tell Jimmy to sit down. So Jimmy sat down. The relief of the toilet was gone and all that was left was a throbbing headache and Hypo, who still looked as if he knew his business, and Jimmy was in no state to play the tough guy.

The bedroom door opened and a man walked in.

'Hello, Mr Costello, nice to see you again. Has he used the toilet?' Hypo nodded and said something in what sounded to Jimmy like Danish. 'Good, you can go now, Bengt. Mr Costello and I need to talk for a while. I'll call you when I need you.'

Hypo, who was also Bengt, left and the new arrival sat in the chair opposite Jimmy.

'I try so hard to keep you alive, Mr Costello, yet you seem to try just as hard to frustrate my efforts. Tell me, is that animosity on your part or your natural bloody-mindedness. Or is it perhaps sheer stupidity? No, not stupidity, I take back stupidity. You are many things, I know, but not usually stupid. My guess would be sheer bloody-mindedness.'

The man sat back with a gentle grin on his face. He'd made his introduction now he waited for Jimmy to make his reply.

'Still playing the comedian, Commander? It is still

Commander is it? That was what you were when you saw me off at Copenhagen.'

'Alas yes, still Commander. I fear I have reached the limits of both my talent and my opportunity. So, to business, why are you trying so hard to get yourself killed? I ask the question professionally, you understand, if you have a death wish then I will of course respect your decision. Have you developed a death wish, Mr Costello?'

'I thought anything outside Denmark didn't concern you. If I want to get myself killed why should you care so long as it happens outside Denmark?'

'Because this concerns things that happen inside Denmark. Didn't you know that? I would have thought you would have known that.'

'No, I didn't know that.'

The comedian manner slipped away for a moment while the man turned over what Jimmy had told him. Then he came to some sort of decision and the act was on again.

'You are not still a member of the Vatican Diplomatic Service I take it?'

'The passport was a fake. I was never employed by His Holiness.'

'No, of course you weren't, but I had to play my part in that little charade didn't I? If I hadn't your Monsignor from Rome would have been gravely embarrassed and in Denmark we take men of the cloth with suitable seriousness, even a Catholic Monsignor from Rome who tells us things that are less than the truth.'

Jimmy stood up.

'Come on, sunshine, you're the one who had me picked up and delivered here so either make your point or let me go.'

The Comedian registered surprise.

'But you are free to go, you are not being held against your will. I have no authority here to arrest, detain, or even question you. Leave as soon as you wish, Mr Costello.'

And he held out a hand pointing at the room door. Jimmy sat down again.

His head still ached and he now had a funny taste in his mouth, but if he really was free to go he might as well stay and do his best to find out why the Comedian had picked him up in the first place.

'I could tell the local police you bundled me into a car and filled me full of some kind of dope.'

'By all means, go to the police and make a complaint if you wish.' He waited a moment to make his point. 'No? Not keen to involve the police? I thought not. However, if you will answer a few of my questions I will do my best to answer a few of yours and our time together may prove profitable to both of us. What do you say?'

Jimmy looked at his watch. He couldn't have been out long, it was only an hour since they'd arrived at Termini. He felt for his phone. The Comedian put his hand in his own pocket, pulled it out, and handed it over to him.

'I switched it off while you were indisposed.'

Jimmy switched it on, after a second it beeped that he had a message. He opened it, read it, and then put away the phone.

'I'm meeting someone in an hour and I need to get back to my apartment and get myself sorted. If we're going to have a heart-to-heart about anything make it snappy.'

'I'll have you driven to your apartment whenever you wish. Your appointment is, I suppose, with Ms Heppert?'

'Yes.'

'Then let that be my first question. What is your relationship at the moment with Ms Heppert?'

'At the moment?'

'Why are you travelling together and why are you in Rome?'

'Those are big questions, the answers might cover a lot of ground. Try something smaller to begin with.'

'Really, Mr Costello, we shall get nowhere like this. Caution is all very well but mutual co-operation requires a little trust from both parties.'

'Go on then, make me trust you.'

The act slipped away again. Now the man sitting opposite Jimmy was anything but funny.

'Ms Heppert is a company lawyer, a very good one. She is a woman of intelligence, ambition, and resource. She is currently employed in a senior position in the Paris office of a small but extremely influential firm based in Manhattan. She has an excellent salary supplemented by what some might call an almost obscene expense account. But she wants more, and when she gets what she wants it will still not be enough. For people like her, it never is. At the moment she is manoeuvring to negotiate a promotion with a rival firm, no, not a promotion, a partnership. She is a dangerous woman, Mr Costello, believe me, I know.'

'How?'

'Serge Carpentier told me.'

The man waited while Jimmy let it sink in.

'Carpentier worked for you?'

'On a casual basis. He came to Denmark a few years ago as part of a European-wide police effort to trace the way Eastern European women were being brought into Western countries to work in the sex trade. The French thought there was a route operating through Denmark. As it happened they were wrong and that left Carpentier with a little time on his hands and unfortunately for him, but fortunately for me, he used it unwisely. A young man died. It was not technically murder, you understand, more a regrettable accident due to an excess of sexual enthusiasm. But it could have resulted in criminal proceedings if it hadn't been dealt with. It would certainly have got him dismissed from his job if it had got back to his superiors.'

'So you made sure it was swept under the carpet, put the screws on Carpentier, and made him work for you?'

'Yes.'

'Why would you need a tame French copper? I thought we were all on the same side these days?'

'Most of the time we are. But not all of the time. Not, for instance, in the case of the Colmar estate. We knew of the US interest in the estate and that Ms Heppert was acting for that interest so I told Carpentier to get close to her.'

'To become her lover?'

'To become whatever he had to be, but as it happened they did develop a sexual relationship. People who are rich, greedy, and selfish usually do not restrain their appetites so it wasn't hard for Carpentier to, as it were, fill a vacancy. Ms Heppert has a very strong carnal urge, luckily Carpentier was a man of talent in that line of work.'

'Did he suggest giving Joubert a going over or was it her idea?'

'Hers. Ms Heppert wanted to remove the lawyer Joubert from his role on behalf of the sisters. She didn't want that complication to get in her way. With Joubert suitably scared off it was easy to take over from him. The sisters needed a replacement lawyer, she came highly recommended, and they took her at face value.'

'So Carpentier hired a couple of thugs and had Joubert put in hospital for her.'

'For her? For me? Let us say it was something that needed doing so I told him to help her do it. When you turned up I was really quite surprised. I shouldn't have been of course, once the matter of the Colmar estate became entangled with the sisters in Paris I should have anticipated that Professor McBride might take an interest, which she did as soon as it was drawn to her attention. I didn't, however, know what it was you were sent to Paris to do, but you were a nuisance at a delicate point in time so I had Carpentier eject you from the country with a warning not to return. With you and Joubert out of the picture all of our energies could be focussed on the Heppert woman. All I wanted, you understand, was to avoid unnecessary complications.'

Jimmy didn't like the way this story was unwinding. He'd had Carpentier down as on Heppert's payroll, a bent copper and, if pushed, a potential killer. If what the man seated opposite was telling him was true he'd been wide of the mark, miles bloody wide.

'Carpentier was your man alongside Heppert?'

'Was being the operative word. Serge Carpentier's body was

found in an alley in a Paris suburb yesterday. He had been savagely beaten then shot though the side of the head with his own gun. Would you know anything about that, Mr Costello?'

The man sat back and Jimmy's mind raced trying to think of what, if anything, he should do or say.

'Why should I know anything?'

It was a poor stall and got what it deserved, a pitying smile.

'Because unless I'm very much mistaken you were the one who shot him.'

And that was that, if he knew, he knew. He was a clever bastard and he didn't piss about. He used that bloody comedian act to put you off your guard but his mind never left the job in hand once it had locked on.

'I thought he'd set me up. I thought he'd got me there to finish me off.'

'No, Mr Costello. I wanted you out of the way, not in the morgue. Nothing more would have happened to you than happened to M. Joubert. A few knocks and bruises, enough to put you in hospital so I could have visited you and put you in the picture. I'm afraid your killing of Serge Carpentier was based on an error of judgement, in fact I'm surprised that you could have made such a mistake, more than surprised, disappointed and extremely annoyed. I spent time and effort to put Carpentier alongside the Heppert woman and, thanks to your blundering, you have undone all of that work.'

Somehow, he didn't quite know how, Jimmy felt he ought to apologise.

'Sorry.'

It didn't help.

'Sorry! That hardly covers what you have done. You have murdered a policeman in cold blood. I doubt any judge would dismiss the case against you on the grounds that you were sorry, that it was all a mistake.'

Jimmy felt confused by the unreality of the situation, by the conversation he was having. Maybe it was the dope in him or maybe it was the Comedian's technique working. This man was too clever for him so he gave up.

'What do you want?'

The man's manner relaxed again and he gave Jimmy a smile of encouragement.

'I want you to replace Carpentier.'

'What, as Heppert's sex machine? You must be …'

Jimmy's outburst got a laugh.

'Good heavens, no, Mr Costello, nothing like that. Up to a point he was trusted by her, the work he did on Joubert ensured that. Now I want you to be trusted by her. Have you told her that it was you who killed him?'

'Yes.'

'And I'm sure she took it in her stride?'

'She cried a bit. I thought they were lovers.'

'Oh no, not lovers. All the rooms of Ms Heppert's heart are fully occupied by Ms Heppert herself. She used him, that was all. If she cried then it was entirely for your benefit, probably to give herself time to adjust to the news and decide what to do. I'm sure she became herself again very quickly.'

'She did.'

Jimmy was feeling out of his depth. He'd got Serge wrong and he'd got Heppert wrong. He was on a losing streak as wide as Piccadilly Circus and had been ever since they gunned McBride. It was slowly dawning on him that he was still only detective sergeant material, a clever plodder who could only work out the little things, like who did the actual job, pulled the trigger, used the knife, or whatever. On his own, without someone pointing him in the right direction, it all sailed over his head and if he tried to figure it out he did more harm than good. No, not just harm, he bloody well killed people. The wrong people. He needed to be pointed in the right direction by one of the grown-ups. By someone who really did know what they were doing. Someone like the Comedian.

'If I stick alongside Heppert how do I report to you?'

'Don't worry, I can easily arrange that. All I want you to do is watch and listen. But be careful, she's as sharp as she is greedy and that is saying a great deal. Don't take any risk that might lead her to suspect you're working for me.'

'It won't work.'

'Won't work?'

'No. I can't act. If I try to pretend I'm on her side in all this she'll spot it. McBride used to hide things from me, tell me half the story and I used to think she was being devious, that maybe she didn't trust me. But now I can see that she knew I had to believe in what I was doing so that anyone I talked to would see I believed it. I can't act. Sorry, but that's the way it is.'

The man stood up and walked slowly round the room and then came back and sat down.

'Then tell her.'

'Tell her what?'

'Everything. I had you picked up, drugged, and brought here. We had this talk, tell it all to her, word for word as you can remember it. I wanted you to replace Carpentier and as I had you over a barrel because of his killing you had to agree. Tell her everything. It won't change our arrangement and there will be no need for any act on your part and nothing for her to find out, you will have told her everything.'

There was a flaw in there somewhere, it was just out of sight, but Jimmy was certain that it was in there somewhere.

'But it will still be a lie, I'll be working for you not her, so it'll still be a lie, right?'

'No. You will be working for Professor McBride, not for me and not for Ms Heppert. That, after all, is the real truth is it not?'

Jimmy thought about it and, to his surprise, he found it was. He *was* working for McBride. He had been all along and he still was. This bloke and Heppert meant nothing to him. He worked for them or against them only in so far as it helped him to do what McBride wanted him to do. Which was …?

And there it was. That was the flaw. What the bloody hell was he supposed to be doing for McBride? It couldn't be as simple as she said, get control of the Colmar Estate and check out the convent? Not with all these other high-powered buggers running around.

‘I’ll need to know what this is all about. I can’t keep flying blind.’

The man sat back.

‘Professor McBride didn’t tell you?’

‘Just to find the heir to the Colmar Estate. If I’m going to do what you want I’ll need to know what it’s really all about. You’ll have to tell me.’

The man thought about it, but not for long.

‘No, I think not. I think you will do very well for me as you are. You can, of course, see if you can get Ms Heppert to tell you, but I have to say I think her attitude will prove to be the same as mine. You may have a certain limited use to both of us but it is, I assure you, very limited indeed.’

‘So what exactly is it I’m supposed to be looking for if I stick with Heppert? I have to have some idea. I’ve made too many mistakes already because I don’t have any idea of where I’m going or why, and your turning up hasn’t made anything clearer. I’m not going to risk killing some other poor sod because I don’t know what everyone else seems to know. Give me something or you can go fuck yourself, Commander.’

The outburst got a gentle smile.

‘Very well, seeing as how you ask so nicely I will give you something, a direction, a purpose. Ms Heppert represents one powerful party which is interested in the Colmar estate. I will call them Group A. There is another party which is also interested, let us call them Group B. Heppert is with A and wants to move over to B taking with her what she knows. That is the partnership she seeks, the one I mentioned earlier. She wants to sell out her employers. But Group B have proved to be a very violent proposition, not something Ms Heppert is used to dealing with. She needs a scout to lead the way, someone through whom to make contact, someone who is used to violence. She needs a stooge to do the dangerous work of locating someone from the top of Group B. She was considering using Serge Carpentier but, as I said, she is clever and she wasn’t convinced he was exactly what she wanted. I think she sensed he was, how shall I put it? He was not someone she could use and dispose of. However, your little bit of back-alley work closed that avenue to her rather suddenly. It did, however, open up a new and better one. She has chosen you to be her scout.'

'She doesn't rate me as difficult to dispose of?'

'Apparently not, although I doubt she sees herself as the actual disposer.'

'So what will she want me to do?'

'You will be in the middle of this affair. Ms Heppert will be able to see you but stay at a safe distance from the opposition. If they react badly it is you who will die and Ms Heppert will withdraw and try again in some other way. That is your position, Mr Costello, you are in the middle. At some point you will be able to see both Group B and Ms Heppert, although they will not be able to see each other. When that happens you will either set up a safe meeting for her or you will be eliminated. There will be no third way.'

It made sense, in so far as anything in this affair made sense. But it didn't sound like it would have a happy ending.

'And if I set up this meeting I'll be eliminated anyway. I'll have served my purpose and be a loose end.'

'I would have thought so.'

'So why should I go ahead? What's in it for me?'

'Group B killed the man in the wheelchair in Munich. They also killed the journalist you sent. More importantly they tried to kill Professor McBride and, if she survives, will undoubtedly try again. That is what is in it for you, Professor McBride's life. Believe me, they won't miss a second time.'

'And you. Which group are you?'

'I represent another group unattached to either A or B. We wish to stay invisible to both sides until we can move in and take the Colmar estate from whichever one remains standing at the end of their struggle.'

'I see.'

He didn't, of course, but he saw enough. He saw how he could get at the bastards he was looking for. At some point, when he had the time, he would have to come to terms with what he'd done to Serge, but that was for later, if he survived. For the moment he knew where he stood. Or, more accurately, he knew where he was going to stand. In the middle, between Heppert and what this comedian called Group B. And if he did get a clear look at any of them, then fuck Heppert and fuck the Comedian, he'd kill them. And this time there'd be no mistake.

Chapter Twenty-eight

They were sitting across the desk from Professor Scolari in his office.

'This is Ms Heppert. She is a lawyer with Parker and Henry in their Paris office. She is acting for the Sisters of Bon Secours in the disposal of their convent. Professor McBride was asked to assist by the superior of the order and sent me to Paris to look into the matter. I liaised with a lawyer, M. Joubert, who was then acting for …'

'Professor Scolari.'

The Professor turned his attention away from Jimmy to Nadine Heppert.

'Yes?'

'Here is my card.' He took it. 'On the back are the numbers of the office of M. Joubert and the sisters at the convent, if any sisters are still there. Please call my office, M. Joubert's office, and the sisters at the convent to confirm that I am now officially handling the matter. If you can contact the superior of the Sisters of Bon Secours here in Rome to confirm that she did indeed ask for Professor McBride's assistance I suggest you do so. Mr Costello tells me there is information relating to the matter in a green dossier in Professor McBride's office. I need to see it and, if I think necessary, to take a copy. I am in Rome only to assess the relevance of this information and I wish to do so as speedily as possible. While I appreciate your giving me access is not without its problems, I hope you appreciate my position. I have given you sufficient information, I think, to confirm my bona fides in this matter and I hope you will be able to make the necessary calls as soon as possible.'

Scolari looked at the card then at Jimmy.

'I'm working with Ms Heppert now. That is what Professor McBride would have wished. I can confirm everything Ms Heppert says and, having seen the dossier, agree with Ms Heppert that there is information contained in it that she needs to support the work she is doing for the sisters.'

Scolari looked back at the card.

'I do not know whether I can …'

Nadine Heppert stood up.

'Then please find someone who does know. I am trying to be as reasonable as I can but my time is limited. Professor McBride is still in intensive care after her latest surgery and will not be in any way contactable for some considerable time. I can, of course, return to Paris and set in motion the necessary legal …'

Scolari stood up, Jimmy sat and watched.

'Please, you must understand, Ms Heppert. I do not doubt your bona fides but I have no legal right to give any permissions …'

She steamrollered over him.

'Then as I say, find someone who has, or I will get my own legal right.' She looked down at Jimmy who was enjoying watching her in action although he regarded the contest as a mismatch. Scolari was nothing more than an academic, he didn't really stand a chance. 'Are you ready, Mr Costello?'

Jimmy stood up slowly.

Maybe it was something in the way she'd spoken to Jimmy that decided Scolari, the nasty edge in her voice, the arrogant confidence of a superior to a menial.

'Perhaps, if it is no more than a sight of the document. I think, yes I think I could …'

'No, Professor. I insist that you make those calls first. I don't want you to agree now and have doubts later if and when anyone should ask you whether you checked you were acting correctly.'

Scolari was finished. She had given him his orders so he

would have to obey them.

'I will make the calls …'

'Good, start with my office then with M. Joubert's office. You will get a response at both of those. Then try the convent and last the mother superior. Mr Costello and I will go and get a coffee and return when you call. Please make your calls as soon as I leave.' There it was again, thought Jimmy, the superior to the menial. First knock the poor bugger down then kick him in the slats. Some did it with boots, she did it with the grand manner. 'Where can we get coffee?'

Scolari brightened. He could provide that information without any reservations. He gave her directions to a café. She led Jimmy out of the office, down in the elevator, and out into the street. Once outside the office block they set off to the café which was close by but which Jimmy had never known existed.

'Nice work. You rolled over him nicely.'

She didn't respond to his compliment but looked around at the office blocks.

'What the hell kind of college is theirs? This all looks more like where I work.'

'It's a college all right. McBride's office is on the top floor. On a clear day you get a nice view of the hills at Frascati.'

'What do they teach there?'

'Nothing. They don't teach. They were founded to study the relationship between religion, power, and politics. They're good at it, they've been doing it a long time. Their founder was one of the Borgias.' Jimmy gestured with his arm. 'This was all farms. The rents went to keep the college going. Now it's offices and the rents still go to the college. Like I said, they study, they don't teach. They can afford to do without students.'

Jimmy could see she was impressed. He'd meant her to be. He needed her to know that he had something solid behind him and he didn't mean one of the Borgias. She wasn't interested in history but money, power, and possessions impressed her, and money did it most because money was usually what gave you the power and possessions.

'That professor guy back there didn't look too hot on power

or politics so I guess he must be the one who does religion.'

Jimmy smiled dutifully, she had made a joke about Scolari to show that she wasn't too impressed by that particular member of the wealthy Collegio. She had obviously enjoyed squashing the harmless academic. The Comedian was right. She could probably be a nasty piece of work when she felt like it.

They found the café. It was a functional sort of place with big windows through which you could see bright plastic-topped tables and shiny metal chairs. At the back was a counter which did the coffee and flanking it were the chiller cabinets of sandwiches and other take-away meals. It was more a snackery for the office workers than a place to eat, anonymous and universal and most of all functional. It was mid-morning, too late for people arriving and not late enough for the quick snack lunchers. It stayed open in case a lucky few managed a mid-morning break but at the moment it was empty. Nadine sat at a table while Jimmy got two coffees.

'I'll give him half an hour then we'll go back.'

'What if he hasn't made the all the calls?'

'It doesn't matter. He'll get someone at my office and he might get someone at Joubert's but the convent won't answer and the superior left Rome last week. We'll give him half an hour.'

'A whole half hour. Why so generous with your time?'

'Because we need to talk.'

'We do?'

'Yes, we do. What is it you're holding out on me?'

'Sorry, you just lost me.'

'No I didn't. When we ate last night I knew something had happened, what was it?'

Jimmy almost laughed. Was it divine intervention, good luck, or was somebody stage-managing the whole thing? Half a dozen times last night when they were eating he had tried to do like the Comedian had told him, tell her about getting picked up outside Termini, and each time he'd fluffed it or let it go because he knew it wouldn't sound right. Now here she was laying it on a plate for him and no acting required. She wanted him to tell her. She'd asked him out loud to tell her. So he told her.

She sat and listened. When Jimmy had finished he waited while she thought the whole thing over.

'Who is he?'

'Intelligence of some sort, Danish Intelligence, rank of commander. That's all I know.'

'And he knew you from Denmark, from some bind you got into there?'

'There and other places.'

She was silent for a moment as she went over what Jimmy had told her.

'I was wrong about you and I'm not often wrong. I don't like that.'

'It happens. No one's right all the time.'

'I thought I'd got you pretty well pegged as no more than a useful leg man but first you kill Serge and then you spring Danish Intelligence on me. To be that wrong makes me think someone worked very hard to get me that way.'

'It's possible but it wasn't me. Until Joubert got smacked around I didn't know you existed.'

'Is there anything else I should know about you?'

'You can have what there is. I got involved in something here in Rome, it doesn't matter what, I was only a bit player. I was out of my depth and got chewed up but with Professor McBride's help I got out alive. There were people after me and they finally caught up with me in Copenhagen. That's where my friend in Danish Intelligence got involved. He was all for throwing me in chokey and losing the key but McBride got me out again and finally squared everything with the people on my tail. I'm clear now so long as I don't go back to Denmark. I'm not welcome there. I owe McBride a lot so now I do odd jobs for her, like finding the heir to the Colmar estate.'

'Except she had one up her sleeve all along.'

'Yeah. She doesn't always tell me everything. She doesn't think I can act. If I'm not telling the truth it shows so she makes sure I only know enough of the truth to get her what she wants.'

She didn't give him an argument on McBride's assessment of his acting.

'Who is this McBride really?'

'An academic. Works for the Collegio Principe.'

'Like that Scolari guy? Don't give me that.'

'No, not like Scolari, not like anyone. As far as I can make out she sort of moonlights for the Catholic authorities. She sweeps things under the carpet for them, in-house stuff they want to be sure stays in house.'

'And you?'

'Like I said, I'm her odd-job man. My way of saying thank you for Rome and for Denmark.'

'So, she's connected and she's no lightweight?'

'Professional killers don't shoot nobodies where I come from.'

'And where do you come from when you're not being chewed up or doing odd jobs for moonlighting academics?'

'London. Detective sergeant in the Met. about a thousand years ago, but I still know how to put two and two together when I have to.'

She fell silent.

The Comedian had been spot on, no lies needed, no acting needed, just tell her the truth, let her add two and two and wait for her to come up with five.

'Why are you telling me all this?'

'You asked.'

'I asked, but you don't owe me anything, so again, why are you telling me?'

'No, I don't owe you anything but I think we need to work together so I've told you.'

'Don't count on it to get you anything. Nothing you've told me gets me anywhere with what I'm working on.'

'Which is?'

'The Colmar estate. That's all you need to know.'

'What's the secret ingredient in the Colmar estate that's got everyone jumping?'

'Does there have to be a something?'

'An old guy dead in Munich, Joubert in hospital, McBride gunned down outside her office, a journalist pushed under a train …'

'What journalist? You mentioned a journalist before.'

'Serge didn't tell you? Naughty Serge. He got me a journalist to visit the old guy's daughter in Munich to see what he could get out of her. They pushed him under a train at a local station and got a witness to say it was suicide.'

'Did he get anything?'

'No idea, he never reported in before he went under the train.'

'So you have no idea what this is all about?'

'Only that the score so far is two murders, one attempted murder, a criminal assault, and Danish Intelligence lifting me here in Rome which to a nasty mind could be classed as kidnapping. I'd say there had to be something pretty exceptional in the Colmar estate for all that to have happened, wouldn't you?'

'I wouldn't say, and it's three murders. You left out the dead police officer in Gagny sous Bois. Don't forget Serge.'

Jimmy wasn't forgetting Serge, he would have a hard time with that, but it would have to come later. Right now he was busy with other things.

'My point is, I think we'd stand a better chance if I know what you know.'

'Your boss McBride never told you what this was all about?'

'No. Just find an heir.'

'Then I'm not about to tell you either. You were a detective, if you want to know then you'll have to find out for yourself. What about our Danish friend?'

'What about him?'

'You said he wants you to get close to me, to report back to him. What are you going to do about that?'

'Nothing, there's nothing I can do. Now you know what he wants you dump me or keep me with you. It's your choice not mine.'

'I should dump you.'

'Yes, that's the safe way.'

'But you think maybe not the right way?'

'It's the safe way.'

'But?'

'But you wouldn't have taken me on board unless you needed me.'

'I took you on board? That's not how I remember it. As I remember it you slapped me about and did all the threatening.'

'OK, you're cleverer than me. You can act and I can't. You got yourself Serge because you needed somebody to handle a bit of rough stuff and I don't mean the sex.' That got a smile. Jimmy was pleased. 'Once you knew I'd killed him you decided I should fill his boots. You still needed someone to look after the rough stuff.'

The smile had lasted.

'The sex?'

'No. For that you'll have to get somebody else. I know what goes where and why but that's as far as it goes with me. With me it would be sex within the meaning of the act, but as for magnificent and wonderful? No.'

She managed to go up as far as a small laugh.

'So, no sex?'

'No, but there'll still be other kinds of rough stuff and it'll need handling so maybe like I said, the safe way isn't the right way. Not if you want to get where you're going.'

'And where is it you think I'm going?'

But Jimmy was finished with the game. He delivered the message like the Comedian had told him. Now he wanted to get on.

'Back to McBride's office to get the address where we can find our candidate, then we go and see her, find out if she's any good. That'll be for you to decide.'

'And if she is any good?'

'Then to Munich to find out who the witness woman is and see if, through her, we can get a line on the opposition. Locating the opposition, that's where I think you're going and that's when things will start to turn nasty if they're going to. But it's just my opinion. You might be going straight back to Paris and tell them that I confessed to murdering Serge Carpentier and try to wash your hands of this whole mess. That would be the safe thing to do.'

The smile came back, but not the same one. This was a predatory sort of smile, like a sexy young lioness might give a tired old antelope who wasn't so quick any more. It said she wanted him, but not for any good reason.

'You're cute, you know that? Innocent cute. Oh, you're a tough guy all right and that's what makes it interesting. A tough innocent. That's a big turn on, you know that?'

Jimmy looked at his watch. Two suits had arrived and were ordering coffee to take out.

'It's not something I think about at ten fifty in the morning. Are we going back to Scolari or are you going to seduce me in here, take my body by force on the table?'

She laughed out loud and the suits at the counter turned and looked at them.

'Damn you, Costello, I hate men who can make me laugh.' She got up. 'Come on, let's go and get what we came here for.'

Jimmy got up.

'Are we still together on this?'

'For now, until I decide otherwise.'

'And do I report to the Dane like he asked?'

'Sure, only you check your report with me first, OK?'

'Any way you like it.'

She stopped and gave him the look again.

'Oh you'd be surprised at the way I like it.'

'No I wouldn't, I'd be shocked and embarrassed.'

And she laughed out loud again as they left.

'Damn you, Costello, damn and blast you. You make that plastic table-top back there look almost tempting.'

Was she flirting with him, laughing at him, or getting ready to squelch him like she'd done to Scolari? Jimmy decided it didn't matter because she had made another mistake about him. He wasn't a tough guy, not any more, if he'd ever been. When he'd put that gun to Serge's head his hand was shaking so much he'd have missed if the barrel hadn't been touching. And when he stood up and looked at the two blokes in the alley he'd been about ready to throw up and piss his pants at the same time he was so scared. She thought he'd kill again, easily, kill her if it was necessary. She admired that in him, that ruthlessness. The problem was, it wasn't there, she was wide of the mark again. He couldn't do to her what he'd done to Serge even though, with her, he was damned sure it wouldn't be any mistake.

Chapter Twenty-nine

Nadine paid for the tickets so they travelled business class and at Genoa airport she hired an Alfa Romeo sports model. She gave Jimmy the map, he would navigate, she would drive. At first he was worried that she'd try to kill them both by seeing what the car could do once they'd cleared the clutter of city traffic, but she drove steadily and well as they travelled down into Liguria. The place they were looking for was on the coast, well away from anywhere. The nearest town was La Spezia, which was also a big naval base, so the road from Genoa was fine. Once past La Spezia they left the main highway and travelled along winding country roads through fields and woodland and began to get views of the blue Mediterranean beyond the fields and trees. Jimmy checked the map and told Nadine to take the next left turn and then take it easy. She turned and drove slowly along the road until Jimmy told her to stop beside a five-barred gate. On the gate was a big sign in Italian. Jimmy didn't need to have it interpreted – 'Keep Out. Strictly Private'.

Nadine punched the horn a couple of times and an old man came out from a small cottage that stood near the gate behind the flimsy wire fence that had run the length of the road. He spoke no English but Nadine soon made him understand that they were expected and they were coming in. He opened the gate and watched them drive through. Jimmy looked back as the man slowly closed the gate. An old woman came out of the cottage wiping her hands on her apron and looked at the car as it travelled away up the concrete road. The road cut through a big field that had something small and green growing in it. It might be Keep Out and Strictly Private but if the old couple and the wire fence were an example of the security then it would keep out rabbits perhaps, but not anything more aggressive or determined. They drove along the concrete road towards a wood. Once among the trees they came to a gate. This time it was a real gate and it was set in a steel fence which was three meters high. Here, nicely out of sight among the trees, was where the serious security began. At the gate Jimmy got out and went to a box set at about head level. He pressed the button. A voice answered in Italian.

'I'm sorry, I don't speak Italian. I …'

'Is that Mr Costello?'

'Yes.'

'Very well. Return to your car please.'

Jimmy returned to the car and as he did so the gates quietly swung open. Nadine drove the car on and the gates noiselessly swung closed behind them. They entered a well-maintained, park-like place which, though apparently empty, gave Jimmy the distinct impression that they were being watched. They drove on without seeing anyone until they came to a T-junction beyond which were six big houses, set well apart, surrounded by well-kept gardens. Beyond the houses was a dark strip of woods, fir trees through which you could just make out the blue of the sea. Jimmy looked at two small boards set on either side of the T. They both had numbers on.

'We go left.'

They drove on slowly until they came to the drive of the last house.

'This is it.'

Nadine turned and they drove up the gravel drive to the front door. They got out of the car and the front door opened.

It was a youngish, rather pretty woman. Certainly not anything like the Veronique Colmar of the dossier.

'Welcome.'

Nadine prepared to go into her act.

'We've come …'

‘I know why you are here. Please come in.’ She led them across the hall to a door, opened it and stood to one side. ‘Please wait in here.’

They went in and the door closed behind them. It was a big living room, elegant in decoration and design. The furniture, however, what there was of it, looked cheap and practical and they’d been sitting in the car long enough for neither of them to be attracted by the hard, upright chairs. They waited until the door opened and the pretty young woman came into the room followed by another woman.

Veronique Colmar did ample justice to her photo. Her hair was still cut in the same way but was lighter because of more grey in it. She still wore glasses. The frames were modern but they made no difference to the overall effect which might best be described as a sort of super-drab. She was wearing a cardigan, plain blue blouse, tweed skirt, and thick shoes. But the overriding impression she had on Jimmy was of a woman with a sort of trampled air about her. It was as if a life spent having people walk over her had led her to expect nothing more than to be used as a doormat. She came straight to the middle of the room and stood looking at the floor until the pretty young woman left and had closed the door behind her. Then she raised her head and looked at them. Nadine was taking her in, the clothes, the figure, the general awfulness of her, but Jimmy was looking at her eyes. Clothes only told you what someone wanted you to know. With Nadine it was, “look how smart and successful I am, how much better than you”. With Veronique someone was saying, “this is a failure, a nobody” but Jimmy thought he saw a look flit through Veronique’s eyes as she, in her turn, looked at Nadine. It was a certain slyness, as if she was quietly laughing inside herself because she had a secret which gave her an edge, something you didn’t know about. The look was there, then it was gone, and Veronique’s eyes went down to the carpet as she waited patiently to be walked on yet again.

Professor McBride had been very careful with Veronique. She had hidden her away in a remote, lay spiritual house run by one of those Catholic Church movements that spring up. The sort that hold out the promise of re-igniting pious passion in the faithful, flourish for a while, then slowly merge into the general melting-pot of the Catholic Church's life.

The house was one of six which made up a private and exclusive estate, each different, but not so very different. They were all substantial affairs and all spoke of wealth and comfort of a high order. They all stood well apart from each other but there were no walls creating boundaries. This was a collective, here no one was could be seen to be better off than their neighbour. Behind the high security fence in the wood all were equals in their wealth. Behind the houses, beyond the narrow pine wood, was a long, empty, sandy beach whose white sand sloped down to be gently lapped by the blue sea of the Gulf of La Spezia. Genoa was eighty kilometres away to the west and Milan one hundred and sixty to the north. In those two ancient and wealthy cities lived the owners of these houses. The men came for a few short weeks in summer, their wives and children stayed for a longer period, especially those from Milan where, being well inland, the annual heat of the summer sun was regarded as a vulgar intrusion to be avoided by the better element of society. The one which housed the lay community had once been the summer retreat of a prominent Catholic Milanese banker who, at the age of sixty-two, ran off with his twenty-three-year-old secretary. He had taken with him a great deal of the bank's money, only to finish up committing suicide after he had killed his pretty young mistress and her secret lover when he'd found them in bed together.

The banker, when still a pillar of both society and Church had, of course, made sure that his property was in the name of his wife while the bulk of his personal wealth was carefully salted away in foreign accounts where the tax people would never get a sniff of it so, although his wife lost a husband, that was about all she lost. The summer retreat had been the banker and his secretary's love nest so the wife decided to dispose of it in such a way that distanced herself, in the eyes of her fellow Milanese Catholics, from her husband's spectacular fall from grace. Having removed anything portable of any value she donated it to the latest popular Church movement. This generous act of Christian charity was very much appreciated by the lay movement and by the Church but loathed by the owners of the other five houses, which is exactly why she had done it. It was the perfect place to keep a valuable but delicate commodity like Veronique Colmar.

Nadine began. It wasn't going to be difficult, she could see that at once.

'Do you know who we are?'

Veronique looked up and nodded.

'You are from the person who sent me here.'

'Do you know who that person is?'

Veronique shrugged.

'A person. She had me sent here.'

'Do you know why we have come?' Veronique slowly shook her head and her eyes went to the carpet. 'We want to talk to you. We want to ask you about your mother. When was the last time you saw your mother?' Veronique studied the carpet in silence. 'What can you tell us about your mother?' No response. 'We have questions, Veronique, it is important that you co-operate. You know you must co-operate? We have come a long way to ask these questions.' Still no response.

Nadine was good in her world but this was Veronique's world and stubborn silence is not so easy to get round in a hurry, not without some leverage, like pain or fear. And they *were* in a hurry. They were due to fly back to Rome that evening. 'Veronique. Look at me. Will you look at me? We have questions …'

Jimmy stepped forward.

'Could we go onto the beach, Veronique? I would like to see the sea.'

Veronique looked up at him and the look flitted through again.

'The sea is nice.'

'Will you take us?'

She hesitated for only a second.

'Yes.'

'And while I look at the sea could you tell us about your mother?'

This time the hesitation was longer and the eyes went back to the carpet. Nadine was about to say something but Jimmy shot her a look that kept her words unspoken. Veronique's eyes came up.

'I can't tell you much.'

Jimmy didn't make the mistake of trying to smile.

'Only what you want to tell, nothing more. Then we'll go away.'

Veronique turned and went to one of the French windows that led out down a few steps into the garden.

'It's through the trees.' She looked at Nadine's feet. 'Your shoes are not suitable.'

Nadine looked at Jimmy.

'That's all right. She likes walking barefoot in the sand.'

Nadine shot him a poisonous look while Veronique thought about it, then opened the door.

'It's this way.'

Chapter Thirty

Nadine and Veronique walked together along the beach, talking. Jimmy was a few paces behind them. Veronique had kept on her cardigan despite the day being pleasantly warm. Nadine was barefoot and had a pair of flimsy, strapped shoes dangling from her hand. She had on a white sleeveless dress belted at the middle. They looked an odd pair.

'The more I think about it the more it seems that I never really knew my mother. I remember her, but now it all seems so very vague, as if we were strangers who met for a time then parted.' She shot a worried glance at Nadine. 'That must be wrong, mustn't it?'

'Wrong?'

'A sin. Not to remember your mother means not to love your mother. It means I never loved my mother. That means I was selfish, thought only of myself. That was a sin. I was sinful and ungrateful …'

Nadine cut in.

'There was no other family.'

'No, no one but Mother and me.'

'No father?'

'Not that I remember and if there was she never mentioned him.'

'You didn't ask?'

'No, children take those things for granted I suppose. When I was little we lived in Saigon, that's where I was born.'

'When would that be?'

'In 1965. I have no idea how long my mother lived there

before I was born.'

'What was it like?'

'I think I was happy, I'm not sure. It's hard to remember. I remember the rain when the monsoons came. I remember I loved watching the rain come pouring down, bouncing about and splashing as if it was dancing for me. But that was selfish too, I loved the rain but for the poor people it was …'

Nadine got her back on track.

'Where did you go to school?'

'With the sisters. Mother said I must have a good education like she had, a good Catholic education.'

It was Jimmy who asked the question this time.

'Your mother was a Catholic?'

Veronique turned to answer the question but they all kept walking.

'A sort of Catholic. She said she was a Catholic, but never seemed to do anything about it. I never remember us going to Mass together but she often sent me to Sunday Mass with neighbours.'

'But she never went?'

'Not that I remember, but I do remember what my mother told me when I began with the sisters,' and she spoke as if making a well-learned recitation, "Try to have a vocation, Veronique, try hard, it will give you a safe place to live your life. See if God will look after you." Even though I was very young, not more than five, her words seemed odd to me. Once I got used to the sisters I told them what Mother had said. They said it was good advice, that I should pray for God to give me a vocation. If I had a vocation God would look after me like Mother said.'

Suddenly Veronique hung her head and stopped. Then she put her face in her hands and started mumbling.

Nadine looked back at Jimmy who shrugged. They all three stood and waited while the mumbling went on. After a short while Veronique slowly removed her hands and made the sign of the cross.

'I didn't pray hard enough, I never accepted the vocation

God had ready for me. I sinned. I thought of boys and dresses and music when I should have been praying. I should have …'

Nadine wasn't interested in what Veronique should have.

'What else do you remember about your mother? Did she have friends?'

They began walking again.

'Mother mixed with all sorts, Vietnamese, Americans, French. She always seemed to be having a good time. I was never with her when she went out with her friends and if they came to the house I was sent round to a neighbour, but I always got the impression she was having a good time, that she was happy, and of course she was away a lot.'

'Away?'

'Yes.'

'Where?'

'I don't know, just away.'

'Who looked after you?'

Jimmy asked the question because it would never occur to Nadine.

'Neighbours, friends. When Mother was away I stayed in their houses. They were very kind. I was very happy when I went to stay with them. When Mother was at home and we were together I was lonely. When she went away I could play with my friends.'

Once again the talk had slipped away from what Nadine was interested in.

'Did you have plenty of money?'

'I think so. We had a nice apartment in a good part of the town but no servants. I don't know why. Most of the Europeans who lived round us had servants.'

'What did she do, what was her work?'

'Mother always had money but never seemed to have a job, not one that I could remember. She said she was a freelance journalist. I didn't know then what that was. All I knew was that it took her away from home a great deal.'

'And what happened?'

'Happened?'

'In the end. You left Saigon at some point I guess. It wasn't a healthy place around that time.'

'No, there were the bombs and there was always talk of fighting …'

'So how did you both get out?'

'We didn't, at least Mother didn't.'

'Tell us about how you got out.'

'There was a lot of noise, I remember that. A lot of people moving. I was with a neighbour but she got a phone call and said she had to take me back to our apartment. When we got there she said she had to leave me, I didn't know why so I waited. My mother was away. People were saying that the Americans were leaving. That seemed to worry them. I didn't know what it was all about so I waited. Then a man came, an American, and said he was a friend of my mother, that she had sent him to bring me to her. He took me in a car to a place with American soldiers and crowds of Vietnamese people all shouting and trying to get in. A place with big gates. I was frightened but he found a way in, I don't remember how. He took me into a big building and we went up to the roof. He gave me to a woman who was in a helicopter at the top the building. I didn't know the woman, she was Vietnamese. The helicopter took us all to a ship, a very big ship with a big flat deck that the helicopter landed on. Then we went down into the ship. There were lots of people. I went with the woman and we found a space to sit so we sat. I went to sleep, I remember that, and when I woke everyone was sitting. We ate and slept and, well, we lived like that. I couldn't tell whether it was night or day so I don't know how long we were there. Then I was taken off the ship somewhere and given to another woman, an American who wore a uniform. I was put with others and we ate and slept and then we were moved on, first in another ship and then on a plane. I was handed on. I felt like a parcel, a parcel being sent to my mother by friends. Eventually I arrived in America. I was looked after by some nurses and slept in a real bed with sheets in what I think must have been a hospital. From there I was sent to a Catholic orphanage. One day a man came and told me that my mother was dead.'

Veronique stopped and put her face in her hands and began mumbling again. Nadine turned back at Jimmy, her look full of impatience.

'Leave her. She's praying.'

'For God's sake, I need to get this done.'

'Let her pray. She'll get going again when she's ready. She's doing well. It all sounds right to me, but what do I know?'

'It sounds right to me as well, but I know shit about all that Vietnam stuff.'

Veronique surfaced again and took it up where she'd left off.

'The man who came said Mother had died in the fall of Saigon. He gave me some papers. He said that they were the papers that had belonged to my mother.'

'What sort of papers.'

'My birth and baptism certificates, I'd never seen them before. Some other legal-looking papers. But the name, the surname on the papers was wrong, it wasn't one I recognised.'

'What was the name?'

'Bailey.'

'What was your mother's name? The one you knew.'

'Colmar, her name was Thèrése Colmar. The name on the papers was Thèrése Bailey. The man who brought the papers explained that Bailey was my mother's legal name – she had been married. They had split up but not divorced. The name my mother had used was her maiden name. He told me that my father was also dead, a US marine officer killed in action in Vietnam, but he had left a will and had left some money to me. After that I was moved from the orphanage to a Catholic boarding school in New York State where I used my new name and began a new life. It was run by sisters again but I didn't pray hard enough for a vocation. I began to think about other things, sinful things so God took away the vocation he had for me. I failed him and my mother and all the sisters who had tried to help.'

'And you stayed at the school?'

Veronique nodded.

'I stayed until I was sixteen.'

'Then you left? What did you do?'

'I didn't exactly leave. I was sort of taken away.'

'Taken away how?'

'I became ill, I heard voices, had memories, said strange things that came into my head. People came to talk to me and I was taken away and spent a lot of time in hospitals. God wouldn't look after me, I had failed him and turned away from him, so he gave me to people I didn't know. God was punishing me because I should have had a vocation but I dreamed of boys and music and dresses.' She did the hands thing again, and again Nadine and Jimmy waited. When she surfaced she looked at Nadine. 'Will you send me back into a hospital?'

Nadine turned to Jimmy.

'I've got all I need for the time being.' She wanted to be gone. 'Let's go back.'

They turned back the way they had just come and Jimmy walked beside Veronique.

'It's not up to us, it's up to other people. Someone will look after you like they did after Saigon.'

Her face, never joyful, took on a little extra sadness and a fear came into her eyes.

'Oh, no. No more punishment. I tried to pray, I really did, but the boys and the music …'

'I know, and the dresses. But that's the way things are, you don't get to choose the people who look after you.'

'Will God go on punishing me?'

Jimmy didn't answer so she looked at Nadine but Nadine wanted to be gone. Her voice was dismissive.

'I can't help you. It's outside my field.'

Veronique looked bewildered and turned again to Jimmy.

'Will He?'

'He usually does.'

The face went into the hands again and the mumbling was noticeably louder.

Nadine's impatience was stretched as far as it would go.

'For Christ's sake, why did you say that? Couldn't you have

said something helpful?'

'She didn't want to be helped. She's been helped enough. She wanted the truth.'

Nadine looked at him. Then she gave up. She took Veronique by the shoulder and gave her a shake. The hands went down slowly.

'Look, I've got to go. Can you get back to the house all right?'

Veronique nodded.

'Come on, Costello. We have things to do.'

Jimmy took Veronique's arm.

'Will you be all right here on your own?'

Veronique looked at him and came as close to smiling as Jimmy guessed she could.

'I'll be all right. I spend a lot of time on my own.'

'Yes, I guess you do. I guess you've had practice.'

'Will you pray for me?'

'Sure, and I'll light a candle, a special candle, one to a secret saint who has a special way to speak to God. One who knows how to get a prayer through.'

The sly look flickered into her eyes.

'You know about that?'

'I'm a Catholic, I know about those things.'

Veronique looked at Nadine who was walking slowly through the sand towards the pine trees.

'She doesn't know?'

'No, she knows bugger all. She only thinks she knows.'

The almost smile came back to join the sly look. This was as happy as she gets, thought Jimmy. Poor bloody sod.

He turned and walked on after Nadine. God knows how McBride had found her or how much of that story she'd had fed into her but she'd done a good job. Veronique Bailey or Colmar or whatever her name was might be away with the fairies, terrified of a vengeful God whose only purpose in her life was to scare the shit out of her, but as a candidate for the Colmar inheritance she certainly looked a very strong contender. If the paperwork stood up she'd walk through inheriting the Colmar estate. Then the people who would act for her as an adult of diminished responsibility could put her away somewhere where she would get more help with her problems while they got on administering everything for her. You didn't have to be a high-flying company lawyer to see how it would work out.

Poor loony sod. The people God was going to let look after her permanently were closing in and He was going to go on giving her hell. But there you were, what could you do? The way Jimmy looked at it, he hadn't started the Vietnam war, some other stupid buggers had organised that almighty cock-up.

The Alfa Romeo sports model she had hired suited Nadine. She didn't need Jimmy to navigate the journey back to Genoa airport, she knew where she was going and she brought the same attitude to her driving as Jimmy assumed she did to her sex. To someone who enjoyed that sort of thing the driving might have been wonderful, even magnificent, but to Jimmy it was simply stomach-churning. She hadn't wanted to talk while she used the country roads like part of a Formula One event but when they had rejoined the main highway she slipped her driving to auto-pilot and was inclined to discuss their visit.

'I like her. She's a clever choice.'

'Will she do?'

'She's perfect. We don't have to worry if she gets things wrong because she's supposed to get things wrong. If she screws up her story and gets confused or contradicts herself that's exactly what you'd expect of someone like her.'

'Is a mentally unbalanced woman a good prospect to put before the Swiss authorities?'

'Don't worry about that, she'll be sane enough when the time comes, or at least sane enough to get the job done. After that who cares?'

'So she'll pass as the granddaughter of the Colmar woman?'

'That depends on what sort of job your boss McBride did on the paperwork. If the papers are as good as Veronique it should be a walk in the park and my guess is the paperwork will be fine. Fixing the paperwork is the easy part, getting the right client, co-operative, and with the right background is the difficult bit.'

'Like your brothers?'

'They might have got through, except of course for their colour, and I made sure a head rolled for that. Their paperwork was good, I know, I arranged it.'

'What will you do with them?'

'Give them some dough and send them back to Chicago.'

'They won't make any trouble?'

'What trouble can they make? They don't know anything except what they've been told and they've been told damn all that they can use. They'll take the money.'

'So what now?'

'Now we go to Munich to find your witness.'

'How will you handle the police?'

'Like I always handle the police.'

Yes, thought Jimmy, I suppose you will.

And she did.

Chapter Thirty-one

When they arrived in Munich Nadine went through the police procedures like a bullet through warm butter. She knew the right buttons to press, the right calls to make, gave the right references to the right people, and made the right half-threats at the right times to anybody who looked a bit squiggle-eyed. Her story was that she was representing the journalist's employers. They didn't want to cause any fuss but they had to be sure that the circumstances of the death were clearly documented. Since the suicide the journalist's partner had suggested that the pressure of work applied by the paper's editor had been preying on his mind and that the paper imposed impossible deadlines. There was the possibility of a claim for compensation. The newspaper's owners needed to be sure exactly where they stood. The police evidence was, of course, perfectly acceptable for a coroner but civil litigation was a different matter. The way the evidence of the witness was presented would be vital to any outcome.

The story worked and they were sitting in the bar of her hotel having a late-afternoon drink when she got a phone call which gave her the name and address of the witness.

She put her phone down next to her drink took a pad out of her handbag and wrote in it then tore out the page and handed it to Jimmy.

'That's that. We see her tomorrow at ten at the care home where she works.'

'The police gave it you?'

'Sure, why not?'

‘Because they’re not allowed to give out that kind of information.’

‘They are if the person concerned OKs it.’

‘They asked her and she said OK?’

‘Of course. What else could she say? She was an innocent bystander, she has nothing to hide. I represent a powerful media company making a legitimate inquiry. If she’d said no she’d only be making trouble for herself.’

‘And what happens when the police find out that you don’t represent a powerful media company?’

‘They won’t.’

‘You sure of that?’

‘Yes, because as it happens one of the clients I represent *is* a media company.’ The surprise sent Jimmy’s beer down the wrong way and he had to put down his glass and cough himself clear. She waited until he was finished. ‘It has nothing to do with the guy you and Serge sent here but, if anyone asks them do they use Parker and Henry, they’ll say they do and that I handle the account.’ Jimmy was impressed. She was thorough. She finished her drink. ‘I’m dining with a friend tonight so your time’s your own until you pick me up here tomorrow and we go and see this woman. Sort out transport and timing. Ring me an hour before you come.

‘Your friend will be stopping over?’

‘Yes.’

‘An old friend?’

‘I’ve never met him, I got him from an agency.’ She stood up. ‘And as you’re so interested I’ll tell you how it went when you get here tomorrow. I guess any details would be wasted on you so I’ll make it a simple score out of ten.’

She turned and walked out of the bar. Jimmy took another drink of his beer. If it had been a man having a girl sent over for the night he’d would have thought nothing of it. Men did that sort of thing all the time. But she was a woman and somehow her sending out for a man got under his skin. Why was that? He didn’t give a damn one way or the other so why did he feel like he *did* give a damn? Why was that?

He got up, left the bar, and went to reception. He told the clerk the name of the district he wanted.

'I need to go there tomorrow morning.'

'Yes, sir?'

'How long would it take in a taxi?'

The clerk told him to allow about three-quarters of an hour if they travelled during the morning rush-hour or around twenty minutes if they went during a quiet time of the day.

'Thanks.'

Jimmy turned away from reception and looked back to the entrance to the bar. He fancied another beer but he didn't like the place. It was too up-market for him, he didn't feel comfortable. He'd walk for a bit, find an ordinary bar, have a beer or two, get a meal at a restaurant, and then go to his hotel and get some sleep.

At eleven the next morning Jimmy was waiting in the hotel lobby. A taxi was outside ready to take them to the residential home. Nadine walked out of the elevator and across to him.

'Nought out of ten.'

'What?'

'My sex report, the one you were so interested in.'

'I wasn't interested, I'm still not.'

They went out of the hotel but she stopped.

'We had dinner together and I could see he wasn't up to the job so I paid him off and did some thinking instead.' She smiled at him. 'Now don't pretend you're not interested because I can see that you are. That you're dying for me to tell.' And before he could say anything she went on. 'He was one of those guys who does it part-time to help him pay his way through college or law school or whatever. Not a professional. He wanted me to like him, he actually thought that was part of the job, being a nice guy, good company.'

'I'm still not interested.'

'You simply can't get quality personnel these days. The amateur freelancers bring the price down, the professionals get squeezed, and the clients lose out because the price is less but the service is lousy. You get what you pay for. Don't you think that's true, Costello, that you always get what …'

'Are you finished, only there's a taxi with its meter running outside.'

'That's OK. I won't be paying. That's what I was thinking about last night. I decided that if you're right, and I think you are, then this might get nasty. The way I look at it, it's more your line of work than mine. If the journalist you sent got thrown under a train, well, who knows what awaits whoever turns up to interview our witness friend? So you go and get what we want then come back and tell me all about it.'

'I don't speak German.'

'Neither do I. I asked the police to find out if she spoke English when they asked if she'd see me. You're in luck, she does. Great isn't it, how many foreigners speak English? Makes life so much simpler. See you.'

And she turned and walked back to the lift.

Jimmy went out to the taxi and told him to get going.

He wasn't surprised, he'd half expected it. It was going to be like the Comedian had said, there was no way she was going to put herself in the front line and the woman he was going to see was connected to an outfit that killed people. If they thought their tame witness was blown they'd probably kill her, but not before killing whoever had come to talk to her. What kind of business outfit could do business that way? And it had to be business because the American side was business. Heppert was business. So it had to be business. Or political. Or both. But what it couldn't be was some kind of gangland turf war. Which was odd because it had all the hallmarks of some sort of gangland brawl. Except that the people who had died were all civilians. But then, he didn't actually have any full account of the casualty list so far. All he knew about were the ones he'd been given. There could be other bodies strewn across Europe for all he knew.

As the taxi moved quickly through the mid-morning traffic Jimmy reflected that it was turning out pretty much as the Comedian had predicted. He was being used as a scout, sent out into no-man's land to make contact with the enemy while

Nadine stayed well out of the frame, where it was safe, well behind the trenches at HQ.

Oh well, this was what he had been told to expect so he would just have to get on with it.

Chapter Thirty-two

The meeting with the witness took place in a small common room in the care home. Jimmy and the woman sat opposite each other across a low coffee table with four chairs around it. She was middle-aged, of middle height, and mild-mannered, a quiet woman, respectable. She wore a blue nurse-like uniform and wouldn't be most people's idea of someone hooked up with a bunch of murderers. But Jimmy had met and questioned people exactly as mild, respectable, and nondescript before, and once in a while they had turned out to be anything but harmless.

She gave him a watery smile and although she spoke with a distinct accent her English was good.

'We won't be disturbed. I've asked that this room be kept free while we talk.' The smile turned into an enquiry.

'The police said I should expect a woman, a Ms Heppert?'

'I'm Ms Heppert's assistant, my name is Costello. Ms Heppert has other business in Munich and this is a very small matter, routine really, so she asked me to deal with it.' Her weak smile returned and she visibly relaxed, so Jimmy smiled as well, to help things along. 'Who paid you to lie about the murder of the journalist? Was it the same people who paid you to leave the old man's wheelchair where their lorry could run over him?' Jimmy didn't wait for an answer, by the look of her she couldn't give one anyway, but he kept the smile going and the calm, friendly tone of voice, just to help things along. 'I think it safe to assume they were the same people. I know they killed the journalist because he had visited the old man's daughter and asked her awkward questions.' The woman had started to breathe in gasps but Jimmy ploughed on. 'They killed the old man because they knew they were more likely to get what they wanted from the daughter. Of course once they find that you also have had a visitor, one who knows that both killings were set-ups, they'll have to kill you. I should also mention that I paid a call on the daughter and asked her questions about her father. I told her my name, Costello, so I suppose that will make it worse when they find out, if it could be worse. Still, there you are, it can't be helped can it? However, it does mean that as soon as they find out I've visited you and we've talked you'll be dead, so I would appreciate a name and contact address or phone number of the people you work for, and I would like it now please. You can see how it would not be wise for me to have to wait for the information. If I don't get what I want …'

The woman gave a sort of moan and slumped sideways. Jimmy stood up and went over to her.

'Shit.'

He'd overdone it. He meant to have her scared enough to talk, before she had time to think, not to make her pass out. He picked up her hand and patted it. He took her by the shoulders and gave her a good shake. She stayed out.

'Shit.'

He looked about the room for some water but there was nothing. Then she moaned and he bent over her.

'Come on, snap out of it. Come on, I want a name out of you, you stupid bitch.'

She moaned again but louder. Jimmy glanced up at the door.

He took her by the shoulders and shook her again. Her eyes opened. For a split second they were confused and unfocussed. Then they clamped on to his face, filled with fear and she began to speak. Unfortunately it was German and Jimmy had no idea what she was saying.

'English, speak in English.'

She stopped speaking. The look in her eyes changed from fear to hate. He'd lost her.

She pushed him back and struggled to her feet. For a

moment she held on to the back of the chair and looked down at the floor, steadying herself. Then she looked at him again. It wasn't a nice look. She was anything but mild-mannered and nondescript now and Jimmy could believe only too well that she could be part of two murders. He could also believe that she would be more than willing to ask her friends to arrange for his death.

She spat something in German at him. This time Jimmy got the gist very clearly even if he didn't know which word meant what. Then she went to the door, pulled it open, and was gone.

Jimmy followed her out of the room; she was walking quickly up the corridor. Another figure in a blue uniform came out of a door and the woman cannoned into her but kept going. Uniform number two shouted after her but she turned a corner and was gone. This new carer, he supposed they were carers not qualified nurses, looked at Jimmy then said something.

Jimmy walked up to her.

'Sorry, I don't speak German. Do you speak English?'

'Some, yes. Greta is upset, what is it that has upset her?'

'Me. I upset her.'

The new carer looked at him for a second trying to be sure of what he had said. Then they heard a car engine revving hard and uniform number two went to the window of the corridor.

'She leaves.'

Jimmy looked. He saw a Mercedes sports car moving away from the drive at speed down the road.

'Her car?'

'Yes.'

'A nice car.'

'Yes, a very nice car.'

'Good wages here? For such a nice car I mean.'

A look of scorn came into her face.

'Greta does not buy such a car from her wages.'

'No?'

He waited. This woman wanted to talk to him, he could tell, but he didn't push it. He'd ballsed up one interview, he didn't want to screw up a second chance.

The woman waited a second before she spoke.

'Did you come for money?'

Jimmy could see that there was no great love between this one and the recently departed Greta, and the way she'd been barged aside made her want to unload some of her anger.

'No, not money. Why would I want money from her?'

'Many people want money from her.'

'They do?'

'Yes. Do you know Greta well?'

'Not at all.'

Number two let the words sink in. Then smiled.

'Not at all is the best way to know Greta.'

Jimmy grinned to show he appreciated the joke.

'Why is that?'

A conspiratorial look came into the woman's face. She was going to dish the dirt on Greta and would thoroughly enjoy doing it.

'You have seen that fine car?' Jimmy nodded. 'It is new. She has money for such a car but not to pay what she owes.'

'She owes people?'

'Plenty of people. When she has no money she is all smilings and friendships and she borrows. Oh, she is so thankful, she vows to pay back. Yes, but when she has money what does she do? She buys herself a pretty car and no one gets paid back what is owed.'

'Does she owe you money?'

A look of disdain that he could ask such a question flashed into her face and voice.

'Me, no. I know better, but others she owes, plenty of others. And her rent, I know she has troubles with her rent. There are other things also.'

'Other things?'

Now she became cautious, her anger was gone, she'd said what she wanted, now she was being careful.

'You are not police, not English police?' Jimmy shook his head. 'But you are making enquiries of Greta?'

'Yes, I'm making enquiries. I was given Greta's name and

her place of work by the Munich police. I am not the police but my enquiries are known to the police.'

That was enough. She was reassured and ready to go on.

'I think she has borrowed from the residents here which is very much against the rules, very forbidden. And there have been missing things. I make no accusations, you understand, I tell you what everyone knows. Small things but valuable have been missed.'

'And she has borrowed from the residents?'

'That I know to be so, I have been told by them. It is expensive, this place, our residents are not poor people, but even the well-off can go childish when they get old, and they can do foolish things.'

'Where does all the money go, when she's not buying pretty cars?'

Reminding her of the car got her going again. Jimmy guessed it might.

'She gambles. She wastes her money at a club. If she wins she spends, if she loses she borrows. Mostly she borrows, I do not think she is a good gambler.'

'Do you know the name of the club.'

'Yes, she has told me. The Schwarz Diamant, The Black Diamond.'

'I see.'

A man came into the corridor. He was wearing a suit and was quite young, either management or a visitor. He spoke rapidly and with authority in German to the woman. He was management. She answered and then he obviously told her to get going because she went.

He turned to Jimmy and said something in German.

'Sorry, I don't speak German. Do you speak English?'

The answer was curt and unfriendly and probably not true.

'Nein.'

It was obviously his way of saying goodbye.

That was that, thought Jimmy so he smiled a farewell and walked away.

Once outside he walked along the quiet road and thought

about what had happened. He'd bollocksed up the interview with the Greta woman, but he'd made real progress with uniform number two. It was a fair bet that the people he wanted were connected with the gambling club she used. They'd probably used her bad debts to get her to do the wheelchair thing and once she'd done that they knew they could use her to set up the journalist killing. That must have been where the money for the car came from. Well, they weren't pikers when it came to pay-offs, he'd have to give them that. The car looked expensive and it had definitely done the trick and bought her silence and loyalty. Even if she hadn't fainted when he sprang what he knew on her he wouldn't have got what he wanted without a hammer and chisel, and maybe not even then.

He saw the busy main road ahead and carried on walking. He'd find a taxi or the station. The woman he'd come to see was pretty much a dead-end now and she wouldn't be taken in with what he'd said about her friends killing her. She'd tell them all right, and probably do her best to see that they came after him. In which case they'd get him. This was their town and even if he moved out of it quickly they'd probably still get him. Distance didn't seem much of a problem for them, not if getting McBride gunned in Rome was anything to go by. No, he needed to stay and contact them, not run. But he had to make it soon, he needed to find them before they found him. Well, he had a name, the gambling club, The Black Diamond. So why not pay it a visit? It was a risky move, but, when you came right down to it, what else were gambling clubs for, except for taking risks?

Chapter Thirty-three

'Yes and no.'

Nadine gave him a look.

'Cut the crap, Costello. Did you get what I wanted?'

'We wanted. I'm in this too, remember?'

'Did you?'

'Yes and no. I know where I can contact the people who used her.'

'So it's yes?'

'But I have no introduction, no safe way in. I can get in all right, but if they don't want to talk to me the question is, will I get out?'

Nadine stood up and took a slow turn round the room. It was a neat sitting room, not big but well done out. She didn't stint herself, thought Jimmy, always a suite. Still, if it was all on her obscene expense account why not?

She came back and settled again.

'I don't like it.'

'I'm not wild about it myself.'

'If you go in and don't come out where does that leave me?'

'That question isn't exactly top of my list.'

Suddenly she was loud and angry.

'Fuck your list. I didn't come all this way for you to finish up in a back alley like Serge. I came here to get a job done. You've screwed up, Costello, I should have known you would.'

Jimmy ignored the outburst. She was just letting the noise out while she figured her options, so he sat and said nothing. Nadine got up took another turn round the room. Jimmy knew what she was working on – go with him to the club or let him go alone? It was a tricky call for her to make. Go with him and she might make the contact she wanted, but she might also suffer the same fate if the contact wasn't welcome. Let him go alone and either he made it or he didn't. If he did then he had what she wanted and that put him in too strong a position for her to feel comfortable. If he didn't she was still on the outside, alive, but in the cold with nowhere to go but back to Paris and the brothers from Chicago. And that would also be pretty much out in the cold now she knew Veronique was waiting in the wings in a place that had enough security to be sure no one could get at her without the right introductions. She'd thought hard but come up empty on how she might get Veronique for herself. To get Veronique she would need Costello and that put her back where she was already. She needed the bastard.

She settled again and gave him another look. It was meant to be a nice look, one which showed Jimmy that she had decided to trust him, one which told him that they were partners in all this. One which hinted that they could be partners in more than this if he wanted. Unfortunately it had insincerity stamped all over it.

Christ, thought Jimmy, she must be desperate to try that game out on me.

'You shouldn't take too much notice of what I say sometimes, I speak before I think,' she lowered her eyes, 'but I guess you already know that.' The eyes came back up. 'Jimmy, I trust you on this, I know you're good at what you do, it's just that, well …' The eyes went down again. God, she was bad at this. But in a way Jimmy was pleased. He was glad she was lousy at something. He finished her sentence for her. It was better than watching her do it.

'You want to stay alive more than you want to make the contact. You want me to go in and test the water. I take a bullet in the head or I get to meet someone, either way you get something out of it.'

She tried to keep the nice going but Jimmy could see it was hard work.

'I only get something if you come out alive. If I didn't think you'd make it I wouldn't let you go.'

'No. If I die you know the people who killed me are the ones you need to talk to and you know where to contact them. All you'll need is another messenger.'

The 'nice' fell away, not that she'd ever been really convinced of it herself. It was something she did when she really had nothing else to do.

'All right, either way I get something.'

'That's OK, I would have made the same choice. I would have explained it differently, that's all.'

'If you make the contact, what then?'

'That, girly, is the big money question.' 'Girly' hurt, he could see it, so he went on. 'And I certainly don't need you with me fluttering your eyes at these guys. It wouldn't work with them any more than it would with me, even if you were any good at it, which you're not.' He could see she was getting up a head of steam. 'I doubt they'll be like your amateur rent boy and think trying to be nice is any part of what they're doing.' Enough. Any more and she'd go pop. Now he'd made it clear he was the one making the decisions he could get down to it. 'They'll only be interested if they believe we can offer a deal and it will have to be a damned good deal and laid out fast just to get them to listen, if they'll listen. To do that I have to be sure I'm offering them more than they've already got. And as I have no idea what it is they've got or are trying to get you'll have to tell me what this game we're all playing is about.'

There. It was out in the open.

The steam was all gone and her brain was ticking. She was good, she latched on to the business as soon as she saw it and put anything else to one side. She'd taken his point and was now deciding how to play it so it was to her own best advantage. Jimmy let her take her time. He wanted her to feel she was in control. That was important.

'They want the Colmar estate.'

'I know that much. What exactly is in the estate that they're so keen to get their hands on?'

'What were you told?'

'Loot, Nazi loot from the war.'

She had the good grace to laugh.

'You didn't believe that, did you? No, you didn't, how could you?'

'So what is it?'

'An island. A smallish island with a big, deep-water harbour.'

'The old whore owned an island?'

'No. She owned most of the shares in the company who own the island.'

'And what does this company do?'

'It processes fish.'

Jimmy had been ready for many things, but not a fish processing company. Who causes all this mayhem to get control of a fish processing company?

'That sounds about as sensible as Nazi loot.'

'Oh it's sensible all right. The people I work for in America have been after that company for over five years, longer if you count all the lead-in work that went on before we got called in officially.'

'Who kills people for a fish factory?'

'Anybody who wants to control the world.'

The laugh came from Jimmy this time but it petered out when he saw she wasn't joking.

'Explain.'

She sat back and let him wait. It was her way of saying she wasn't giving up control so easily.

'I'll tell you enough to make you understand what this is all about because you're right, you need to know how big it is and because your boss was also right, you're a lousy liar. When you talk to them they need to know you understand how far everyone will go in this thing.'

'And how far is that?'

'All the way because a war is coming. In many ways it's already started, but at present it's very low-level and the casualties are small and peripheral. Your boss McBride, the old

Nazi, the journalist, even Serge, are all casualties of this war. And more people will get killed, eventually lots of people, and in the end there will be winners and losers. But this time the war isn't being left to countries or politicians. No one is going to use military muscle, well, not much anyway and nowhere that it really matters. The real strategic fighting, the fighting that matters, will be done between businesses, multi-national corporations. It will be planned in boardrooms and carried out through stock exchanges. Countries don't matter any more, they're a leftover from a bygone age. Politicians are irrelevant. They can be bought and sold like any other commodity. You see, Costello, no one in their right mind wants a war that kills business and leaves everyone with some great, God-awful mess that has to be cleaned up. The people who want to run the world, to own the world, don't want it smashed to pulp first. Nuclear weapons are as far as military muscle can ever go and have proved as useless as all the other miracle weapons, expensive, unreliable, and in the end no damned good. The only real difference is that nuclear weapons don't even leave anything to the winner.'

'All of which means?'

'Large-scale military wars are over, but the aim of war remains – occupy your enemy's territory, subjugate it, and you've won! Nothing else works. Occupation means bring him to his knees on his own soil and have the means to keep him there.'

She waited, did he understand, was he convinced she was making sense? It mattered, it was important that he felt in control.

'And this fish factory can do all that?'

She knew it wasn't a joke, it was a genuine question. He wanted to understand but unfortunately he was stupid.

'Controlling energy does the job and does it without destruction of physical things or the economic fabric – only people die and then only the poor or unimportant, those who are neither serious producers nor mass consumers, the unnecessary, the unwanted, those surplus to economic requirements.

Whoever has control of the energy will have the industrial might, a might greater than any military force. Machines need fuel, people need fuel, without fuel everything stops and we all go back to the Stone Age. Masses of cheap labour are useless without energy. Control the energy and you control the people. Control the energy and you have occupation. You win.'

Jimmy believed her, at least he believed big business was behind it all. He also believed that the fish factory island was part of it all, an important part. But was he right to believe? What would McBride have made him believe? And that brought him back to the most important question and the one he couldn't answer – what was it that McBride wanted out of all of this? Not control of a fish factory!'

'Why is the island so important?'

'No, you've got enough to be going on with. If you believe what I've told you then you know what the stakes are and that's enough. The people you will contact want the island. Colmar must have stashed some shares with the old man, he wouldn't deal, so they killed him and got them from the daughter. Now they want the other ones held by the Colmar estate. You have to convince them I can get the estate. That we have a cast-iron candidate whom we can control absolutely.'

'If they've gone this far they must be sure they can get the estate somehow. What's my offer of Veronique Colmar likely to be up against on their side?'

'Work it out for yourself, you're supposed to be the shit-hot detective. I'm just a girly who flutters her eyes badly, remember? Just get me what I want. If you set up a meeting for me, a safe meeting, I'll tell you the rest. If not, if you don't come back, well, I won't say it was nice knowing you.'

Jimmy wasn't happy. He'd done badly with Greta at the residential home, now he'd done badly with Heppert. He knew a bit more but nothing that really helped, nothing that he could honestly say he even understood. What would McBride want him to do? And what did he want? Did he still want to kill the bastards, did he still want that? Maybe, maybe not, but even if he wanted to kill them, was he still up to it? If the business in the alley with Serge was any indicator the answer was no.

'Do I tell the Dane what's happening?'

'Nothing, not this time. Let's keep this to ourselves. Does he still trust you?'

'I don't think he ever did.'

'Don't get smart. Does he still think you're feeding him straight information?'

'How the hell would I know? I call him and tell him what I know. He listens. End of story. You two are the ones who know what's going on, not me. In case you hadn't noticed, I'm the one who does as he's told. I leave you two big brains to figure out who believes what.'

'When will you go to the club?'

'Tonight. No point in putting it off or hanging about. I'll go early, about nine. If I'm not back by midnight …'

She waited.

'Go on.'

But there was nothing to go on with. If he wasn't back by midnight he was never coming back at all, so what the hell did he care what she did? It all had to end sometime but he'd always hoped it would end for a reason, for some reason he'd understand. If he didn't come back he would have died without knowing why or for what: a stupid, pointless death. Then he thought of his wife Bernie, dying in a hospital bed from cancer with him useless, watching, with nothing he could do and nothing he could say. All death was pointless, why the hell should his be any different?

'If I don't come back let McBride know what happened.'

'Sure, I'll see that she knows.'

Jimmy knew it was a lie. It had come too quickly, too easily. But it didn't matter, one more lie among so many lies made no difference and in the grand bloody scheme of things, what the hell ever did?

Chapter Thirty-four

The Black Diamond club could never be mistaken for anything other than what it was, a cheap and nasty dive where small-time gamblers went to lose money. The entrance was down some steps off a street that was, at night, bright with harsh, coloured lights that flashed, flickered, and flared among the bustle of people desperate for fun and laughter, desperate to tell themselves they were having a good time. Daylight would reveal the reality, and it wouldn't be a pretty sight.

'The membership charge is a one-off payment of two hundred Euros.' Jimmy handed over some notes. The young man counted them, slipped them into a drawer, and pushed across a form. 'Fill this in using a name you will remember. It is the name that will appear on your membership card.'

'If it's on my card why do I need to be able to remember it?'

'In the event of your losing your card we would need the name to replace it.'

Jimmy wrote his own name and looked through the other information they wanted. He put the street of the residential home as his address and the telephone number of Nadine's hotel. For references, they required two, he put Nadine Heppert with her Paris office address and M. Joubert with his Paris address, then pushed it back to the young man who examined it.

'You have a Munich address but your references are both in Paris?'

'I'm an international playboy.'

The young man made a face that said he didn't care one way or the other so long as he had the money in the drawer. He filled out an elaborate membership card and pushed it across. Jimmy slipped it into a side pocket and went on into the club.

The place wasn't big and it wasn't busy. There were half a dozen tables each set out for up to six people to sit at and play cards. The lighting over the tables was adequate, elsewhere in the room it was about enough to get around without falling over anything but not so good the management would have to spend much on keeping the place decorated. Around the walls were pools of light in which stood gaming machines. In a dark corner a light shone weakly on the sign for the toilets and the emergency exit. The only other well-lit place was the bar. Jimmy walked through the tables, stood at the bar, and looked round the room. Two tables were in action, one was full, five players and the house dealer. A young man in a white shirt and black bow tie. The other had a young woman in a low-cut evening dress and two middle-aged men sitting talking. The young woman had a deck of cards in front of her so Jimmy assumed she was the dealer waiting to get a game going.

Somebody behind him said something in German. Jimmy turned.

'I don't speak German.'

'There is no problem, I speak English very well. What do you want to drink?'

'Beer.'

The man went and got a bottle out of a chiller cabinet, snapped off the top, and picked up a glass. He put them before Jimmy on the bar.

Then he told him the price.

Jimmy's eyebrows went up. It was a small bottle even by small bottle standards.

The barman smiled.

'Yes, I know, a good price, you are surprised, you expected to pay more.' He took the note Jimmy put on the counter. 'The prices go up after eleven. This is what you in England call happy hour, yes?'

'Happy hour, yes.'

The man went to the till, put in the note, and brought back

the change.

'Put it wherever you keep your tips.'

He nodded thanks and he went off.

Jimmy poured the beer into the glass and took a drink. It was, he supposed, beer under even the loosest interpretation of any trades description act, but it was gassy and really too cold to tell what taste it had, if any.

Another man came in and sat down at the table where the girl was the dealer. He shook hands with the other men. Regulars, thought Jimmy. For God's sake, why not play at home with friends with no cut going to the house? But no, people were people. They were funny and did things you never could explain. If you could explain why everybody did what they did there'd be no place for coppers and crimes would solve themselves.

'Another?'

Jimmy turned back to the barman. The bottle was empty but he still had beer in his glass, not much, true, but there wasn't much to begin with, not with bottles that size. Jimmy decided the bloke must be on a percentage.

'Is there a manager?'

'Sorry?'

'A manager, someone in charge.'

'You wish to talk with the manager?'

'Yes, I wish to talk with the manager.' If he was going to do it there was no point in hanging about until he had a bigger audience. 'I have a message for him from a customer, Greta Mann. I don't know if she uses that name here but her first name really is Greta. He'll know who I'm talking about. If he's not sure tell him she's in the residential home business and drives a neat little Mercedes sports model that his friends bought for her.'

The barman's English obviously wasn't good enough to follow and even if it had been he didn't seem to like Jimmy's attitude.

'Tell me your message and I will see that it gets to the manager.'

'OK. I visited Greta today and we talked. We talked about two friends of mine, an old soldier who died in his wheelchair a few years back and a French journalist who sadly passed away under a train here in Munich not so long ago. Greta told me that the manager could tell me all about it and before you ask I'm not the police, not German police, not any police. I'm a businessman, I represent an office in Paris which has a proposal to put to his,' Jimmy paused looking for the right words, 'his associates.'

'Associates?'

Jimmy reckoned the barman was making a genuine enquiry, he couldn't imagine the man was any part of what was going on.

'Yes, the people the manager works for or with, his business associates. They know all about my two friends here in Munich, the old soldier and the journalist. It's a long message, do you want to write any of it down or will you remember it all?' The barman wasn't in the mood for any kind of humour. He'd understood the general idea of what Jimmy was saying, Jimmy could see that by the way he looked at him. 'And no more beer, thanks. It's too cold.'

The barman turned and went to a phone behind the bar. He talked to someone and then came back to Jimmy.

'You wait.'

It was spoken like an order.

'Sure.'

Another customer had come to the bar. The barman switched back on his smile and happy manner and went to serve him. Jimmy guessed that later on, if and when the tables got busy, there would be waitresses to do the fetching and carrying so the games wouldn't get interrupted. At the moment, as it was happy hour and the beer at almost give-away prices, it was self-service. Jimmy stood and looked at the room. Somewhere the manager was probably making a call, checking, finding out what to do.

After about ten minutes the phone behind the bar rang. The barman answered it then put it down and came to Jimmy.

'Who in Paris do you represent?'

'Parker and Henry, corporate attorneys, they're an American firm. I'm working with a Nadine Heppert who is in their Paris office. Nadine Heppert, Parker and Henry, got that?' The barman didn't answer, he went back to the phone and picked it up and spoke again. Jimmy waited until he'd put the phone down. 'You can tell your boss that Ms Heppert is staying in Munich, he can check what I've told him if he likes. I put Ms Heppert's hotel number on my application form.'

The barman gave him a nasty look and for the first time Jimmy noticed what a well-muscled, fit-looking, young bloke he was. You wouldn't have thought they'd need much in the way of muscle in a club like this, still, I suppose they got a few bad losers who needed to be escorted from the premises now and then.

The barman was back on the phone. When he put it down there were two more men waiting at the bar. He served them and they took their drinks to the table with the young woman dealer. The table was full so the woman was shuffling the cards and there were chips in the centre of the table. There were dealers at two more tables, one had one punter, the other two. All men so far. Jimmy looked at his watch, quarter to ten. The night was getting going.

The phone rang again. The barman apologised to the man he was serving and answered it then came to Jimmy. He nodded to a dark corner.

'That door over there, up the stairs, there is a door at the top. Knock.'

He went back to the man he was serving and Jimmy crossed the room to the dark corner. When he got really close he saw a door peeping out from behind some sort of heavy drape. He pulled the drape aside and opened the door. In front of him was a narrow, uncarpeted wooden stairway lit by a solitary bulb in a wall-bracket half-way up. The top of the stairs was in darkness. He began to climb, passed the bulb, and went on. With the bulb behind him the top of the stairs became a little clearer and he could see a door. When he reached it he knocked and a voice answered. He went in. It was a small, shabby, cluttered office lit by another single bulb, this time hanging from the ceiling. There were two people sitting at a desk. One was a well-turned-out woman in a business suit, the other an older man, flabby and bald, in an open-necked shirt with a gaudy tie hanging loose. It was the woman who spoke.

'Please, Herr Costello, sit down.'

There was a chair facing the desk so Jimmy sat down.

'You the manager?'

'No, Herr Schmidt is the manager but he speaks no English so he asked me to come and talk to you. I speak English.'

'I thought everyone spoke English, most of the people I've met did.'

'I assume you have not come to talk about whether people speak English or not, so please explain what it is you have come to talk about.'

'What about Flabby? If he doesn't speak English what's he here for, decoration?'

There was nothing in the way of a reaction on the flabby man's face so Jimmy accepted that he wasn't an English speaker. Not that it mattered if the woman could negotiate.

'I've come to offer you a deal on the Colmar estate business. My partner, a woman of influence who has an interest in the matter, feels sure it will be a better deal than the one you think you have.'

'I was informed you wished to talk about two friends. I know nothing about any Colmar estate.'

'Of course you don't. But I bet you know someone who does.'

'I was told you had a message from a customer of ours. Do you have such a message?'

'No, I told you, I want to talk to someone about the Colmar estate.'

'I'm afraid we know nothing about this Colmar estate and if you do not have a message then I think we have no more to talk about.' She turned and said something in German to the flabby man whose face didn't change and who said nothing, just kept looking at Jimmy. 'If there is nothing further, Herr Costello, the manager is a busy man and I also have things to do.'

'Is that it?'

'Unless you have anything further you wish to say.'

No, he had nothing further he wished to say. He wished he wasn't there, he wished he hadn't come in the first place, and he wished he'd done a better job of making his pitch. All of those things he wished. But there was nothing he could think of that he wished to say.

He stood up.

'Thank you for your time. If you or your friends change your minds I'll be around for a day or two.'

'Goodbye, Herr Costello.'

She didn't get up to say it.

Flabby said something in German.

'The manager says that your application for membership is not acceptable. I'm afraid you have been refused membership.

'Why is that?'

'There were irregularities in the form you filled. This is a respectable gaming club. We cannot allow irregularities.'

'Of course not. Where would we all be if we let the irregularities pass?'

It was the manager who answered.

'We would all be where you will soon be, Mr Costello.'

So, Flabby spoke English and spoke it well. Another mistake.

Jimmy went to the door and left. The light bulb on the stairs had gone out. It was total darkness. Jimmy felt for the wall and began to negotiate the steps slowly. Suddenly the light came on beside his head. He stopped and looked round. At the top of the stairs Flabby was looking down at him.

'You were in the dark, Mr Costello, but look, I have returned the light so you can see your way out. Take my advice, Mr Costello, leave all this alone, get out while you can still see a way out.'

'Or else?'

Flabby raised his hand and Jimmy found himself once again

in total darkness. He waited for more advice from the voice but nothing came so he felt his way to the bottom of the stairs and opened the door. Compared to the dark of the stairway the room looked bright. Two more tables had gone into action during his short visit upstairs. At one of them a face was looking at him. Greta's face. She was smiling. Whatever they had planned for him pleased her and that was not a good sign. Jimmy walked across the room to the exit and out to the desk where the young man was still sitting. This time the barman was standing beside him.

'Your card please, Herr Costello. Your membership has been refused.'

Jimmy pulled the card out of his pocket and tossed it onto the table. The young man took it, tore it in half, and dropped the pieces on the floor.

'How about a refund of my membership fee?'

'Oh no, that was a standard administration charge. Membership is free for those who are accepted. There can be no refund.'

Jimmy left the club and walked up the stairs into the street and headed quickly for the main road where it was brighter and noisier and there were plenty of people, witnesses. Before he could reach the lights and the people a car pulled in beside him the front door opened and a man quickly got out and looked around while he opened the back door. He said something in German. Jimmy guessed he was being told to get in so he got in. If he was going to die he didn't want to hurry it up by causing a fuss, and he didn't want it to happen on a grubby side street. Once in the car it pulled away, nobody spoke, there wasn't much to say. They all knew what they were doing so they got on with it.

Chapter Thirty-five

The Comedian put a beer on the table beside Jimmy's chair then sat down opposite him and poured a beer for himself.

'I'm sorry you could not be told what was happening but I had to use the men that were available and none of them speaks English. It was all something of a rush.'

'What was planned for me?'

'There is a young boy in your bed at your hotel, a young immigrant boy. An illegal of course. There are a couple of reporters and a photographer. The police have been primed and I expect someone has been told to be ready.'

Jimmy poured his beer and took a drink.

'Well, it's not as drastic as I was expecting.'

'No, not perhaps what you were expecting but effective. You would have been a paedophile, a man who travels abroad seeking out the young and vulnerable to serve his perverted sexual desires. The boy, of course, would have been beaten as well as sexually assaulted. He would have earned his money, I assure you.'

'I think I'd have preferred a bullet.'

'The outcome would have been a serious criminal charge which would have been splashed over the media and the job would have been done. No one, no one at all, would want to listen to anything you might say. When the visitors at your hotel realise you will not return they will leave and I will arrange for your things to be collected and find you somewhere to stay until you leave Munich.'

'I'm leaving Munich, am I?'

'Oh yes, Mr Costello. Keeping you out of trouble is taking up too much of my time. I think you will have to go back to Rome.'

'Who told you?'

'That you were at the club?'

'Yes. Was it Heppert or the people at the club? Who?'

'I was told and now you are safe. How I came by that information is no concern of yours.'

'Like hell it's not. I trust you about as much as I trust the people I met at the club. How do I know you're not in with them on this?'

'Even if that were the case it would still be no concern of yours. You invited yourself into all this, Mr Costello. You have no idea of what you are doing or what is going on, yet you still blunder …'

'Those bastards kill people, two to my certain knowledge and they tried damned hard to kill Professor McBride. Is that the company you keep? Is that the way Danish Intelligence works?'

'More to the point, how do you work, Mr Costello? I have to say I find your methods opaque. I cannot see what it is you are trying to do. You are here with Ms Heppert. Why? She is pursuing her own ends in this matter and I assure you she is not at all interested in helping you. You interview Greta Mann. Again why? Given that she is involved in two murders she is hardly likely to prove co-operative when questioned, especially by a foreigner with absolutely no authority. You barge into a gambling club where you know you will not be welcome and put yourself in danger. Again why? What is it you hope to achieve?'

He was right of course. He was ex-Detective James Cornelius Costello, not James bloody Bond. He wasn't one of those blokes in books who crash into stuff like this, kill the baddies, and save the world.

'I want to save the world.'

For the first time ever Jimmy saw exasperation in his face. The Comedian had finally run out of patience. Jimmy also had run out. What of he wasn't sure. This bloke might be the only friend Jimmy had at the moment so he decided to give him what he wanted.

'I came here to kill as many of the bastards as I could.'

This time the look on the face was surprise but it soon faded.

'Please, don't joke, I am not in the mood.'

'I'm not joking, that's as far as my plans went.'

The Comedian paused to think about it.

'Explain.'

'There's not much to explain. They tried to kill McBride, that was before I got told what any of this was about. With her in hospital I didn't know what I was supposed to do so I decided to do what I could, which was kill some of the bastards who'd blown off McBride's arm and as near as dammit killed her.'

The Comedian sat with a puzzled look on his face.

'You're serious, aren't you? This is not a joke or some story, you actually meant to come here and kill someone.'

Jimmy nodded. It was only when someone else said it out loud that you saw how bloody stupid it all was. When it was inside his own head he could pretend that it made some sort of sense. Out loud you had to see it for what it was, fantasy.

'It was a stupid idea but there was nothing else. Without McBride I'm just crashing about, filling in time, trying to play the good guy. I don't expect you to understand but after what she's done for me …'

'But I do understand. She has saved you more than once. One of those occasions was in Copenhagen and it was I that she saved you from. After that incident I undertook considerable research on both you and Professor McBride, so I do understand. What I don't understand is exactly who it is you were thinking of killing. The club manager, perhaps? The lady who spoke to you? Who exactly?'

'I hadn't got that far.'

'You hadn't got anywhere at all, it seems to me.'

And Jimmy had to admit that he was about right.

'So where am I in all this?'

'That depends on what you know. What has Nadine Heppert told you?'

'That it's a war, World War Three, but without the guns or rockets.'

And Jimmy told him what Heppert had said. The Comedian listened quietly.

'And Professor McBride? What do you think her interest is in all this?'

Again he listened while Jimmy told him about the Nazi loot story and the claimant stashed away. When he had finished the Commander gave a small sigh.

'For an supposedly intelligent man, Mr Costello, you are remarkably susceptible to fairy tales. Ms Heppert's was less imaginative than your Professor's but they were both no more than stories. But putting fairy stories to one side what have you actually found out for yourself? What do *you* think this is all about?'

'I think there probably is an island, Heppert had to have a bit of truth to set the lie going because she had to come up with something quickly. If there is an island then I think it's Danish because you're involved. If it's owned by a company that processes a lot of fish it might very well have a deep-water harbour so factory ships can unload. If the island exists then it's become important for some reason and, as it can't be because of fish processing, it must be because of its location and the fact that it has a deep-water harbour. Fish and Denmark could mean Greenland and that could mean something to do with the Arctic. That's about as far as I've got.'

The Comedian sat back and raised his glass.

'Congratulations, Mr Costello.'

'I'm right?'

'That there is an island and that it's Danish, yes.' Jimmy felt surprised but also pleased. 'Now that you know you are correct does anything else suggest itself to you?'

One thing did.

'Is it oil, stuff like that? Heppert said this was all about energy, getting control of the energy. A deep-water harbour means big boats which could be supertankers and tankers mean oil.' He waited for a response but none came. Jimmy mentally laid out his pieces. He was missing something. A Danish island to bring out oil or something else just as valuable that was still in the ground, and enough of whatever it was for people to kill each other over it. That was the question that niggled, why the killing? Why not do it like they always did, with money? Why not grease the right palms, slip enough money to whoever could … Then the pieces locked together. Because they couldn't, there were no palms to grease on this one. No one was even supposed to be gearing up to get the stuff out of the ground never mind getting ready to build a place where they could load it ready for transport. 'They're going to get the oil that's in the Arctic, aren't they? And they're fighting over control of the way it's going to come out.'

A look of mock surprise came to the Comedian's face.

'But surely you know that mineral exploration is forbidden by international agreement in the Arctic regions?'

'A lot of things are forbidden by international agreements but they still happen. If there's oil or gas or any other bloody thing that governments and businesses want under that ice they'll be looking. I would say they've been looking for a very long time and now they know what's there and they're all argy-bargying each other to get control of how it comes out when the international agreement goes pop. This island must be earmarked as the best place for something like a pipeline terminal to get the stuff onto tankers. The Americans want it, so do the Russians, and if you're sitting in, maybe Europe wants it as well. Old Ma Colmar must have got wind of what was going on and bought up the processing company. She must have used Young Hitler and others to buy the shares and either sit on them for her or hand them over. She was a whore and a blackmailer and a double-crosser. Her sort never change and they never give up. She was at it to the bloody end. Ma Colmar was a tough old bitch and crafty with it so everybody waits. No one's in a hurry, the oil won't flow for a few years. But when she finally croaks the starter's flag drops. Unfortunately before anyone gets past the post the sisters in Paris start looking for an heir and things get sticky. That's where me and McBride come in and all the rest you know.'

'Very good, but this person Young Hitler is?'

'My little joke. It's the bloke in the wheelchair. Your Group B crowd found out he had a block of shares and went after them.'

'But he died some years after Mme Colmar's death. Why wait?'

'No idea. They had to find out he'd got them and when they did maybe he got bloody-minded, maybe he was still obeying orders – sit on them until you are told otherwise. I don't know, but one way or another they decided they could deal with the daughter more easily than her dad so they had him run over. The daughter started selling off his books and anything else that would give her cash to spend on all the things she'd missed out on so they probably got the shares without too much difficulty. Getting Ma Colmar's wouldn't have been so simple. They had to wait to see if an heir turned up. When one didn't I guess everyone interested began to hunt around for someone to fill the vacancy.'

'Hmm. You've got quite far, haven't you? I can see why Professor McBride uses you. Maybe I should have left you to go back to your hotel, then you would not be a problem.'

'Am I a problem?'

'Yes, I'm afraid you are.'

'A bullet in the head problem not a little boy in the bed problem?'

'Yes, I think so. Before tonight you were simply a nuisance, it was only a matter of getting rid of you and making anything you might say of no value. Now you may be thought of as a threat.'

'Like McBride?'

'Professor McBride was a very serious threat, she has powerful connections and could do considerable harm.'

'And the journalist? Was he such a threat, did they have to kill him? Couldn't they have shut him up?'

'He found out about the shares from the daughter. She is a very silly woman which is why it was decided to deal with her and remove the father. The journalist had the key, the shares gave him the location, he would have followed things up and come to the same conclusion you did and there could have been considerable and damaging publicity. No one wanted any publicity.'

'No, I can see how that would be a problem rather than a nuisance.'

They both sat for a moment, each with their own thinking to do.

'Well, you can stay here tonight, there are two bedrooms. You will be safe here and tomorrow we can decide what is to be done with you. Now, if you will forgive me I must retire, it has been a long day and in its own way quite difficult. I'm sure you too must be tired. There's plenty more beer in the fridge if you want it. Goodnight.'

Jimmy watched the Comedian stand up and leave the room. He picked up his beer and looked at it, then put it down. He wasn't in the mood. He was tired and he was ready to go to bed but first he had to think about the Comedian. Whose side was he on? He also had to think about Heppert. And there were other things as well.

He pulled out his phone and made a call.

McBride was improving, if she continued to improve she could be out of intensive care in a few more days. There would still be further surgery but the worst looked like it was over. Soon she might even be able to have visitors. Jimmy put the phone away and went to find a bottle of beer. He felt like one now. It was good news and he needed some good news. It was like the Comedian said, it had been a long and difficult day. And he couldn't see tomorrow getting any easier.

Jimmy sat and thought. He went over what he knew, or what he thought he knew. He thought about Heppert and the Comedian and Flabby & Co. Flabby was definitely one of the bad guys, or was he? He only had the Comedian's word that there was some sort of set-up in his hotel. Was Heppert's story a fairy tale? Again it was only what the Comedian said. McBride's story he discounted, she never told him the truth but she was definitely one of the good guys. So, what did he really know? He got up and fetched himself a couple more beers and tried again. But nothing happened so he gave up and thought about tomorrow and the days that would come after that, the future. He thought about when there was no future, when you closed your eyes for the last time, or someone closed them for you – what then? The same old question. Was it finally the end or was it another beginning? And which did he hope for? It was a tough call.

Chapter Thirty-six

Somebody was gently shaking his shoulder. Then he was awake. The Comedian was looking down at him.

'There was a perfectly good bed in the bedroom. Why did you choose to sleep in the chair?'

Jimmy struggled to sit up. He felt awful. He was stiff and his mouth was dry and he felt as if he hadn't changed his clothes since his sixteenth birthday. Suddenly he was taken by a fit of coughing. The Comedian stood back and waited until the paroxysm had spent itself.

'Are you well? You do not look so well.'

'No, I'm not well, I'm old and tired and bloody fed up. Can I make myself a cup of tea in this place or do we have to send down?'

'I have coffee ready and warm croissants but I can send for tea if you wish.'

'No, coffee will do.'

The Comedian went to a sideboard where a jug of coffee and something under a white napkin was on a tray. He brought the tray across and put the plate on the table in front of Jimmy. He picked up the glass and empty beer bottles from the table and floor, put them onto the tray, took them away then came back and sat down. He poured them coffee and took a croissant from the plate. Jimmy took his cup and sipped at it. It wasn't much but it helped.

'I should imagine that your hotel room is now free from problems. Would you like to freshen up here or go straight back to your hotel?'

‘I’ll go straight back. I need a day in bed as much as anything, but I need to let Nadine know what’s going on. I told her that if I wasn’t back by midnight …’

‘I wouldn’t worry about Ms Heppert. She sent out for company yesterday evening, that doesn’t sound like someone who was overly worried about you, does it? I think you can be back by the time she is up and taking an interest. I’m afraid I have no car to take you to your hotel, my men are occupied elsewhere. I can order a taxi for you.’

‘No, don’t bother. I’ll sort myself out.’

‘As you wish. Do you want a croissant?’ Jimmy shook his head. ‘Then I will take another.’

Jimmy drank some more coffee then stood up. His legs, especially his knees, registered a formal complaint but then reluctantly got going. He walked about a bit before coming back to the Comedian.

‘What will happen now? Will they come after me again?’

‘How should I know?’

‘Because you’re mixed up with them somehow. You knew about me being at the club, you knew about the hotel. You …’

‘All right, Mr Costello. I am mixed up with them as you put it. In situations like this one cannot be too choosy about one’s allies.’

‘So, will they come after me?’

‘Yes.’

‘And you? What about you? Where do I stand with you in all this?’

‘You are a problem only to them. To me you are still a nuisance. If you can get yourself out of Munich and back to Rome and leave this business alone you are of no concern to me.’

‘I’ll see what I can do. Thanks for the use of the chair and the coffee.’

The Comedian dismissed the thanks with a wave of his croissant and Jimmy walked to the door and left.

Outside the hotel it was the beginning of a pleasant day. The sun was already well on its way into a clear blue sky. He decided to walk for a while to blow away the feeling of being a pile of dirty laundry left in the basket too long. He didn't think about anything, he didn't want to think about anything. He wanted a shower and then to get some real sleep. He walked for a few minutes then began to look for a free taxi. He spotted one, flagged it down, and asked for his hotel. He picked up his key at reception and went up to his room.

It wasn't a big room and most of it was taken up by the double bed. On the bed on her back, naked except for a pair of black, patent leather high-heeled shoes, with her long legs splayed wide apart, was Nadine Heppert. She was looking at him, but she didn't see him. He knew this because of the bullet hole in the right side of her forehead.

Jimmy stood for a moment trying to take it in. Nadine Heppert was on his bed. She had been shot in the head. What did it mean? What should he do? What the fuck was going on?

He sat down heavily in the one small armchair and looked at the body. There was blood around the wound and it had run down the side of her face. There was none that he could see on the pillow and none on her body below the face. She had been shot while clothed and undressed before she was put there. He looked around, he couldn't see any of her clothes. It wasn't an easy thing to do, undress a dead body, and people tend to notice if you carry a naked, dead woman from one place to another. Even a fully clothed body isn't exactly inconspicuous, especially if you have to get it through a small hotel lobby and up in an elevator.

Jimmy stood up and went into the bathroom. Her clothes were bundled into a pile beside the toilet and there were smears of blood on the floor. Someone had wiped the blood-stained clothes across the floor before piling them where they were.

He went back into the bedroom and sat down again. Now he knew what had happened. She had arrived alive, come up to the room, been shot, stripped, and dumped on the bed. The blood had run onto her clothes and then they had been wiped over the floor in the bathroom to make it look like a hasty attempt at cleaning up. But if he was being set up for the killing there would have to be a gun. He began to look and then stopped.

'For Christ's sake, think straight. Call the bloody coppers.'

The sound of his own voice in the room finally gave him the shove his mind needed. He picked up the room phone and called reception and gave them his name and room number.

'Call the police, quickly. There's been an accident, an accident with a gun. Yes, it's a serious accident, as serious as it can get. After you've called the police you can call an ambulance but it won't do any good. I'll wait here in the room until the police arrive. When they come bring them straight up and let them in.'

He put the phone down and went back and sat in the chair. There was nothing he could do until the police came so he waited.

It had to be the Comedian. The Comedian had picked him up and told him yet another fairy tale which, like the others, he had believed and all the while he was being set up. Why? Where did it get him?

Jimmy's brain circled the problem while he waited. He had got exactly nowhere when the door opened. A man came in and looked at him then at the bed. Another man came in and stood by the door and outside Jimmy caught a glimpse of the receptionist.

It was going to be another long, difficult day.

The man who had come in first said something to him in German.

'Sorry, no German, only English.'

The man turned to his colleague who shrugged.

Marvellous, thought Jimmy, now I find a couple who speak no English.

The man came into the room and looked at Nadine, then had a quick look round the room. He went into the bathroom and came out again. Then he made a simple gesture with his hand. Jimmy knew what it meant, come with us. He stood up and walked to the door and went out followed by the two men. One closed the door and said something to the receptionist who left them. The man who had come in and had a look around took out his phone and made a call then they all stood and waited. It took about five minutes for the sirens to arrive during which time they stood where they were and said nothing. Once somebody came out of a room and walked to them. It was a businessman leaving his room to begin his day. He said something but was sent back to his room. When the sirens stopped the man who'd phoned said something to his partner. He gave Jimmy the sign again so Jimmy walked with him to the elevator. The partner stayed by the room door. They went down into the lobby where the police were arriving to turn the place into a scene of crime. Outside there was an unmarked car. The man with Jimmy called to a uniformed officer who was standing by the doors of the hotel. The officer joined them then took hold of Jimmy's arm. It wasn't much, just enough to let him know that the officer was there. Jimmy and the uniform got into the back of the unmarked car, the detective got into the driver's seat and called in on the police radio. When he'd finished his call the car pulled away and the uniform let go of Jimmy's arm.

Jimmy let his head go back onto the seat. He was dirty, dog-tired, and had a headache. There was a naked, dead woman in his room and he had no idea how much trouble he was in or what he was going to do or say.

He let his head turn sideways and watched the traffic and the buildings passing by. The day was bright, a nice spring day and he was going to spend all or most of it in a police interview room if not a cell. The only idea he had in his head was that life could be very shitty sometimes, no, correct that, life could be very shitty most of the time. But the truth was you probably ended up with what you deserved. Not in the little things like money or success, but how you saw yourself, the kind of person you knew you were.

He let his mind run on, he was too weary to stop it. They were pointless thoughts but he didn't care, he let them run.

That's why so many people top themselves, I suppose, but it doesn't put anything right or make anything better or even change anything, it just stops it going on for one person. Who knows? Maybe it doesn't even do that.

And there his mind decided to stop so he looked at the passing scenery until the car pulled into a police station and he got out. Uniform gently attached himself to Jimmy's arm again and he was taken inside.

Now, he knew, his day would really begin.

Chapter Thirty-seven

He had provided them with everything they had asked for, personal details, a potted version of his life-history emphasising his unblemished career as a detective sergeant with the London Metropolitan Police and his retirement with full pension. He had given them a complete explanation of what he was doing in Munich with Nadine Heppert, or, as full as he thought they could get if they checked.

He gave them the business of the wheelchair and the journalist and how he and Heppert had agreed to come to Munich to find out if there was a connection between the two deaths and if so what it meant for the case they were working on. He told them about his visit to Greta at the home and what the other woman had told him when Greta had ran out on him. He even gave them everything he had about his meeting at the gambling club and how he spent the night with the Comedian. That bit had been sticky. The best he could manage was that he was a friend of a friend and that he'd promised to have a drink with him. It wasn't too late when he left the gaming club so he'd contacted him and gone to his hotel where they'd sat in his room and had a few beers. It was weak, it was worse than weak, but he hoped it would hold them until he could get at the Comedian and sort out something better. Whoever's side the Comedian was on they were alibis for each other. Unless it was the Comedian's men who had killed Nadine, in which case Jimmy guessed he was well and truly fucked.

Now he sat and waited.

He was used to waiting, one way or another he'd done a lot

of it. And he was used to interview rooms, both sides of the desk. He'd interviewed and been interviewed, he'd had a go at people and people had had a go at him. The great thing was to let the time pass, not try to hurry it and not worry about it as it passed. He would get company again when they were ready. Until then he waited.

The officer who eventually came was the same one who had interviewed him when he'd arrived at the station with the escort. A woman, late thirties, short black hair and good at her job. She had a man with her, a bit older, balding at the back of his head and not so good at his job. Jimmy had seen the sort a thousand times before. One of life's eternal sergeants. One of those who made the rank on time served rather than ability or effort and would now stick there until he drew his pension.

The woman sat down and said something in German into the recorder.

'That is the …'

'I know, interview resumed.'

'We have checked the information you gave us about where you say you spent the night. The room is indeed occupied by a Danish national,' she opened a plastic folder and read from a sheet in it. 'Krista Dahl, twenty-six from Copenhagen. She works for the Danish Tourist Office and is in Munich on business. Yesterday morning she left but she is due back later today, probably this evening. You said in your statement that the person you visited was a man. The hotel are not aware of anyone else using Ms Dahl's room and no one has any recollection of you're having been there.'

'Did you check whether anyone ordered breakfast sent up this morning? Coffee, two cups, and croissants?'

'No, but I will have that checked.' She made a note on the sheet. 'Earlier I asked you if you could think of any reason why Ms Heppert would have come to your room. You said you could not. Can you still think of no reason?'

'No, still no idea. Have you interviewed Greta Mann or the other woman who I spoke to at the retirement home.'

'Everything will be done in due course, Mr Costello. You

say you were a policeman, you will know how these things work. They take time.'

He knew they did. They took exactly as long as the police wanted them to take.

'How long will you hold me here?'

'Do you wish to leave? At the moment there are no charges, you are helping us with our enquiries into a serious crime, a murder. You are here of your own free will. Do you wish to leave?'

'No, I don't wish to leave but I would like to go to the toilet and after that I would like a cup of coffee.'

She turned and said something to the sergeant.

The sergeant beckoned him so Jimmy got up and followed him out of the interview room, along a corridor to a door with a gents sign on it. He went in, used the urinal, then gave his face and hands a thorough wash in soap and warm water. It wasn't much but it helped. He went back out and the sergeant took him back to the interview room. Jimmy sat down again. In front of him was a cup of coffee.

'I asked for milk but I didn't know whether you took sugar so it has none. I can send for …'

'No, it'll be fine as it is.'

He took a sip. Like the wash he'd just had, it wasn't much but again it helped. She started on the folder again

'We have checked your service in the London Metropolitan Police, it is all as you said. Ms Heppert's office in Paris confirm that she is working on establishing the identity of the claimant to Mme Colmar's estate and that you visited Ms Heppert at her office. They were unaware that you were working together or that she had come to Munich. She simply said she would be away for a few days on business. M. Joubert's office confirmed all you told us.' She flicked the folder closed. 'I tell you this so you are aware that we are doing all we can to establish the correctness of all information you have given us. We keep nothing back from you, you understand. We share with you the information as we receive it. If you wish to challenge any of it please do so.'

‘No, I do not wish to challenge any of it. Ms Heppert and I had a common interest but we were not partners in any formal sense. That is to say I was working with her not for her.’

‘I see, yes, it is a point cleared for us, thank you.’

She opened the folder and got to work again for a second. Then there was a knock at the door. The sergeant opened it and Jimmy caught a glimpse of a uniformed officer. The sergeant went out and moment later came back in and said something to the woman. She spoke at the recording machine again then got up.

‘Excuse me, please.’

She picked up the folder and she and the sergeant left the room.

Jimmy sat back, picked up his coffee, had another sip, and settled down to wait again.

He didn’t wait long. The door opened and the woman came in alone.

‘You are free to leave, Mr Costello. Your hotel room is a crime scene so you will understand that you may not enter or take anything away. I suggest you find another room and buy whatever you need for the next few days. When you have arranged another room please let us know at once where you are staying.’

‘Can you suggest somewhere?’

She thought for a moment.

‘Yes, I can suggest a hotel.’

‘Great, why don’t you get someone to call them and book me a room then you’ll know exactly where I am and I’ll know there’s somewhere I can go and finally get a shower and some sleep.’

He was sure it wasn’t what they usually did for someone they were questioning but if he was being kicked out of his own room and they wanted to keep tabs on him it made sense.

‘Yes, that will be a good idea. Please follow me.’

‘And who pays for the stuff I’ll have to buy?’ She turned and Jimmy saw at once he’d pushed it too far. ‘Never mind. I’ll sort it out myself.’

She left the room with Jimmy in tow.

It was efficient service. In not much over half an hour he had a room in a small but comfortable hotel in a quiet street. He had showered and was in bed with the curtains closed waiting to fall away into oblivion. His life as a copper had taught him to put aside whatever he was dealing with, no matter how bad it was, and give his body the rest it needed. He would do his thinking when he woke, when he was capable of thinking straight. He lay still and let the sleep seep into his brain.

Then his mobile went off. It was on the table beside the bed. He tried to ignore it. After the right number of rings it went silent and somebody got told to leave a message. Then it began again. Again he ignored it, again it went silent and again it went off so he sat up and answered it. He knew the voice.

'Hello, Mr Costello. I think we need to talk, don't you?'

It was the Comedian.

'I need to sleep, go and talk to someone else. Better still, go and talk to the police and tell them I was with you all of last night.'

'Of course I will, Mr Costello, but only when you and I have talked things over. You really do need to talk to me, I think you know that, so please don't be difficult. Turn left as you come out of the hotel doors and walk, keep walking and I'll find you. Goodbye.'

Jimmy threw the bedclothes off his legs, got out of bed, and began to dress. At least he'd had a shower. He went down into the hotel lobby, out of the doors, turned left, and began to walk. He'd gone about a hundred metres when he came to an intersection, he crossed the road and kept straight on. He hadn't gone much further when someone came from behind and fell into step alongside him. It was the Comedian.

'I didn't think the police would be watching you but I didn't like to take the chance.'

'The hotel lobby was empty, there wasn't even anyone on reception. Did you have it cleared?'

'Me? No. I do not have the resources for that. It's hard enough to get approval for two men and a car.'

‘And a woman who works for the Danish Tourist Board, Kirsten Dahl. Don’t forget Kirsten.’

The man ignored Jimmy’s remark and started into his act.

‘You haven’t shaved. But it suits you. These days I understand it is fashionable to have a certain amount of stubble on the chin. Why that should be so I couldn’t say, but there you are. You are fashionably dishevelled, your face and clothes match perfectly.’

Jimmy kept to the point.

‘Did you kill her?’

‘Me? No.’

‘I didn’t mean you personally. Did you have her killed?’

‘I’m afraid that is a very direct question and not one I am sure it would be wise for me to answer, even assuming my answer would be that Ms Heppert’s death was not of my doing.’

The Comedian’s manner was losing conviction. Jimmy had seen it often enough now to recognise that he was having to work at it. He got the feeling the man walking beside him was working his way slowly to something so he let him take his time. Finally the Comedian spoke, there was still a trace of his act but it was almost gone.

‘In some ways you could say that Nadine Heppert committed suicide.’

‘Will that be your defence if it comes to court? She killed herself. She shot herself in the head in my bathroom, undressed herself, wiped up some of the blood with her own clothes, and then went and threw herself on my bed.’ The Comedian didn’t answer. ‘Oh yes, and while she was at it she hid the gun she used or took it away with her. No, she couldn’t have done that, could she, not take it away? She was dead on the bed.’

‘I use the word suicide in a metaphorical sense, as an image to enhance the reality.’

‘I did my share of murder investigations but I never came across a metaphorical killing.’

The Comedian gave up his act. His voice was flat and direct.

‘Ms Heppert came to Munich to contact the people whom she knew had committed two murders and attempted a third.

She knew the sort of people she would be dealing with and, unlike you, she fully understood what the stakes would be in the game she wanted to play.'

'And her game was?'

'I told you, to sell out her own side, the American interests her firm represented.'

Jimmy stopped so the Comedian stopped.

'Is that another fairy story I'm supposed to swallow because I'm just a fucking gullible foot-soldier? Because I warn you, if you or anyone else in this stupid bloody farce pushes me very much further I'm pretty sure I'll find I can kill the fucker without my hand shaking like it did with Serge.'

And the funny thing was, that although he had thought he didn't mean it, that it was only a try-on to see where it might get him, it came out sounding like the truth. Then he suddenly realised that it sounded that way because he meant it. He really was angry and lost and ready to lash out at somebody and because of that he still might kill. They began walking again. The Comedian stopped and put his hand on Jimmy's arm.

'Let's go in there.' Jimmy looked. It was a bar. It wasn't busy, most of the tables were empty. 'We can sit and talk and I can explain what it is I want. No fairy stories, I promise.'

Jimmy nodded. He wanted the thing explained. He wanted to be brought back from the edge he'd found himself at. Or maybe there was no edge, maybe it was just lack of sleep and too long doing God knows what and worrying about McBride. Maybe the tough-guy outburst had been nothing but his own fairy story and, like all the others, for a second he'd believed it. He could feel the weariness seeping through him. He wanted to sit down. Better still he wanted to lie down for a very long time, maybe for ever.

'OK, buy me a beer and tell me what it is you want.'

Chapter Thirty-eight

'You were, in part, right about the Arctic resources. However, it is not a question of getting anything out. Before anything can be got out a great deal has to be got in. To get in all the equipment that will be needed to extract the riches of the Arctic requires a deep-water harbour preferably ice-free all year round and an airport capable of taking the largest transport planes. Needless to say the people who will eventually litter the Artic with oil rigs, gas pipelines, mining equipment, and all the other paraphernalia of energy and resource extraction began looking for places to bring in the equipment some time ago and did so under the greatest secrecy. Mme Colmar still had friends in America and through these found out that there was an island off Greenland that was ideal. She moved quickly and bought up as much as she could of the company that effectively owned the island and, had she not died, would have played one party off against another. I cannot imagine how much money she expected to make, the figure would be too great to guess at.'

'So it's the Americans and the Russians fighting over …'

'The Americans have some interest, yes, but not the Russians.'

'No?'

'No. They have ready access to the Arctic through their own borders. They do not need an island. No doubt, quietly, their plans are already well advanced.'

'But surely the Americans have access through Alaska?'

'They have some access, but not as much as they would like, and certainly not as much as Canada – and the Canadians have made it clear that this time Canada will, so to speak, freeze onto their advantages of an Arctic border and exploit the situation for themselves. They will not be America's partner nor puppet in this.'

'The Americans and who, then?'

'Come along, Mr Costello, who has the wealth to be a player in this and has absolutely no access to the region by proximity?' Jimmy thought. 'If you don't own the actual land which holds the resources then be the people best placed to bring it up and get it out. Ms Heppert was not telling fairy tales when she said this was all about big business. Nations may own the rights but it will be multi-national companies who exploit those rights.'

'The Saudis? They're the only ones big enough to try something like this.'

'Are they? Who knows how much oil money is sitting in accounts around the world, and, with their oil reserves diminishing each day, who could say which particular oil-rich state might not back such a project. And if it is oil money then why only the Saudis or any of the Gulf states? The whole thing probably won't cost more than a few billion, a small price to keep the revenues flowing in and have a seat at the councils that really matter. The technology already exists to bring it all up. All that is lacking, for the moment, is the political will to exploit the region. But when competition for resources raises the spectre of engines slowing down or even stopping the politicians will fall into line and any opposition will be trampled into silence, so why wait for the inevitable? It's all there and it will be brought out. The only question is, who gets to bring everything in and who gets to bring it out?'

'And you? Which side do you represent?'

'Denmark. The island is Danish and we have our share of Arctic territories through Greenland. We are by no means a disinterested party in all of this. Apart from that, my government takes considerable exception to people who try to effectively annex Danish soil, especially when the methods they use are criminal.'

'But you said you were mixed up with the crowd who had

McBride shot.'

'Mixed up is a vague and imprecise term. They are under the impression that I am working with them. The reality is slightly different. I am, in fact, spying on them. That is why you posed such a nuisance. Unless I had stepped in when you made your presence felt in Paris I fear they would have eliminated you. As you already know they are great believers in direct action. I felt I could not let that happen but preventing it made my position somewhat equivocal with my temporary friends. They appeared to accept that getting you put on a plane and told by the police not to return was satisfactory but they are suspicious people. Unfortunately that couldn't be helped. For Professor McBride's sake I couldn't let them kill you, could I?'

Jimmy thought about the naked body spread over his bed. He was supposed to the one who handled the violence, took the big risks, and got a bullet in the head if things didn't go right. But he was sitting here drinking beer and she was the one in the morgue with a hole in her head. It wasn't where she'd expected to end up. He felt sorry for her in a way. But not too sorry.

'She didn't understand violence. She thought it was something that happened to other people, something you pay someone to deal with.'

'Do not shed any tears for Ms Heppert. Her aim was to go right to the top, to become a person of international consequence. Being a part of making all this business happen would have put her well on her way to where she was going.'

'If she picked the winning team.'

'Yes, she had to judge which of the parties involved would serve her purpose best, which side would give her the best deal. She was very much a loose cannon and the stakes were too high to wait and see what damage she might do.'

'OK, it's all a big deal, as big as it gets, but I'm not trying to climb any ladder. I'm one of the little people, so for me it still comes back to the little questions, like did you kill her?'

'Yes and no.'

'For God's sake give me a straight bloody answer. I'm too tired for any more of your fucking act.'

‘I arranged for her to be where my friends wanted her to be. While they were busy I was able to pick you up and ensure that you would be out of the way while they did what they did.’

‘But why kill her? Was she such a danger? Why not listen to her and then tell her to bugger off? It was a deal she wanted, a crooked deal perhaps, but still a business proposition. There was no need to kill her.’

‘Yes, I’m afraid there was.’

‘And what was that?’

‘You.’

‘Me?’

‘Ms Heppert told me that she had a claimant for the Colmar estate who would be completely acceptable to the Swiss authorities. Not only that, this claimant is mentally unbalanced and all her affairs would have to be handled by someone with power of attorney. Naturally she proposed herself as that person. She also assured me that the claim submitted by her own firm would go ahead as planned and would fail.’

‘She told you? She’d made contact with you?’

‘Yes, Mr Costello. You don’t honestly think she relied solely on your efforts in this matter? If you succeeded with the people you approached, well and good, but if you failed, and she felt there was a strong possibility of that, she had to be sure of another avenue of progress. I was that avenue. I think your role in this was to act as her stalking horse. If you survived a face-to-face meeting with those she wanted to contact she would feel safer in arranging such a meeting for herself. That would bring one more option into play for her. If not, well, she had made contact with me and no doubt would explore other avenues as well. She was a careful woman who knew the value of what she was offering.’

‘So why didn’t you take up her offer?’

‘Because she would have wanted more. She would try to use me just as she used you and Serge Carpentier and everyone else. She would have been worse than Mme Colmar who wanted nothing but money. As I said, Ms Heppert wanted power, she wanted a place at the top table of business. No, she would have been totally unreliable. But I wanted what she offered. That meant disposing of her but keeping you alive. If I told my friends that I had been approached by her I knew their response would be simple and brutal, they would want her dead.'

'And you told them?'

'Yes, and offered to arrange what they wanted done. What I didn't explain to them was that it would be done in such a way that you would be left in a co-operative frame of mind, a mind open to suggestion and persuasion.' The Comedian waited a moment to let what he had said sink in. 'The situation now is that either I disappear and Ms Dahl denies all knowledge of me and the police investigation takes its course, or I tell them that you and I were together in a hotel room lent to me by my good friend Kirsten Dahl who will return and confirm what I have said. But you must decide quickly. My power to assist you ticks away as we speak. Once my friends realise what has happened they will no doubt arrive at the inevitable conclusion that I have my own agenda in this matter.'

'And in return for your alibi I give you the claimant?'

'Yes.'

Jimmy didn't have to think about it. A police investigation into him at this point in time would turn up too much even if it didn't manage to pin the Heppert killing on him. There was still Serge Carpentier to consider. He just wanted to be free of the whole mess.

'OK, get me out of the Heppert thing, clear of the Munich police and your friends, and I'll give you the claimant.'

'I'm afraid I will need more than your assurance of that. If you could give me some details of who she is and most importantly where she is at the moment.'

'Her name's Veronique Colmar, or at least her papers say that's what it is, and she'll say that as well. God knows whether it's true. She was born in Saigon and her mother was Colmar's daughter. She has the right kind of paperwork, even including a baptismal certificate, and she's like Heppert said, a bit away with the fairies. She thinks God's got it in for her, that he's punishing her for turning down a vocation. The place she's staying is …'

And Jimmy gave the Comedian all he had and the Comedian listened.

'Very well, it all seems suitable. I never doubted that it would be otherwise. If Professor McBride arranged for a claimant I knew there would be no problems, except finding her of course. Now I think we should be going, don't you?'

As the Comedian was in a giving mood Jimmy had one more question.

'Did you have McBride shot?'

'No, but if I had been responsible I would not admit it to you. You are a violent man, Mr Costello, however much you try to suppress or deny it. People who get near to you have a habit of dying. I found that out in Copenhagen.' The Comedian waited but there were no more questions. 'We really should be going if we are to see the police. On the way we can fill in the details of our story. What did you tell them?'

They stood up.

'You're a friend of a friend, I said I'd get in touch and we'd have a drink.'

'Not good, Mr Costello, in fact positively weak. I expected better.'

'I know, but I didn't have time to think of anything better. I wasn't exactly expecting what happened.' They left the bar and began to walk back towards Jimmy's hotel. 'You got the police to spring me, didn't you?'

'Not me personally but I made sure the call was made. I needed us to have our little talk. I will confirm your story that we met last night after you left the club and invited you to Kirsten's room for a drink. You stayed the night because you fell asleep in a chair after we had been drinking. I woke you early the next morning. You see, it is almost as it really happened, no lies, no acting.'

'But it's still weak.'

'Yes, but the police have no murder weapon and no motive. If you can account for your time when the murder was committed I don't see how they can build any sort of case.'

Jimmy couldn't put his finger on it, but it was all going wrong somewhere. The whole thing seemed to be turning into one great, bloody fairy story, but if it was, who was the storyteller? He desperately tried to separate what he knew as fact from what might very well turn out to be fiction. Heppert was dead, her body had been real enough. The Munich police were real as well, there'd been no play-acting there. Greta Mann and the gambling club, probably, but he wasn't so sure about them. He mentally pencilled it in as a grey area. That left the Comedian. There had to be something wrong with the Comedian. He said he'd ordered the killing of …

It happened too quickly for Jimmy to realize what was going on. There was the blare of a horn and the scream of a motorbike's engine as it roared away, the Comedian grabbed his arm and half pulled him to the floor. Jimmy shook off the hands and pulled himself upright and the Comedian slipped to the floor and sat there. A car skidded to a halt with its front wheel up on the curb. By the time the two men in the car were out the bike had disappeared. The men from the car pushed past Jimmy and knelt down beside the Comedian. A crowd began to gather, people came out of doorways and across the road. One man from the car stood up. He was talking on his mobile. The other was supporting the Comedian who was sitting on the pavement holding both hands to his right side just below his ribs with blood beginning to show between his fingers and a sort of blank look on his face. Jimmy knelt down beside him.

'Is it bad?'

The Comedian turned his head and his eyes blinked a couple of times then focussed.

'I have no idea. It doesn't hurt yet but that is no sign.'

'Is there anything I can do?'

'No, these men will have help here very quickly.' He managed a half smile. 'I didn't realise how quickly …' but the words stopped and his face twisted and his eyes screwed shut. The pain had arrived, but that was still no sign, it was just pain.

Jimmy stood up. There was nothing he could do. It all

depended on how much damage the bullet had done. Everybody waited. After a short while a siren sounded, far away but coming fast. The man who had done the phoning cleared everybody away from the kerb to give the ambulance team clear access. He ignored Jimmy who stood alongside the Comedian and the man squatting down supporting him. The man was talking urgently but gently, probably trying to keep the Comedian from slipping into unconsciousness. Jimmy felt useless, like a privileged spectator with a ringside seat, but uninvolved in any of the action. Then the ambulance arrived and the paramedics got to work.

Jimmy forced his mind to work. There was another siren, more than one, and they were also coming fast like the ambulance. In a few minutes the place would be crawling with police, putting out tape, taking names, setting up a serious crime scene. He stepped back into the crowd. The Comedian was being put into the ambulance. He edged back through the bodies until he was at the back of those trying to see what was happening. The siren of the ambulance went off and it pulled away. Jimmy turned and began to walk down the street towards his hotel as the first police car arrived. He walked slowly and didn't look back. Act normal, blend in, be one of the crowd.

What the hell had happened? More important, why had it happened? The team on the bike had got a shot off and hit the Comedian but the bike was already moving away because of the car. So did they hit the one they were aiming at? Was the bullet meant for him or the Comedian?

Jimmy turned the thing over in his mind until he came to the doors of the hotel.

Why was he still alive? They'd tried for McBride, they'd killed Heppert and the journalist, now they'd shot the Comedian. They'd had a go at everyone who'd poked their nose into this Colmar thing. Except Carpentier. I, God forgive me, did that job for them. Everyone except me. Why am I the exception? What keeps me alive in all this carnage?

There were answers somewhere, there had to be, but this was all someone else's story and the thing about stories was, you only got told what the storyteller wanted you to know.

The flush of adrenalin from the shooting had worn off, the weariness was flooding back. He felt old and worn out. He felt too tired to go on caring what it was all about, too tired even to be frightened. All he cared about was rest. He went into the hotel and up to his room where he threw off his clothes and climbed into bed. He just wanted to sleep. He closed his eyes and closed down his mind. And slept.

Chapter Thirty-nine

He woke the next morning at six o'clock. He couldn't remember what time it was when he had gone to sleep so he didn't know how long he'd slept. All he knew was that he felt one hundred per cent better. He showered and got into his clothes, yet again. He might have felt better but from what he saw in the mirror he looked considerably worse. The clothes were deteriorating as quickly as his face, where the thick, greying stubble spoke more of homelessness than any fashion statement. He was certainly beyond what anyone could mistake for designer dishevelled. Unkempt and soiled on the outside he felt much more well ordered on the inside. Somehow things had clicked into place while he slept.

Why go to the trouble of planting Heppert's body in his room if later in the day they were planning to kill him? The Comedian had indeed been the target. But did that mean he had been telling the truth about arranging the killing of Heppert, or was he being clever, using what had come to hand when he saw he could use it to apply pressure? Either way somebody wanted Heppert dead and was using her murder to get him out of the way. That had to mean something, didn't it? Jimmy began to put his ducks in a row.

The old Nazi wouldn't play ball so he had to go. McBride had been a target because she was gearing up to get control of the estate. The journalist was unlucky, when he turned up to talk to Young Hitler's daughter the suicide was their idea of a neat and simple solution. Heppert must have overplayed her hand somehow and that was that. Now the Comedian had been targeted. Did that mean they'd been friends and fallen out or wasn't he ever on their side. And who were "they"? The Americans? Unlikely. The Americans were working through law firms like Henry and Parker, not blokes with guns on motorbikes. The Saudis? The Chinese? India? God, it could be anyone, anyone with enough money to be a player and no bit of the Arctic of their own to play with.

Which leaves me. Why am I still standing?

And finally he got somewhere. 'They' didn't know about Veronique. If they'd known they'd have used him or Heppert to go and get her. But they'd killed Heppert and framed him. They didn't know about Veronique! But the Comedian knew. And if he knew it had to be because Heppert told him. Who else knew? All of which meant he was been telling the truth, Heppert had contacted him, or the other way round.

He was pleased with himself, he was thinking at last, getting somewhere. But thinking cuts both ways, it shows you everything, not just the things you want to know. If he was right, then Heppert probably hadn't gone to the heavy mob and overplayed her hand. The more likely scenario was that he'd given her to them by trying to be clever, by trying to play Jack the Lad at the gaming club – 'Parker and Henry, an American firm, I'm working with a woman of influence from their Paris office. Nadine Heppert, Parker and Henry, got that?' Another bloody brilliant judgement that managed to get somebody killed. The brief feeling of self-satisfaction passed. God this was a mess, a total, bloody disaster.

His thoughts were interrupted by a loud internal call. His stomach reminded him that though he might have slept he hadn't eaten. Jimmy took the call. He left his room, went out of the hotel, and found a café where he ordered breakfast.

What would McBride want him to do? The very last thing she'd told him was to carry on, to keep going. Well, he'd certainly kept going and the result was two dead bodies and the Comedian in hospital with a bullet in him. True he now had some idea what it was all about, but that still didn't tell him what was it she wanted as an outcome? Did she want the

Colmar estate and, if so, why? He thought as he ate but got nowhere. This wasn't detective work, it was big business, finance. He knew as much about that as he did about wonderful, magnificent sex. And even if he found out who 'they' were, if he put names and faces to the killings, where would that get him? It wouldn't stop any of it. At best, at very best, he might give a couple of people to the Munich police for murder or complicity to murder. But he would never get within sniffing distance of whoever was giving the orders. What more could he do? And to that question he still only had one answer. There was still Veronique, and if the wound wasn't too bad there was still the Comedian. That was enough. With that he could try to do what McBride had told him to – keep going.

Once he'd silenced his stomach with breakfast he went back to the hotel and got Reception to call him a taxi. When it came he headed off to the police station where he'd been interviewed.

If the Comedian was on the side of the good guys then he had to be working with the Munich police, which made sense if he'd been the one who got him sprung, and who else was there who'd do that? In the taxi he made a call to McBride's hospital.

The improvement slowly continued but she was not yet allowed visitors or to receive calls. Maybe if she continued to improve, but there was no way they could say how long that would be. There could be further surgery and …

He put away his phone.

There was no help coming from McBride, not for the foreseeable future. He was on his own so he'd do what she'd told him to do, keep going.

In the police station they put him back into the same interview room. An hour passed but he waited. It was the only line of enquiry that looked like it might get him anywhere so he'd wait for as long as it took. The door eventually opened and the same woman officer as the previous day came in and sat down opposite him. She was on her own and said nothing into the recording machine. She sat and looked at him and waited.

'I need to speak to …' but he still didn't have any name and he could hardly call him the Comedian. 'I need to speak to the

Danish commander, the one who was shot yesterday.'

He got a blank look. He would have to do better.

'The Commander and I were co-operating on a matter of great importance, great importance to Denmark.' Nothing. He tried again. 'Important to Germany and to Europe. He told me he was working with the knowledge and support of the Munich police, he said that if anything happened and I was unable to contact him I should come to the police and they would see that some sort of contact would be re-established. How is he by the way, was he seriously wounded?' The blank look had gone but it didn't go beyond that. He had done enough to get her thinking, maybe even interested but not enough to get her to speak. The trouble was, he'd gone as far as he could by lying. Any further and he'd cock it up in some way. 'Look, I can tell you what this is all about. If that's what it takes I'll tell you. I don't think you're supposed to know any of the details but I need to re-establish contact with the Commander.' Nothing. He was getting nowhere. 'When you last questioned me, when I was last here, there was a call that got me released. Find out who it was and tell them I need to re-establish contact. Tell them it's urgent.'

There was a knock at the door and a uniformed officer came in carrying a holdall. Jimmy recognised it. It was his. The officer put the holdall on the table and left closing the door behind him.

Stoneface finally found her voice.

'These are all your belongings from your hotel room. Please check them.'

'I'm sure it's all there'

'Please check.'

'I'm still sure it's all there.'

'You will be asked to sign for it.'

'Then I'll sign for it, won't I?'

He reached across and pulled the holdall in front of him.

'You will be taken to the airport, Mr Costello, where you may take a flight to anywhere you choose so long as your destination is not in Germany.'

'And who pays?'

It wasn't a serious question, just something to say to get some sort of response. She ignored it.

'I have been asked to advise you not to return to Munich.'

'Only Munich?'

'The matter of the death of Ms Heppert is still under investigation.' A look of distaste came over her face. Whatever she was going to say she didn't like having to say it and she wasn't about to hide her feelings. 'Early indications are that she committed suicide. At the moment the police are not seeking anyone else in connection with the matter.'

'So all charges against me have been dropped? Lack of evidence is it?'

There never had been any charges against him, he knew that and so did she, he was still winding her up. He had to take out his frustration on somebody and she was to hand. If he could have hit her and got away with it he would have hit her. He wanted to hit somebody.

The look of distaste stayed but this time it was directed at Jimmy.

'You seem to have influence in high places, Mr Costello. We both know that Ms Heppert did not kill herself and we both know that you were implicated in her death. You have been told to leave Munich and not to come back. For myself I would like you to return. If you were to do that, Mr Costello, not all the important friends in the world would protect you.'

'You don't like me very much do you?'

'I don't know you, Mr Costello. I do not wish to know you. I only wish to know what, exactly, was your involvement with the killing of Ms Heppert.'

Jimmy stood up.

'Is my taxi ready?'

She stood up and went to the door.

'Sign for your belongings at the desk before you leave.'

She opened the door.

'Tell the Commander I've gone to Paris.'

'I am not your messenger.'

‘The people you call “my influence in high places” would want him to know. Tell them.’

Jimmy left the interview room and went through the corridors into the main reception area where he signed a paper which the man at the desk pushed in front of him. It was in German and could have been a confession to murder for all he knew but he signed anyway.

Outside there was a taxi waiting. Jimmy got in and it pulled away. The driver knew where he was going.

At the airport Jimmy checked his holdall. Everything was there. He went into the toilets and washed and shaved, changed his shirt, socks, and underwear. The ones he’d been wearing he put in one of the bins then he went out into the main concourse, found out which was the first flight to Paris, bought his ticket, and went through Security into Departures. There were no problems. His flight would leave in fifty-five minutes. He would be in Paris by late afternoon. He looked at his watch then took out his phone and made a call.

‘M. Joubert, please. No? But he *is* back at work after his accident? Good, then tell him I called, my name is Mr Costello. I would like an appointment to see him. As soon as possible. I’m arriving in Paris today and would like to see him tomorrow if that can be arranged. Please tell him that I still represent Professor McBride and she wishes him to act for her in the matter of the heir to the Colmar estate. No, this is nothing to do with the Sisters of Bon Secours. She is acting as agent for the claimant. You have all of that? Good. I look forward to hearing from you.’

Chapter Forty

Jimmy stood at the window of his hotel room looking down at the Gare de l'Est. He'd booked into the same hotel and had been in Paris over twenty-four hours but Joubert hadn't called to set up any appointment. He'd phoned the office twice and each time he'd been stalled. He was getting restless. He had no way of knowing if anyone had submitted any kind of claim to the Swiss authorities and no way of knowing how urgent it was for him to get Joubert working on putting in a claim for McBride's nominee.

He picked up his phone and called Joubert's office once more. This time there'd be no stall.

'It's Mr Costello, I've phoned twice and I … He is, good.'

Joubert's voice came on.

'Good afternoon, Mr Costello, I'm sorry I haven't been able to speak to you before but I have been busy re-arranging my schedule so that we can meet. Can you come to my office now?'

'Yes, I'll be there as soon as I can.'

'Thank you, good day.'

Jimmy left the hotel, crossed the road and headed for the taxi rank by the station. As he approached the rank two men suddenly stood in front of him blocking his way. One said something in French. Jimmy didn't need to get it in English because he also flashed a police warrant card. The other man waved his arm and a car slid up alongside them. The arm waver opened the door and the other man pushed Jimmy towards the car. Jimmy got in and the two men got in with him, one on each side. The car pulled away. There was no siren, now they'd got him they didn't seem to be in any hurry.

Jimmy didn't need any detective skills to see that Joubert had got in touch with the police and told them he was coming to Paris. The thing he couldn't work out was why they'd got Joubert to set him up for a pickup? Why not simply come to his hotel and lift him if they wanted him? He'd told Joubert's office where he was staying. Why all this lifting him off the street business? Then he gave it up. It made as much sense as anything else in this mad farce so he sat back and watched the traffic as the driver made his way to wherever he was going.

Where he was going was to the back entrance of a police station. They stopped and got out of the car. The driver pulled away, Arm Waver went first and opened the doors, Warrant Card came behind and gave regular shoves to keep him moving. They didn't say anything and there was no one in the corridor they went along. There was no one on the stairs they went down or by the cells they came to. For a police station it was an empty place.

Arm Waver went into one of the cells and Jimmy followed, as he went in Warrant Card gave him a hefty shove in the back. Jimmy stumbled forward and fell against the wall. He pushed himself off the wall and turned round.

Turning round was a mistake because it meant he came right onto the punch. He fell back against the wall again and raised an arm to ward off the next blow. It was a useless gesture. Warrant Card's fist landed on his cheek anyway and Jimmy fell sideways.

Don't go down.

He knew the score, if he went down they'd start kicking. It was the kicking that did the damage. He knew, he'd done it often enough himself, or watched as others did it. He leaned against the wall and covered himself with his arms as best he could.

Don't fight back. It only makes things worse.

Then Arm Waver, he thought it was Arm Waver, but he couldn't be sure, kicked his legs out from under him. A fist to the back of his head put him all the way down and he tried to roll into a ball and get his back to the wall as he felt the first boot go in.

Find a place where there's no pain, a place deep inside where the pain can't reach. Find a place …

But there was no place. The pain reached everywhere. He felt the first few kicks then it all blurred into one massive pain that consumed his whole body and he knew he was losing consciousness.

Then, far away, in some foreign country because the words made no sense, he heard shouting. It came and went but the pain stayed. Then he realised no one was kicking him any more and consciousness, if it had gone, was coming back. The voices were closer but outside the cell. He opened his eyes. The shapes of two men were shouting at each other outside the doorway. One might have been Warrant Card. He was doing most of the shouting and, as he came back into focus, pointed to Jimmy a few times.

Then the other man said something. Warrant Card stopped shouting and looked into the cell at Jimmy. He came into the cell. Jimmy kept his eyes open and looked up at him. Warrant Card stood over Jimmy and looked down, then spat at him, turned, and left. The other man looked in, then turned away and he too was gone.

Jimmy lay on the floor trying to feel whether any real damage had been done. It hadn't been such a bad kicking and there'd been no science about it. In fact the whole thing had been a shambles. They'd hit him twice on the face before he went down which meant he'd be marked and the marks would last long enough to have pictures taken. From what he remembered of the kicking it was wild stuff and most had landed on his arms or legs where it would do the least damage but leave the plenty of big, photogenic bruises. It was a fucking shambles, and what for? They hadn't asked him anything and hadn't said anything he could understand. Jimmy dragged himself up onto all fours. He felt the blood on his face and as he looked down a drop of blood dripped from his chin, or it might have been his nose, onto the concrete floor of the cell.

I'll look a fucking mess, he thought.

He pulled himself upright into a kneeling position and held on to the bed. The blood dripped onto his shirt and he tasted it in his mouth. Fucking hooligans. Why? Coppers beating the shit out of people should serve some fucking purpose, shouldn't it? It always had when he'd done it. He slowly stood up.

Fucking amateurs.

He put his hands on his hips and tried to breathe deeply but stopped straight away and clutched at his chest. They must have hit his ribs at least once then. He tried to breathe carefully through his nose but the blood got in the way. It must be broken. He sat down on the hard wooden bed and felt his face. He took his nose in his fingers and squeezed to get his nose back into the right shape.

'Oh fuck me!'

The noise of his shout bounced off the cell walls. He gingerly felt his nose. It seemed to be the right shape or close enough, but only time would tell. Not that it mattered, his face was never much and for a few days it was going to look more like a glorious sunset elaborated with a bit of cross-stitch than anything else. He continued his explorative work. He was cut above his left eye his left cheek was bleeding as well. He slowly and painfully took out his handkerchief and held it to both places and then looked at it. It had turned dark red. He held it to his chin and tried to stop the blood dripping onto his shirt. He was too late. He slowly slid sideways, painfully pulled his legs onto the bed and lay stretched out looking at the light in the ceiling with his head resting on the folded bedding. At least this way, he thought, their stuff gets the blood stains for someone to clean. Then he closed his eyes and waited.

Chapter Forty-one

He didn't know how much time had passed when he heard the man come in and he opened his eyes and looked at him. It was the same one who had pulled Warrant Card off him. He was smoking. He pulled a packet of cigarettes out of his jacket pocket and held them out and said something in French.

'Fuck off.'

The man nodded, put away the cigarettes, and left.

Jimmy closed his eyes again and went back to waiting.

He didn't have to wait long. A few minutes later the man was back, still smoking. There was another man with him. A non-smoker.

Non-Smoker spoke English.

'Sit up.'

Jimmy slowly sat up.

'You wish to make a complaint?'

'Why, what happened?'

'Do you wish to complain about the officer who did this to you?'

'I cut myself shaving.'

'Mr Costello, you have been …'

Jimmy coughed and then spat some blood onto the floor.

'Look, sunshine, nothing happened because if I say anything did happen I would have to fill in God knows how many forms and then hang around in this pisshole of a town while you lot arrange to lose the forms and generally fuck about until, in the end, I drop the charges or you make counter charges or whatever it is you coppers do over here when one of your own fucks up. We both know this won't go to court or anywhere else so don't piss about pretending you give a shit. Just let me get cleaned up and out of this place.'

It was a pretty speech and he meant enough of it to make it almost convincing, but the man listening had heard better speeches delivered by better liars so Jimmy could see he didn't think much of it.

'Mr Costello, you murdered a police officer. We have two witnesses and enough forensic to charge you. We do not need to, as you put it, fuck about.'

'So charge me and when you do I'll fill in your complaint forms and we'll get on the roundabout together.'

'No, there will be no charge, your friends have seen to that. You must have very important friends to walk away from the murder of a police officer.'

'Yeah, well your chum with the boots made sure I didn't get away scot free, didn't he?'

'Mr Costello, in a moment you will leave this cell and a car will take you back to your hotel. After you have cleaned yourself up the car will take you to the airport and you will leave. Those are my orders. Now I will add my own orders. When you leave, stay away, don't return to Paris. In fact don't return to France. If you do there will be consequences.'

'Consequences?'

'You understand perfectly well, Mr Costello.'

'Am I being threatened?'

'Oh yes, be clear about that. I am threatening you and my threat will be acted upon if you ever set foot again in France. Now get up and this officer will take you to the car and then go with you to the airport.'

Jimmy stood up. He felt like a standing bruise but all in all he knew he'd got off lightly. He'd killed one of their own and the bloke was right, you needed very important friends to crawl out from under that sort of thing. Who were they, these friends? And why were they watching him and keeping him going?

Non-Smoker left the cell and his companion stood to one side as Jimmy limped out. While they walked the man lit another cigarette.

'You want to be careful, mate, those things will kill you.'

The man said something in French. From the way he said it Jimmy didn't really need an interpreter to get the gist. He didn't think it wasn't going to be a chatty journey to the airport. He was right, it wasn't.

He got a few odd looks when he bought his ticket to Rome and again as he went through Security but his companion made sure no one interfered with his departure and finally his flight taxied out onto the runway and took off. It was a clear sunny day and as the plane ascended into the blue sky Jimmy looked out of the window at the city below.

It was still April in Paris, still Paris in the spring, and he was leaving it and France for good. He didn't care, he wouldn't miss it. It was a city for locals or tourists, for ordinary people, happy people, for lovers. He wasn't any of those. He was a man with important friends, the sort of friends who got you kicked out of countries and told to stay out or else. He looked out of the window again as the great city fell away and the plane turned to head for Rome. That was that for Paris in the spring, or Paris at any other time. It wasn't that it was overrated, it just hadn't worked out. Things didn't sometimes.

Chapter Forty-two

'Mr Costello, I can barely believe what you have told me. You seem to have gone across Europe trying to start your own private war. What on earth inspired this fit of madness?'

'You did.'

'Me! I have been in hospital throughout your … your …'

But words failed her. It was that bad and Jimmy knew it. He'd tried to keep going like she'd said. He'd tried to do what he thought she wanted, but all he had done was cause her pain. She sat for a moment with her eyes closed. If she had put on a black cap and pronounced his death sentence he couldn't have felt much worse.

Jimmy looked at her sitting upright in a neatly made bed in her private room in the clinic. There were no machines now nor any flowers or cards. It was a private room in a private clinic and she sat in bed with a crisp, white nightdress which emphasised the blackness of her face. She looked like she used to, straight from the laundry. Except that one sleeve was neatly folded up and pinned shut above where her elbow would be if she still had her arm.

But Jimmy could see she was tired. She was better but she wasn't anywhere near well. He'd told her everything, even about Serge Carpentier and how it might have been a misjudgement on his part. She had listened and now he waited for her verdict but she kept her eyes closed.

'You should lie down. You're still not strong. I'll go if you like.'

She opened her eyes.

‘The aim is to get out of bed as soon as possible. People die in bed. Normal people that is, not however people who get close to you. People who are unfortunate enough to meet you seem to increase their chances of a violent death by a considerable margin.’

‘It was a misjudgement, I admit that. It had all the hallmarks of a set up and it was. How was I to know he only wanted me turned over? People were already dead when I got involved and you, as near as dammit, were one of them.’

‘But why go back to Paris in the first place?’

‘Because you sent me. You told me to carry on, to keep going.’

Jimmy could see his answer made no sense to her.

‘As I said, I was in hospital. From the time of the shooting until several days later I have no clear memories of anything and even when I became conscious of my surroundings. I have no memory of us talking. I had no visitors or phone calls. How could I have told you anything? Did I appear to you in a vision?’

Jimmy ignored the sarcasm.

‘The doctor said I had to see you, you said my name. You were hooked up to all sorts of things. It was touch and go whether you’d make it. The doctor said you were fighting the medication, that he needed you to settle and rest. You’d been asking for me and the doctor reckoned you’d calm down if we spoke so he arranged for it. You told me to keep going. That’s all you said. You were in a bad way and what it cost you to tell me was, well, it could have killed you making the effort so I guessed it was bloody important, worth dying for, so I carried on. I went to Paris and did what I did.’

‘And now I know what it was you did.’

‘I did my best, but I was running last from the word go. The thing had gone too far for me to get anywhere, but I tried.’

‘Mr Costello, you were an excellent detective. I think you are still an excellent detective despite the evidence of your recent actions. But you are no medical diagnostician. Did it not occur to you to consult with anyone, with any medical person, on how reliable whatever it was I said to you would be?' Jimmy shook his head. No, he'd not thought of that. Right now he wished he had. 'I was, as you say, in a bad way. If what I have been told is correct I was barely alive and very nearly dead. I was shot full of drugs and when I felt anything it was pain. If I did what you say I did wouldn't you think it might have been influenced by my condition?' Yes, Jimmy could see that now. 'Why would any rational person put any reliance on what I said never mind act on it to the point of murder and general mayhem across two countries?'

'I suppose I wasn't thinking straight. The bastards had gunned you and the chances of you making it weren't good. I wanted to do something about it. I wanted to get the bastards.'

'I see. All this was about you, about you being upset that I had been shot, is that it?'

No, that wasn't it. But Jimmy was beginning to see it was a big a part of it.

'I tried to get your woman in for the claim. I knew that was what you wanted so I tried to make it happen. I may have started out because I was mad but once I got going it was all about doing what you wanted and all I knew was that you wanted Veronique Colman to cop the estate.'

'You knew what I wanted?'

'I thought so, part of it.' She looked at him. 'A bit of it.' She still looked at him. 'Well, you never tell me what it is you really want. You point me at something and set me going. You'd pointed me at this thing in Paris and so I kept going. What else was I supposed to do? You weren't there to say anything, you were in intensive care, you couldn't tell me what you wanted so I had to do the best I could.'

'And what was it that you think I wanted?'

'To make sure that whatever came out of the Arctic got to the right people.'

'The Arctic?'

'Yes, it's all about getting stuff out of the Arctic, isn't it?'

She closed her eyes and shook her head.

Jimmy began to get the feeling it wasn't all about the Arctic, not for her anyway. She opened her eyes.

'And the right people would be?'

'Well, not whoever tried to kill you. And not the Yanks, you were setting up a claim against theirs. Look, I don't know who you wanted to win. All I knew was that you wanted the estate. When the Commander turned up I figured he might help. Then he got shot so I tried to get Joubert back on the case so he could put Veronique into the frame and that's when I got the shit kicked out if me in a Paris cell and bounced out of the country. With France and Germany closed to me it was all over so I came back to Rome and waited until you were well enough to see me. That's it. That's all of it.'

She thought it over.

'Did you work all that out by yourself?'

'Yes, once I'd been told what it was really all about. You told me it was all about Nazi loot, remember? Once I knew that was a load of balls one thing followed on from another. I just didn't make it to the finish, that's all.'

'No, Mr Costello, you didn't make it to the finish. In fact you were in the wrong race.'

There it was, he'd been wrong all along. Shit.

'Not about the Arctic then?'

'No.'

'So who'll get the island, the Americans, the bad guys? Who?'

'Someone, if there is an island.'

'You don't seem too worried.'

'I'm not, not about any island or Arctic exploitation. It is true that when I ask you to carry out work for me I tell only you what I think you need to know, but it is also the case that what I tell you is always substantially the truth. What I told you was the truth, Mr Costello. I was not interested and am still not interested in who does or does not benefit from any future resources exploitation from the Arctic.'

'You're not telling me that nonsense about Nazi loot was true?'

'Yes, substantially true.'

Jimmy turned it over in his mind. It still didn't make sense.

'But what if the wrong people get the oil and stuff?'

'I'm sorry, I don't understand.'

'They kill people, they're nothing but a bunch of thugs and gangsters. They may put out like billionaire businessmen but that doesn't change anything. They take what they want with guns. You can't seriously expect me to believe you want them to have the oil.'

'Why not? It is of no interest to me or those I represent who gets what in the way of natural resources. I cannot see any greater moral good in the resources going to people in the West rather than in the East or going anywhere else. A great deal of money will go into comparatively few pockets whichever way it flows. The oil and gas and other valuable resources will be brought out, who profits from that is a matter for politicians and business to decide. It is no concern of mine and was never supposed to be any concern of yours. That scenario existed in your head alone, Mr Costello.'

'So why send me to Paris in the first place?'

'To confuse and misdirect. I needed a small amount of time to present Veronique Colmar's case to the Swiss authorities. While that was being done I wanted other interested parties to be looking elsewhere. You were my elsewhere. You were supposed to do as I asked, make your contacts, ask your questions, and, in your inimitable style, generally make your presence felt and provoke a response. The assault on M. Joubert was regrettable but I anticipated some such outcome. Once you had engaged their attention you were supposed to withdraw. By the time they had come to the conclusion that you were no sort of threat and resumed their efforts Veronique's case would have been presented. Unfortunately my activities were not as discreet as I had anticipated and there was an overreaction from one of the interested parties.'

'They tried to kill you.'

'We all make mistakes, Mr Costello. Considering what happened to Serge Carpentier you should be more alive to that than most. At least I was the only direct victim of my error of judgement.'

Jimmy's mind circled everything he knew.

'So you're saying that, among all the rest of it, there really was Nazi loot?'

'No, not loot exactly. Mme Colmar was involved exactly as I described to you. Her business associates in America used her as I said. The payments she supervised were not, however, made in loot, not artefacts anyway. They were made in untraceable liquid form, gold, precious stones, anything that could be turned into cash regardless of who won the war.'

'But there had to be something in the estate that you wanted that would hurt the Church?'

'Yes.'

'What?'

'Think, Mr Costello, think like a detective. You have all the information you need. You had it all along. If you hadn't become obsessed with delusions of violent revenge and one-man justice like some comic-book hero and then blinded by all this stupid energy business you would have seen it.'

Jimmy pushed to one side anything connected with fish processing islands. What was left? Mme Colmar and her ill-gotten gains. She was all there was. Whatever it was it had been under his nose all along. Mme Colmar and the work she did for the Americans with the Nazis in Paris. Mme Colmar and her American friends …

Then he saw it. If he'd stuck to thinking like a detective sergeant instead of playing at being a bloody TV tough-guy hero he'd have seen it long ago. It was there and it was simple street stuff, detective sergeant stuff, run-of-the-mill villainy. She'd been a whore, a blackmailer, and a go-between. It was as simple as that.

'She kept records. She kept records and accounts and all the proof she needed to make sure she stayed safe and she had it salted away where no one could get at it, in a Swiss bank. So long as they were safe, she was safe.'

'Records, accounts, a diary, details of names, dates, transactions. Everything.'

'She would. She was a blackmailer. She'd want to be sure she'd have a few powerful friends firmly by the balls if the allies came out on top, which after the D-Day landings looked likely. God, she was sitting on a gold mine.'

'If she'd have chosen to use it. But she never used it, did she? It was her insurance for a trouble-free life.'

'OK, she had all the protection she needed so that what she did in Paris would never catch up with her. But that's all ancient history now. Anyone she could finger must be dead and the companies might not even exist any more, gone out of business, taken over, merged. And even if they do exist they're not responsible now for what happened a lifetime ago. Why do you want it, this diary or records or …' And the last piece fell into place. 'It's one of ours isn't it? Some bloody high-up Catholic whose family were involved. Some Catholic family who made a fortune by screwing their own side while their own soldiers died. What is he, a cardinal?'

'One is. The other is a senior politician who could, conceivably, become president.'

'My God. All you wanted was to get the evidence and bury it.'

'Yes. Mme Colmar made no provision for what would happen to her records after her death. She didn't care what would happen to them. She would be dead so any damage they might do would not have concerned her.'

'The sins of the fathers, is that it? Old Ma Colmar is like some sort of unholy ghost who's waiting to come back from the grave through her estate and haunt the Catholic Church in America.'

'That is one way of putting it. The men concerned are themselves innocent of any involvement but that would not stop ill-disposed people, of whom there are many, from using what Mme Colmar kept. The damage such people could do would have been considerable. However, the matter now, thankfully, will never come to light.'

'What?'

'Veronique Colmar's claim is progressing and she is in the

care, legally as well as physically, of people who will see to it that the matter is closed. Mme Colmar's records will never see the light of day.'

'But, I thought …'

'No, Mr Costello, you didn't think, you acted in a spirit of violence and revenge. A moment ago you took the trouble to think, to think carefully like a detective, and look how long it took you to see what this was really all about. You were never important in the matter, a muddier of waters, a sideshow to slow and confuse, a pawn. Unfortunately your old self, the self you have been at pains to put away from you, is still too close to the surface. Do as you are told, Mr Costello, and behave like a detective sergeant, then what you think may be of use. Anything else is dangerous and destructive. From the very beginning Veronique Colmar's case was in the hands of suitable people, people whom I could trust.'

She closed her eyes. Jimmy could see she was tired now. The interview was over or very nearly over.

'So what happens now?'

She opened her eyes.

'Now I rest, you may go.'

'About me? What happens about me?'

'I'm not sure. You were already barred from Denmark, now we can add France and Germany. You cannot safely return to the United Kingdom, your old friends there have made that abundantly clear. I'm not sure you are of any further use to me, Mr Costello. I had hoped that you might change, but I now think that might have proved a false hope. I will think about it.'

'Will they kick me out of Rome, out of Italy because of this?'

'They might.'

'I'd have nowhere to go if they did that.'

'No, you wouldn't, would you? But I'm not at all sure you have anywhere to go if you stayed. I'm not sure you have anywhere to go wherever you go.'

Jimmy knew what she meant, he was going nowhere, but how much more damage might he do on the way. Suddenly he felt as if he were the one who had lost an arm. There was something missing in him, what was it?

'Did the Comedian die?'

'The Comedian?'

'The Commander, the Danish bloke.'

'I doubt it. If he had I would have been informed.'

She closed her eyes again. There were no more questions and nothing more to say. He was dismissed. He got up quietly and left. The clinic was in central Rome so he walked until he came to a church. It wasn't far, it never was in central Rome.

He went in and found the nearest statue. It was a friar, you could tell by the long, hooded habit and the tonsure on the top of his head. Maybe it was St Francis or St Dominic, but Jimmy didn't care who it was.

He put some money in the box and took a candle, lit it from one already burning and put it with the rest.

'It's for Serge Carpentier. It's something I owe him, this and a lot more, only now it looks like this might be all he'll get. Tell him, sorry.' But it was never that simple. 'If you're there, if he's there, if any of you are still there.'

And then he realised what was missing in him – hope.

There was no one there. There was no St Francis or St Dominic to carry his message. There was no Bernadette, no Michael waiting for him. There was no one and nothing. When it ended it ended. There was nothing else, nothing to look forward to, nothing to hope for, no reason to go on. Somehow it had all slipped away from him.

Jimmy left the church, a crumpled, middle-aged man, anonymous and alone, a man of sorrows familiar with grief. A man going nowhere, because nowhere was the only place left for him to go.

More titles from
The Jimmy Costello Series

Corrupt ex-copper, and fixer for the Catholic Church, Jimmy Costello is sent to Spain to investigate when a senior cleric is accused of being part of ETA, the Basque terrorist movement.

Unsurprisingly, perhaps, a murder occurs as soon as he gets to Santander, and it's not the last as Jimmy encounters some unwelcome reminders of his violent London past.
His enigmatic boss in Rome may not approve, but Jimmy, as always, decides to see things through, to the end.

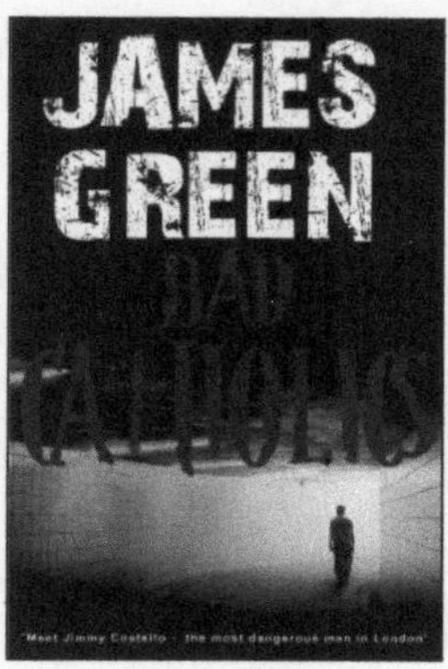

Jimmy Costello always thought he was a good Catholic, a good father and a good copper. But he is a man with a past, a violent, criminal past.

Following the death of his wife, this corrupt London CID Sergeant put the wrong villain in hospital, got himself the quickest retirement on record and then disappeared.

Now he's back on his home turf in London for a reason and there are some very important people who are going to be upset by his return.

But why has he come home? And what does he want?

Jimmy Costello has come home for a reason, a good reason, but he has to get in, get what he wants, and then get out again before he finishes up where he's put others, in the ground. And time isn't on his side. In fact nobody is on his side. Go careful, Jimmy, this time you're not a copper and it's you they'll be after.

Other titles by James Green

Boston, 1802, Lawyer Macleod is a man full of hate, a dangerous man. When a newly arrived young lawyer is mad enough to insult him, the consequences spin out of control and Macleod is caught up in a web of danger and intrigue.

With England at war with France, some powerful Americans feel that the USA's best chance of remaining independent is to throw in their lot with France– even if it means accepting a French king – for a while.

To counter their plot, Macleod is sent to New Orleans, where he meets Marie, wife of Etienne de Valois, aristocrat and fop, and through her learns a terrible secret.

Together, unable to trust anyone, they race to uncover the traitors at the heart of the American Government.

James Green uses fictional characters to illuminate the real events that lead to the birth of the American Intelligence Services and culminated in the extraordinary Louisiana

Purchase, which doubled the size of the USA – at the cost of 3 cents an acre.

Packed with action and fascinating historical detail, *Another Small Kingdom* will appeal both to those interested in the history of the USA and to aficionados of intelligent spy thrillers.

1850 and America is violently divided on the issue of slavery. When President Zachary Taylor dies, suddenly and under questionable circumstances, it is left to his Vice President, Millard Fillmore, a weaker man, to find ways to keep the North and the South apart.

In New York, child of Irish immigrants, Matthew O'Hanlon is fired from his job as a newsman on the Herald but, surprisingly, finds work as Foreign Correspondent for the Associated Press in Panama City. There he is given accommodation with a Dr Couperin, his wife and beautiful daughter, Edith, but finds himself caught up with the secret agents protecting America's commercial interests during the struggle for control of Panama's trade routes and, as it crashes about him, realises that he has been living in a house of cards.

Set against the Gold Rush and the opening up of California and the Oregon Territories, when the United States walked a narrow and dangerous line, *The Eagle Turns* charts the course of history as America's Secret Services struggle to bring prosperity amid the conflict.

For more information about **James Green**

and other **Accent Press** titles
please visit

www.accentpress.co.uk

BILLY SAVES THE DAY

BILLY GROWING UP SERIES: SELF-CONFIDENCE

James Minter

Helen Rushworth - Illustrator

www.billygrowingup.com

MINTER PUBLISHING LIMITED

Minter Publishing Limited (MPL)
4 Lauradale
Bracknell RG12 7DT

Paperback ISBN: 978-1-910727-21-8
Hardback ISBN: 978-1-910727-23-2
eBook ISBN: 978-1-910727-22-5

Printed and bound in Great Britain by Ingram Spark, Milton Keynes

>>>>>

DEDICATED to those who don't believe in themselves, self-belief can be acquired. When you do believe in yourself, you can do more than you might think.

<<<<<

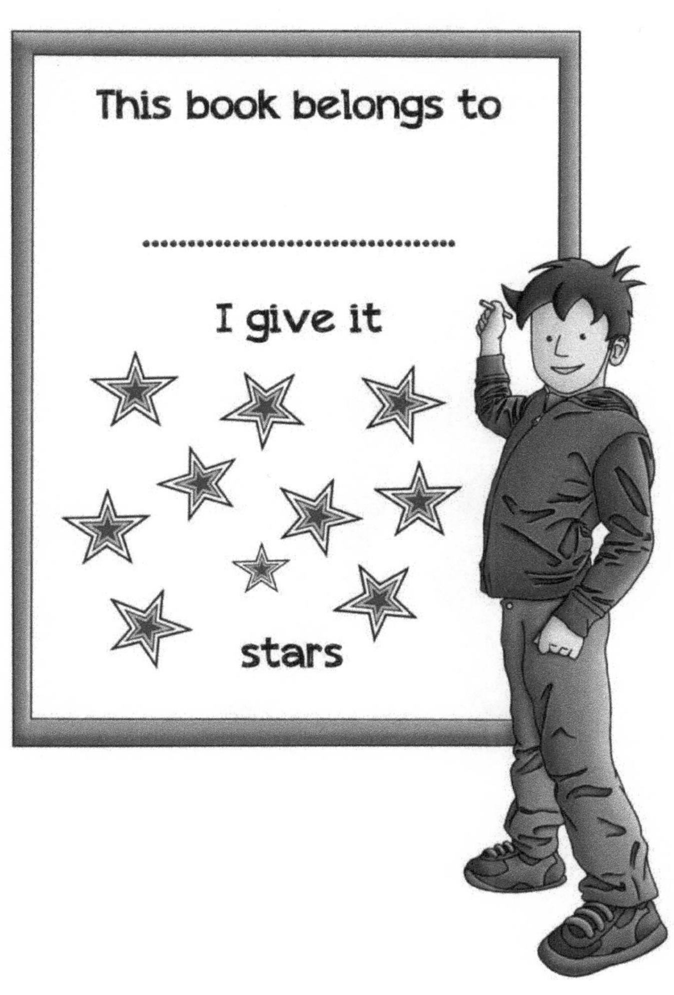
This book belongs to
....
I give it
stars